CURIOUS OBSESSION

ELORA NICOLE RAMIREZ

AWAKE INDIE PRESS

Pleasant Bitches, this one's for you.

PROLOGUE

We're standing by the ocean, the foam washing our feet in a joint baptism, when you tell me you can't see me anymore. You give all kinds of excuses: it doesn't make sense, there's no more mystery, you aren't attracted to me — but I know they're all lies.

I watch your eyes roam my face with desire. It's obvious you want me, you're just fighting innate impulses. I reach my hand out and caress your arm, but you pull away, a snarl on your lips.

I smile. You're so feisty when you resist.

I watch you turn and walk away, studying the fabric of your sweater blowing in the wind as you maneuver through the sand back to your car. You didn't even offer me a ride, but maybe that's because you haven't broken up with your boyfriend yet and you don't want to raise questions.

I understand.

I drove here anyway.

I watch you until you turn invisible behind the sunset and then wipe my face. Fucking tears. I breathe deep and notice a starfish on the sand by my feet. I pick it up, fingering the indentations and grooves. I remember you telling me once that starfish symbolize infinite love...or was it vigilance? Either way, I lift the creature to my lips and give it a kiss before snapping off each arm and throwing it back into the sea.

If you want to play cat and mouse, Juniper, we can play.

But you need to know — I always win.

.::.

OVER THE LAST FEW MONTHS, I've watched you. I've learned your habits and who takes up most of your time. I've left you notes, but they fall wasted. But here's the thing: I know. I saw how much they meant to you. How they would make you pause and re-read them. So I kept leaving you messages and sending you texts. You kept pretending to not be moved by them. I know they mean something. So over the next few days, I wait. I watch. I see you lock one of the notes into the drawer of your night-stand, glancing around as if someone would see you hide our love. As if you knew I was watching you from my perch.

When you end it with Simon, I know it's for me. You tell him it's not working and that he can't control you and I fall in love all over again. I watch as you both pace your living room, Simon being the obtuse man that he is, tries to reason with you.

"You're too smart to waste your intellect teaching high school kids who won't even remember you!"

You throw a book at him and I smile. There's your sass. You walk toward the front door and open it.

"I think you should leave. Now."

He stands there, shell-shocked. I roll my eyes. It's not like you haven't done this dance before — although this time I can tell you're really done with him. I wait for you to tell him about me — to not let him off gently and to cut to the marrow of why you're ending it — but you don't. I frown. You care too much about what other people will think.

I need to remind you.

I need you to remember.

So I leave a note for Simon, letting him know you found something better.

Then I follow you into school one morning and you don't even notice because you're talking into your phone — telling your sister you need to talk to her about something. Is it me? It's too bad she won't ever know. I hang out in the hallway while you teach your classes and chat with your students about some gala this weekend that you won't make it to but don't know yet. It's noble, really, how you give. How you refuse your own desires.

How you refuse me.

You won't be able to for long.

In between classes when you run to the teacher's lounge for a refill on coffee, I sneak into your room and find the perfect spot in the water heater closet. How convenient. I leave the door open just a crack and know you will never see. It's not that you don't pay attention, you're just focused on other things.

People.

Your students.

I watch you as you finish your day, resting your head in your hands at your desk and breathing deep before diving into the pile of papers still needing to be graded. You stretch. You massage your neck. And finally, you give up and decide to leave.

You told me once you worried about your students walking home after school — how they paid no attention to their surroundings because they were too busy looking down at their phones to see oncoming traffic or a potential rapist. So I note the dramatic irony in how I catch you: head down, looking at your phone, paying no attention to the cat behind you, finally about to catch his mouse.

1

One moment Juniper Reese existed, and the next she vanished into thin air.

At first, I chalked up her not answering my phone calls to being busy. We normally chat every single night, but we also both have full time jobs that tend to weave into our daily rhythm. Work life balance has never been a thing for the Reese women, plus I knew she was organizing a gala at the school where she taught, so I waited for the typical text that followed up a missed call. Probably something like....

HEY. *I'm busy but I'll call you tonight. Love you.*

BUT THIS TIME, there was no text. I told myself it was okay, there wasn't anything to worry about, any moment now I would hear from her and she would be apologizing profusely because *ohmygosh I had no idea what time it was...*

But then I went more than 24 hours and didn't hear from her, and I couldn't ignore it anymore. That was Sunday. Yesterday. I called her multiple times, each time hoping that she'd breathlessly answer, nonchalant about the stress I endured. Even though I knew that wasn't Juniper. Even though I knew she would never just not call me back. So here I am, trying really hard not to freak out, and failing miserably.

Come on, Juniper. Text me, dammit.

I stare up at the fan in my room, trying to determine just how much of an emergency this is when I feel a familiar pain blossom in my chest that feels a lot like grief.

If mom were here, she would know what to do. I swallow the tears ballooning in my throat. Ten years later and her absence still felt like a gaping wound that wouldn't ever heal.

I scrape the edge of my hairline with my finger, anxious for some type of clarity. Instead, it's just the standard brain fog coupled with anxiety and grief. I groan. Who am I kidding? I'm not going to be able to accomplish anything until I get coffee. I take a deep breath, willing myself out of bed. A glance at the clock lets me know it's not even five in the morning.

Not surprising. Sleep and me aren't friends, especially when my sister isn't responding to texts.

I sniff and push myself up and out of the covers, stretching and watching the lights outside my window blink in iridescence. I chose this loft for a reason — it overlooks the San Francisco bay. Throwing a chunk of my monthly salary toward the minuscule living space that functions as a bedroom, living room, and kitchen seemed rational at the time. Now I'm just lonely.

Lonely and worried.

My feet grab the coolness of the wood beneath me as I sleepily move from the bed in the corner to the kitchen counter a few feet away. Bonus of living in a true loft: the coffee is literally steps from your sleeping space. I turn on the espresso machine and choose my roast for the day, tampering the grounds and hoping my mind being somewhere else entirely won't effect the taste of the brew. At this point though, I guess it doesn't matter. The coffee will be more about clarity and energy than enjoyment. I grab a cup and pour the shots, mixing it with almond milk. Juniper would be laughing at me right now and reaching for the full fat cream I leave in my refrigerator door in case she ever comes to visit.

She's only come once.

I grab a blanket draped off the side of my bed and carry it with me to the couch that sits against a brick wall and in perfect view of the sun beginning to stretch over the horizon. I try and think back over my conversations with Juniper.

Wednesday, a week ago, she talked to me about Simon. They were ending it for real this time — his pursuit of a career getting in the way of her desire for normalcy.

"What's more normal than brow beating your way up the corporate ladder while your wife stays home and pops out babies?" I joked with her. She didn't find it funny.

Later that night I called her crying, completely in my feelings. My day had taken a complete turn and a project at work was running away from me. I didn't know how to fix it. Like always, Juniper came in and offered her logic and practicality. By the time we got off the phone, she could barely form a sentence she was so exhausted and I was downing a shot of espresso, fully inspired. I finished the project in a few hours. I texted her my celebratory photo of taking shots...this time full of vodka. She texted me that she was afraid I was becoming unhinged.

Even still, that day was no different. We texted until we couldn't anymore and then she told me she was going to be busy working with another teacher on the Gala the next day but she would try and call me that weekend.

Thursday morning when I woke up, there was a text waiting for me saying she needed to call me about something and to be expecting to hear from her the next morning because she'd be working on the Gala again that evening.

"This is important. Please answer," she said.

Meaning: *this is important. Please get your ass out of bed and be ready to talk.*

Friday morning I got up early — I remember stumbling out of bed and making my coffee and properly attempting to do some sort of yoga before getting a notification that she'd sent me a video message in Marco Polo. I clicked on it, confused. She stared back at me, smiling and in her classroom. It was completely empty.

"Hey. I know I said I was going to call you tomorrow but I am still working on the Gala and I imagine we'll be here pretty late," she rolls her eyes. Who is *we*? Who's with her?

"We still need to talk, though." She's out of breath even though she's sitting down. Her eyes keep darting in front of her, to what I imagine is her door. I frown as I watch it again for the thousandth time. There's a shadow that crosses her face when she tells me she still wants to talk and her eyes are definitely swollen, as if she's been crying. She left me a similar message back when she was telling me she needed to talk and it was about Simon.

I swipe up out of the app on my phone before my response starts playing and rest my head on the arm of the couch.

Friday morning. Last time I heard from her. Is this grounds for calling the local police? I try and think back to all the missing persons cases I watched on *Unsolved Mysteries* and keep coming up blank. No wait. Maybe I'm thinking of a murderino podcast.....

My phone vibrates in my hand and I startle, my heart racing. I glance down at the screen and feel the crashing of my energy when it's an unknown number. I recognize the area code though — Providence. Where Juniper lives.

"Hello?"

"Hi. This is Tracey from Sacred Heart. We're looking for Juniper and you're listed as one of her emergency contacts. Have you spoken with her recently?"

I close my eyes and start massaging my forehead.

There are moments in life where you experience something in technicolor. Everything around you turns luminescent, a built in bokeh-effect around the moment. Finding out my mother died is filed under this category.

So is finding out my sister is missing. Truly missing — not just ignoring my calls and texts. It feels like cement has lodged itself into every corner of my being. I'm frozen. I force myself to speak.

"I'm - I'm her sister. I haven't heard from her since Friday. Did she not show up today?"

For Juniper to not show up to one of her obligations, let alone her job, is definitely out of character. A cold realization hits my limbs and I'm glad I'm sitting down. Tracey wouldn't be calling me if Juniper had waltzed through the doors this morning like she always does. I can feel my pulse staccato out a rhythm that's unfamiliar. Something is wrong.

Tracey clears her throat. "She's been great with communicating in the past if she would miss, and so when she didn't show, we thought we would reach out in case you had heard from her. You are her emergency contact." She repeats this last fact as if it would magically unlock the whereabouts of my sister.

I get up from the couch, nervous energy beginning to bounce around my limbs. I need to pace.

"I haven't. I-I haven't heard anything, actually. Like I mentioned before — last time we spoke was Friday." I take a fistful of hair from the messy bun on the top of my head and squeeze until I feel the pressure against my scalp. I'm beginning to come undone and I need some type of tactile reminder that in this moment I am okay, that I can breathe and focus on what's next. I glance out of my window and watch the sun begin to creep over the horizon of the bay.

I feel my hair.

I see color in the sky.

I smell my coffee.

All reminders keeping me present, but I am dangerously close to the precipice. Right here in the middle of my living room, I'm going to unspool and collect like dust on the hardwood. I reach for another branch.

"Have you spoken with the the teacher she was working with on the Gala? Would they know?"

"He's not in yet this morning. I haven't been able to ask him."

I rub my tongue across the top of my teeth and am surprised at the shock of how organic the thought pops into my brain, *she was working with a man?!*

As if this were any other phone call.

I shake my head and force the thought into the back of my mind to retrieve later. Not that it matters. Well, yes it does. This is the type of information in which sisters give each other hell for, and I would have given her the worst kind in the form of third degree questioning.

I *will* be able to give her hell. I wince at the tense change, resisting it.

Tracey hums absentmindedly, "is there anyone else who might know where she is you think?"

I think through any other options — any other person I know she might have been working with on something or another. Conversations about the teachers and their close-knit community come back to memory. Juniper had a hard time connecting with the cult-like mentality there. She was always telling me about an awkward conversation or an invisible rule she knew nothing about within their culture.

I sit down again, this time on my bed, and shake my head.

"There's no one. She...she had a boyfriend, but they broke up and she wasn't - *isn't* - very close to anyone at the school...."

Tracey clucks her tongue, the judgment evident in her voice. "I see."

I remove my hand from the tangle of hair and spread my fingers out over my knee, pressing down as hard as I can and breathing like my counselor taught me so many years ago after Mom's death —

Inhale one two three
Exhale one two three

It calms the panic attack that I can feel brewing underneath the surface, but I know it won't work forever. That's when I know I need to leave. I need to be there.

"I'm coming," I say. "I'll be on the next flight."

I hear Tracey mention something incoherent and I speak over her, "my sister wouldn't miss work. Something must be wrong. I'm coming. We'll find her."

I hang up the phone and let the adrenaline move for me: I need to find a flight out of San Francisco, call the local police station out in Providence, and shove as many clothes as possible in my carry on — I'm not too concerned about how many outfits to bring. Juniper and I are the same size. I can always borrow her clothes if needed. Thankfully, job perks means I have miles I can use for a last minute, very expensive flight. I call the police station in Providence and report my sister missing, but the conversation is frustrating at best. As soon as they know she's been missing less than 48 hours they refuse to do much. I'm persistent though, and manage to snag the number of a Private Investigator they promise will "look into it."

I don't believe them for a second.

I'll call him as soon as I get there tonight.

I send a haphazard email to my team at work letting them

know I'm making an emergency trip and will be out of pocket for a few days. Immediately, Jack responds.

REALLY? *I find out via email?*

I ROLL MY EYES. I can deal with him later.

.::.

WHEN I LAND IN PROVIDENCE, I'm shocked by the chill coming off of the coast. I wrap my scarf closer to my skin and put my head down to avoid the way the wind cuts into me. I take an Uber to her house out in Newport, feeling the apprehension settle in my throat as we turn on her street. The entire ride, it's been silent and now suddenly the driver wants to try and have a conversation.

"Visiting family?"

When I don't answer, he just nods to himself and turns up the music — a tired country song that sounds like a mixture of Clint Black and Montgomery Gentry. I roll my eyes and stifle a groan.

When we reach her house, I notice the lights are off. I pay for the drive and close the car door behind me, standing on the sidewalk for a beat before moving up the steps of the porch. I blow out a series of short breaths, hoping to gain control of my emotions. What happens if she doesn't answer? What happens if I find her inside? I swallow those thoughts, shoving them as deep as I can, and try the doorbell.

Nothing.

I look around me, noticing the lack of other houses nearby — it's a quaint neighborhood on the edge of the coast. I can see the waves crashing over each other from here. I try knocking, and when I don't hear any footsteps, I try the doorknob.

It's locked.

I bite my lip, trying to remember where she put the key for drop in visits, attempting to encourage me to come and stay for a bit. It isn't something obvious like underneath her door mat. She doesn't even have one. I look around her porch, trying to determine where I would hide a key if I were Juniper.

Oh.

I reach over and feel the underside of a nearby sconce. My fingers brush up against the familiar shape of a key and I manage a smile.

The key goes into the lock and within seconds I'm in the entryway of her home. I glance around, trying to ignore the overwhelming scent of my sister that permeates every surface.

"Juniper?"

My voice sounds scratchy and foreign. I clear my throat and take a few steps into her living room, noticing her bedroom door ajar. I walk toward the kitchen counter, my head tilted in the direction of her room. There's no response.

Nothing.

I spend a few moments walking through every room and checking every closet, making sure that I know with everything left in me that she is not here. I glance out her bedroom window and notice the path winding up the cliff and hugging the coast. It's her walking path. I almost walk outside and straight onto the loose gravel, mimicking her movements and wanting desperately to retrace her steps. But I'm not familiar with this area, and it's the dead of night. I may want to find her, but I don't have a death wish. I decide to pull out my phone and call the detective the police said would help me with a missing person's case. I glance at the clock at the wall after dialing and only after I recognize the time do I hesitate — 11:00pm. I shrug.

They did say to call any time because he keeps weird hours.

The phone rings twice before he picks up, groggy.

"This is Dan."

I wrinkle my nose without thinking. First, because it sounds as if I woke him up. Second, his name. *Dan.* Such an ordinary name.

My mother's voice echoes in my memory and I remember Juniper and I sitting on either side of her on the bed eating ice cream out of the carton one Friday night. I can't remember what happened, but I remember being in middle school and devastated by a boy who played Juniper and I against each other. His name was Matthew.

"Don't ever trust a man with an ordinary name, girls. He'll be so bored by the ordinary he'll purposefully shake up his life and create chaos on a whim."

It probably doesn't bode well for my relationship with this man that I already have a suspicion of how he'll handle the case because his name rhymes with *van*.

"Hi, Detective. It's me. Lavender."

"Ah yes. The spice girls. Someone told me you might be calling."

I roll my eyes. It was bad enough that Juniper and I were identical twins right down to the part in our crystal blonde hair and the freckle on our left cheek. Names meant so much to my mother that she chose Lavender and Juniper: intuition and healing, respectively.

Despite this, Detective Dan is not the first to call us the spice girls. As if both Lavender and Juniper are spices. As if there is nothing else to be pulled from our names other than it being some type of decoration. I think of the first time we came home fuming because of the nickname. We didn't even know there was a girl group attached to the name first — all we knew was that being dubbed *spice girls* felt wrong and misplaced.

"You are not a decoration, girls," mom said. "You have all the sass you need, but you are not regulated to the spice on a dish. You are more than that — so much more. You hear me? Your names come from here." She'd patted her chest, signaling her heart and soul. "Don't ever let anyone take that away from you."

And then she looked into our eyes and spoke the meaning we knew then by heart.

Her hand on my cheek, "intuition," she whispered.

Her lips on Juniper's head, "healing," she echoed.

I sigh.

Mama, I sure wish you were here.

I sniff and Detective Dan takes my silence as approval to continue.

"It's late," he says.

"I know." I rub at my face, anxiety already starting to settle in and make a home with dry patches and mini-breakouts. "They told me to call you any time — said you kept weird hours." He gives a noncommittal grunt and I take that as a cue to keep going.

"I wanted to let you know I'm here in town. I flew in tonight and am at Juniper's place now."

"Is she there?"

I blink at his question. Is she...what?

"Would I be calling you if she was had magically appeared?" I hear another slight grunt on the other end.

"Just checking. Sometimes family just likes to...you know... disappear for a while."

Something in his voice makes me pause. I pull at my ear, feeling the weight of my earrings stretch the skin.

"Not Juniper."

He hums for a moment as if he's thinking and I swear I want

to reach through this phone and punch him where it hurts the most. Instead, I close my eyes and reach for patience and ask a question.

"Have you...." I pause to give my voice a minute to strengthen. "Have you looked into this at all? I know this is the first time you've heard from me, but you knew about her missing from the station when they called you. Have you checked in with any of her coworkers yet?"

"Well, you reported her missing today and it is almost midnight so...no. I haven't. I was working on other cases."

I breathe in quickly and he jumps in, "your sister is an adult. It's very possible she needed to get the heck out of dodge, if you know what I'm saying. We can't force her to come home. If I had a dime for every time someone told me *it wasn't like so and so to just up and leave,* I would be a rich man. Sometimes, we just don't know our people like we think we do."

"I know what you're saying," I whisper, the words tight in my throat. I fall into Juniper's leather couch and pull a pillow into my lap. "But I know my sister. And what I am telling you is that Juniper just doesn't disappear. Something isn't right and I'm just asking for y'all to help me find her."

"Okay. I'll take a look at the school tomorrow. See if we can't get a feeling for where she might have wandered off. But for now, Ms. Reese, I suggest you try and get some rest."

I laugh under my breath because like *that* is going to happen. We hang up and I twirl my cell phone around in my hand, trying to determine how nosy I want to be with my sister's belongings. Her space is immaculate: nothing out of place. It wouldn't be hard to find anything that feels as if it doesn't fit. I start in the drawers on her nightstand.

"Alright, J." I whisper to the air around me, "show me where you are...."

2

Her drawers are filled with innocuous things: receipts, magazine subscription cards, pens and other plethora. But the difference is that Juniper's drawers are *organized*. Like, she has partitions and dedicated boxes and a receipt holder labeled *2018 Taxes*. I spend hours pilfering through her documents and belongings, opening up mail and cracking her windows so I can hear the waves crash in the distance. She organizes with precision. It doesn't take me long to understand her process. Bills go in the mail holder by the door. Magazines pile up on the shelf below her nightstand. Books are alphabetical. She'd probably have a fit at my books currently organized by the color of their spine. I smile, remembering the moment she tried to show me her undoing by organizing her books in a chaotic fashion.

I wipe at my cheeks.

That was the week Mom died.

I run my finger along the titles and realize I am familiar with absolutely none of these authors. In a different world, Juniper would chastise me for my lack of memoirs or creative nonfiction. I purse my lips and grab one that looks enticing and throw it on her bed to read.

Maybe, just maybe, it will be a proper distraction. I wrinkle my nose.

Probably not, though.

After hours of searching, I still feel lost. I have no idea where else to look and part of me feels crazy for expecting her to turn up at any moment. The other part anticipates it like my next breath. Her presence is so heavy in these rooms I keep thinking I'm going to hear her voice bounce across the hallway.

"What the hell are you doing here?"

I wait, and I search, and I glance at the door, willing her to return.

She never does. I never hear her.

She didn't leave anything important behind: cell phone, computer, purse, keys — none of them are here. I bang my forehead against the wall in frustration. It's not that I expected to find out where she was based on something she left behind, but I was hoping for some sort of clue — something that would let me know she was okay. Something like a plane ticket or travel plans.

At least then I would know she just didn't want to be here anymore.

But again: I know better.

Our entire life, Juniper has been the practical one. She would often complain that I got all of the creativity and sass and she got all of the logic. Nothing is happenstance with her. Even down to where she lived, she intentionally created a life that existed from her goals. It's why she chose to teach in Providence and live in Newport — enough distance between us to live our own lives without any overlap. Even more important: enough distance between her work life and students and the space she made her home.

"I need to find my own identity," she said.

So she left California and moved across the country, from one coast to another. She chose Providence because of it's big-little-city vibe and Newport because she could still live by the ocean. I remember her balking when I mentioned the name — how it felt like *providence* that everything was falling into place.

"Please. That's not a thing."

And now she was gone.

Something grates at me though about her nightstand, like I missed something. Or maybe I *saw* something but it didn't register. I return to the drawer, opening to find the same receipts and mail outs and pens. I stare at it for a few seconds before sighing out of frustration.

Nothing.

I'm just about to slam the drawer shut again when I see something strange: a tiny latch in the side corner. I push in and something gives, releasing a secret area where you can hide valuables. Instead of valuables, there's a solitary piece of paper. I pull it out and unfold it, noticing the rudimentary way it's haphazardly creased. I smile, thinking of the many ways Juniper would fold our notes in middle school and high school — before cell phones were an expected accessory and text messaging the preferred method of communication. It's obvious Juniper had nothing to do with the folding of this note.

The handwriting is also a giveaway. Large and splotchy, the letters fall over each other in their attempt to form a word. It's a simple message: five words. I get a dryness in the back of my throat when I read it, even though the contents are relatively innocent.

WHY DO YOU IGNORE ME?

I frown. Who would write this? And why would Juniper save it? I stuff the note in the pocket of my bag. I plan on heading to the school tomorrow morning anyway and I can show Dan. It might mean nothing. It could have something to do with her and Simon recently breaking up for good. But I saw nothing of his when I was searching the place — no signs of a relationship, either. No keepsake boxes, no pictures, no memories stashed behind the clothes in her closet for when she's feeling lonely.

Not that I know anything about that.

I walk to her bed and collapse into the covers, exhaustion taking over. My thoughts aren't even making sense anymore, so I know I should probably call it a day, despite the way my insides are colliding against each other. The fear I have for her is palpable, like a taste on the edge of my tongue — bitter and sharp. I still feel her, still know she is somewhere waiting for us to find her– I just have no idea where. The note I found feels weighty and important. I look out the window and try to decipher the horizon from the sea and there's no discernible difference: it's all black expanse. I try not to find the metaphor in that, but it's already there, lodged in my mind.

There is no difference. It doesn't matter. You can't save her.

I grab a pillow and throw it over my head, groaning. For the first time since I realized she was missing, I let myself cry. The tears come hot and fast and spill down my neck, forming wet spots on the sheets. I can't stop. The grief and fear and not knowing feels as if it will swallow me whole. And perhaps it will — perhaps I won't exist anymore, just like Juniper.

Just like the horizon being consumed by the black expanse.

There's nothing more I can do tonight, so once the tears subside I finally let myself breathe deep and settle in as much as possible. At least I *am* breathing. At least I can feel my heart beat at a normal pace. For the past 36 hours, I've felt like my heart has been beating a steady rate fit for cardio. The fear is still here. The grief and worry continue to consume. But for now, my exhaustion wins. My heart rate continues to slow as my eyes grow heavier and heavier and my breathing deeper and deeper. My mind is still racing, but I've effectively worked until I cannot move anymore. Sleep comes quick.

.:::.

The next morning I'm woken up by seagulls. For a brief moment, I've forgotten about the particulars of why I'm within earshot of the coast and I allow a slow smile to creep across my face.

My body remembers before I do.

I feel the tension in my neck and my heart begins to race in anticipation. It's a desperation: a *please please please* tap of staccato that jolts me awake as memories resurface.

Juniper. Missing.

I rub my face and try to blink the night away, feeling the soreness settle in my joints. I'm suddenly very thankful I decided against the unopened bottle of sparkling wine I saw in Juniper's fridge last night. I wanted to open it so bad — wanted to dull the sharp edges of how my mind was playing tricks on me and crafting worst-case scenarios over and over and over again. Ultimately, I left it in the fridge. If I had started drinking, this morning would have been even more miserable.

It doesn't take me long to get dressed and find a taxi to take me to Sacred Heart. Once I get there, I'm struck by the architecture. No wonder Juniper spoke about the tight-knit community of the school. It looks like it's only the elite who are able to step through the iron gates guarding the property. I see her car in the parking lot and chills cascade down my arms. There's no way in hell she would leave her car anywhere. Juniper is not someone who fights for material things, but she saved for years to purchase her own car and completely splurged with an all-leather-interior Subaru. She takes meticulous care of it. I notice students and teachers parking and greeting each other with smiles and laughter and I grimace involuntarily.

How life continues to move on with normalcy in the midst of chaos and trauma is beyond me. It's as if my sister never disappeared. I blink and turn my attention toward the school as the car slows to a stop. I see a man talking with a woman who has a badge around her neck — clearly someone who works here — near the entrance of the school. As they talk he nods and looks down, writing down notes in a small note pad. That must be Dan. I pay the driver and step out of the car, waving in his direction. He looks at me and widens his eyes in surprise then purses his lips. We've never met in person and I don't even know if he knows it's me, but it feels like he doesn't want me here.

Tough titties, Sherlock.

He's ending a conversation with the woman when I walk up to him.

"Thanks. Let me know if you hear anything."

"Of course," she offers half a smile and squeezes his arm. "We're all worried about Juniper and hoping she's taking care of herself, wherever she is —" her voice falters and her hand flies to her throat as she glances my way and freezes.

"Oh. I'm sorry. You startled me for a moment — I th-thought you were..."

I give her a reassuring smile and hold out my hand. You would think that being an identical twin sits in your psyche at all times, but there are so many moments I forget to other people, I'm not my own person. I'm one half of a whole. I glance at Dan and notice boredom behind his gaze. I feel my defenses rise.

"Lavender. I'm Juniper's twin."

"Yes," the lady says, refusing my hand. "the resemblance is...striking."

"So I've heard," I widen my eyes, hopefully as an invitation. "And you are?"

"Oh!" She laughs nervously but still doesn't take my hand.

Well this is incredibly awkward.

She doesn't meet my eyes when she replies, "I'm...I'm Tracey. We spoke on the phone. I didn't realize you'd actually come."

I frown. If coldness had a body, it would be Tracey.

She turns her attention to Dan.

"I need to get inside. We'll talk later?"

He nods before turning to me and Tracey walks up the steps into the building without a backward glance. Only then do I remember hearing about her. I squint my eyes in distaste as I watch her retreat. She actively makes Juniper's life a living hell. And...I think....do I remember Juniper telling me about suspecting her having an affair with the principal?

My brain is lost in thought when a voice at my side startles be back into the present.

"What are you doing here?"

"Hi," I blink and move my attention to Dan. I shift my weight so my outstretched hand is facing him now.

He rolls his eyes and limply shakes my hand.

Gross. Another thing our mother always taught us: don't trust men with a limp handshake. "Limp handshake, limp soul." She would tell us. Then she would smile a mischievous smile and shrug, "among other things, of course."

Juniper hated that rule.

Hates.

Shit.

I inconspicuously wipe my hands on my jeans and offer a smile.

"What's the latest?"

He looks at his watch for a brief second before throwing me a cursory glance.

"Nothing."

"Have you checked her car? I saw it in the parking lot. It's still here. That's weird, right? Maybe you could dust for finger-prints or something? I don't know." I'm rambling but I can't stop — the nervous energy is flying up and out of my mouth before I can censor anything.

"We could also check security tapes, see if she ever showed up yesterday. If her car is here....that means she had to have been here at one point, right?"

He chews the corner of his lip and rolls his eyes. "Sure. I don't know if I will find anything, but I can check it out."

"Okay. Because, it's just odd to me that her car is still here. Did she leave with someone? Someone doesn't just disappear."

"Some people do. Also, Sacred Heart doesn't have security cameras outside. They've never had a reason to, really."

My eyes widen in shock.

"They don't," I repeated, unsure I heard correctly.

Who doesn't have security cameras outside?

He avoids eye contact, kicking at a rock by his shoe.

"Nope."

I can tell by the gravel in his voice that I'm annoying him, but I don't care. I can feel my emotions gathering in my chest, threatening release. I don't know how to make him understand that this isn't Juniper. That something had to have happened.

"On my worst day in high school, I hitched a ride to Tijuana and didn't come back for three days. On Juniper's worst day, she came home and hid under her blankets for a week. She doesn't disappear."

He looks at me now, questions in his eyes that weren't there before. I keep pushing.

"Is it okay if I go into her classroom?"

He looks at his watch again, clearly wanting to get rid of me.

"Right now?"

I nod. "I know her schedule. Classes won't start for another 30 minutes. I just want to see if there's something that looks out of place." I pull at a strand of hair and twist it around my finger, suddenly nervous that he might say no. Never mind that I've never been in her classroom and so I couldn't necessarily find what's *out of place* — but I do know I would be able to spot something decidedly not Juniper. He squints off in the distance, thinking. Finally he shakes his head and waves me by as he starts walking toward the parking lot.

"It's not a crime scene. I can't stop you."

I'm already walking up the steps. I pause for a moment before walking in, noticing Dan making his way to the parking lot. He's either curious about her car or making his own disappearing act and leaving me to wander these halls alone. I turn back toward the double doors and take a deep breath. I recognize them from all of the videos Juniper's sent me. Not wanting to waste any more time, I step foot into the halls and look around.

I feel closer to Juniper than I have in days. Almost as if I walk where she has walked, I can conjure her presence through the footsteps left in the hallway.

"Ms.. Reese?"

I blink, realizing someone is talking to *me,* and turn toward the voice. It's a young man, his backpack flung over his shoulder haphazardly. When I catch his gaze he tries to hide the shock but it crosses his features in a flash.

"Hi," I respond. I offer a smile. "I *am* Ms.. Reese but probably not the one you're looking for — my name is Lavender."

He looks really confused now.

"I'm Steven."

"Hi, Steven. Listen..."

He chuckles, interrupting me. I stop talking, swallowing the question I was about to ask.

"This is weird. You look...you look *exactly* like her."

"Yeah. We're twins. Identical." I tilt my head, explaining the obvious. I feel like I need to go super slow with this man-boy standing in front of me and I'm completely lost as to how to handle logical explanations — or just a simple conversation — with him.

"Cool. I'm a twin."

I nod in encouragement.

"Oh, really? So you know how it is," I wave my hand in front of me, a cue that I really don't want to sit here and talk about this. "I'm actually looking for her classroom. Could you show me?"

"She's not here." His hand grips the strap of his backpack, the other hand dangles by his side holding a cell phone. He's still staring.

I start to sigh and then stop, not wanting him to see my frustration.

"I know. That's why I'm wanting to find her room. I'm thinking I might see something letting me know where she went."

He stares at me for a few more seconds before his sneakers start squeaking against the linoleum. I'm not sure if he's running away or leading me to her classroom, so I stay frozen for a moment, realizing how unsure I am of how to interact with teenagers.

"Follow me," he says, calling over his shoulder.

My lips push together and I raise an eyebrow. Right. I'm fairly certain by now that I would lose my ever-loving mind working with this age group every single day, not knowing what was going on in their heads at any given moment. As I shuffle my feet a few times to catch up with Steven, I consider the patience of Juniper and am thankful all over again for my advertising job back home.

Her classroom is empty when we get to the door, and I say a quick thanks to Steven who is muttering about needing to get to his first period study hall. I give a half wave as I walk through the threshold, and pause for a moment. I run back into the hallway.

"Hey Steven!"

I barely catch him before he turns the corner. He turns and looks at me, eyes wide.

"Yeah?"

I walk over to him, my arms crossed. "You said my sister wasn't here today."

He nods and glances around and I notice the students watching us and whispering to each other. It's clear he doesn't want to be anywhere near me, but I persist.

"How did you know?"

He bends his eyebrows together. "What do you mean?"

I widen my own eyes to match his and point in his direction. "You were walking in from outside when you called me Ms.. Reese. How did you know she wouldn't be here today if you had just gotten to school?"

He clears his throat and slightly takes a step toward the hallway behind him. "Uh. I don't know, miss...really. I just...I just said it. I don't know. She never misses and I knew she was out yesterday so I just thought once I knew you weren't her... she must be gone."

His circular logic might just send me over the edge. I roll my eyes and wave him off again and put his name in the back of my mind for later. Walking back into Juniper's room, I watch the groups of students pass me by and whisper.

Sorry, sis. You might have some damage control to do when you get back.

As soon as I walk into her room, though, I'm overwhelmed with the sense of Juniper that permeates the space. There's her diplomas — a BS from Brown University and the M.Ed. she received from Stanford. Next to it is a bulletin board full of pictures of her travels — Paris, Hawaii, the Alaskan cruise we took two years ago. We loved it so much we decided to extend our stay and turned the second half of the cruise into an Alaskan vacation. Memories come quickly. Her wanting to read in the hotel watching the snow fall while I wanted to hike, the quirky locals, the grizzly that roamed into the street as we were trying to make our way to the airport. I fight from grabbing the pictures for myself and focus on finding something that feels out of place. I walk to her desk and move the chair to sit. I grab a pen and twirl it in my hand, flipping through the calendar she has opened to Friday's date. There's nothing scheduled for that evening, but on Saturday she missed a hair appointment. The pen freezes mid-roll as I lean closer to read over the appointment again.

Juniper never misses her hair appointments.

I'm leaning back in the chair, staring out the window, when I hear footsteps. It's Dan. I look at him as he pauses in the doorway for a second before walking toward me, a toothpick dangling from his mouth. He pauses for a moment and points to something behind me. I turn to look and notice notes stuck to the whiteboard. Different sizes, some on sticky notes, some actual cards. WE MISS YOU! is scrawled next to them in dry erase marker. It's only been a few days and her students are creating a makeshift shrine. I wrinkle my nose at the thought, but am also touched by the display.

"Your sister was popular."

"Is," I correct. And then nod, a small smile playing on my lips. "She loves her job."

He clears his throat.

I swivel the chair back to face him.

"What."

I can tell there's something he's not saying.

"Did you find something in her car?"

He swallows for a moment before pulling something out of his pocket. It's a piece of paper. Something about it jolts a memory, but my brain is still so foggy I can't pull it into clarity. He's avoiding eye contact. When he begins talking, his voice is strained.

"Was Juniper stressed?"

The corners of my lip drop downward before I straighten my face, remaining stoic despite the panic rolling through my veins.

"As stressed as any teacher would be at the end of the year. Why?"

"You said on her worst day she came home and hid under her blankets for a week. Did she suffer from depression?"

I wait a moment before responding.

"No. Only when she found out our mother was dead." My breath catches at the end of the sentence and I pull my thumb up to my mouth and start gnawing at the cuticle. I wonder if I will ever be able to talk about it without crying — without wanting to run away so I can feel as if I'm not living in this skin without my mother for just a moment.

He looks down at a desk briefly before deciding to sit in it, and folds his hands in front of him. My nerves are at a peak right now trying to decipher his body language.

"Tracey mentioned she had a hair appointment on Saturday."

I look at him.

"How does she know that?"

He shrugs.

"Maybe they talk?"

I laugh. "My sister does not talk with...with her." I point toward the door and fight a look of disgust from crossing my face. "She had it in for Juniper from day one."

Surprise clouds his face for a split second before making a sound as if he's thinking. "I can still reach out to the salon. See if she made it."

"She didn't."

He looks at me.

"And you know...."

"She would have sent me a picture. She always sends me pictures when she gets her hair done." He looks at me with doubt and I shrug.

"I haven't heard from her since Friday. She didn't go."

"What about her relationship? Didn't you mention to me that she had recently ended things with her boyfriend?"

I nod. "Yeah." I flick my wrist as if throwing away the thought. "He got adamant about everything, gave her an ultimatum, and Juniper doesn't work with ultimatums. She ended things."

"How torn up was she about the break up?"

I laugh again. This guy.

"She wasn't. She and Simon are notoriously hot and cold, so for her this was the last straw." I remember the conversation we had that night — her exclamations at finally feeling free and able to live her life. My eyes widen.

"Oh. She said something about traveling to Morocco finally. Maybe she booked a ticket and left?"

Dan flicks his eyes toward me and then back down again.

"What are you trying to prove, detective? You obviously found something but haven't said anything about it."

"I didn't find anything about a trip to Morocco." He fingers the piece of paper in his hand. "But I did find this." He taps it against the desk and looks at me. "If I didn't know any better, I would say she wanted to disappear. For good. I've seen these kinds of notes in dorm rooms and households and offices where people were seemingly happy and loved their life and did a fantastic job hiding how they really felt until they just....couldn't anymore."

I blink.

You've got to be kidding me.

I don't know what scientific explanation there is for what

happens when identical twins are separated by death, but I imagine it has something to do with your molecular structure shifting into second gear. And if I listen hard enough, I can still hear the second beat to the rhythm of my heart. I know Juniper is still alive because I feel her.

A laugh escapes me and I bring my hand up to cover my mouth.

If you could only hear this guy talk, J.

"You okay?"

I cross my legs and shrug. "I'm fine. Juniper isn't dead."

He drums his fingers on the desk in front of him, a toothpick poking out of his mouth, bouncing up and down. He says nothing. I glance at the clock and realize we don't have very long before students start filing in, expecting to learn something about math.

"She was quiet, but even more so before she disappeared, had recently been through a breakup, didn't really have anyone close to her...."

I shake my head. Refusing to believe it.

"Assuming someone is upset or disappointed or sad or whatever from a note seems a lot like conjecture. Especially because you haven't even told me what it says." I hold out my hand, wrinkling my fingers for him to give it to me. I need to see it. I need to read what she wrote. He just looks at me, frozen.

"Let me see it."

He hands it over, and I grab the paper. Opening it up, something snaps free in my mind and I stare at the handwriting. It's not hers. It's not her handwriting. I breathe out relief while feeling a sense of curiosity and dread take over. It's not hers, but I know this handwriting.

I CAN'T TAKE IT ANYMORE.

That's all it says. It's another note with five words. I push aside the anger at their inability to care and their willingness to assume she ended everything over five words because there's something in the note I wasn't expecting.

"Wait," I breathe out.

The way the letters collapse over each other — I stumble for my bag where I shoved the other sheet of paper last night. I pull it out and shake it with my hand, motioning for Dan to grab it.

"There's-there's something here. I know it. She was getting notes. This has the same handwriting. I found it stashed in a compartment in her nightstand drawer."

Dan looks at me, his eyebrows bent inward. He reads the note I found and takes the note he found in Juniper's car, comparing them.

"They're definitely written by the same person," he says.

"Yeah. But who?"

He studies the pieces of paper again.

"You found this in her nightstand?"

"Yeah, it was hidden in a box where you keep valuables — I almost missed the latch until I went back and looked again. Why would she hide that? She didn't say anything to me about someone writing her..."

I need to talk to you....

Her words echo back to me and I pause. Is this what Juniper wanted to talk to me about on Friday? I push back the unease forming a brick in my throat as I remember the shadow that crossed her face in the Marco Polo message.

I need to talk to you...

She didn't get to me in time. Whatever these notes are, it's why she's gone.

"Are you with me, Lavender?"

I glance up at Dan. "Huh?"

He waves the plastic bags. "I said I needed to make a

meeting back at the office but I would take these with me and see what I can find."

I shake my head to free myself from the bad feeling that just snaked its way up my back, the uneasiness a smoke filling the spaces in my thoughts.

"Okay, thanks. Yeah."

I massage the back of my neck and manage a small smile before he turns and walks out of the classroom. I glance at my watch and realize I only have a few minutes before Juniper's students will begin filing into the room. I gather my things, my heart tripping over herself in my chest. Something is wrong. For the first time, I'm not just worried about finding Juniper. I'm worried about finding her alive.

3

I walk outside, checking my Lyft app to see if my driver is here. It's freezing. I pull my jacket closer to guard against the wind, running right into a chest that smells of sandalwood and smoke.

"Oh. Gosh. Sorry." I mutter, embarrassment coloring my cheeks. I avoid eye contact and move out of the way, but feel a hand wrap around my wrist. I freeze.

"Juniper?" I hear my sister's whispered name just as I am about to start ramming my knee into an unsuspecting crotch. Slowly, my heart starts beating normally from the rush of adrenaline when I was grabbed. For now, I appear safe. I turn and look at the face that belongs to the chest.

Up. I look up because this guy is so damn tall.

"No. Not Juniper. I'm her twin, Lavender." I pause. "You know her?"

His eyes blink in confusion for a moment before he remembers his hand around my wrist. He lets go and his face grows red.

"I'm so sorry. I thought..."

"We're identical down to the part of our hair and the freckle

on our left cheek. Trust me. It's common. Don't worry about it."
I brush the hair out of my eyes.

"You look...*so* much like her."

"I mean, if we're getting technical, she looks like me. I'm two minutes older. I'm sorry. Who are you?"

He shakes his head. "Right. It's Jasper. I'm...clearly not in my right mind. I saw Dan was here earlier and I wanted to catch him before he left. I saw you and thought I was looking at a ghost."

I nod in understanding. "Unless he stopped somewhere else on his way out, I'm pretty sure he left before me." I ignore him calling Juniper a ghost.

He twists his lip, turning his head and squinting toward the parking lot, probably looking for Dan's car. "I saw something between Juniper and one of her students. I thought maybe — possibly — it would help in some way."

I open the door behind us and motion for him to go first. "I guess we can check the office to see if he checked out before leaving."

So much for getting to his meeting on time, I think.

"He's probably talking with Tracey." He turns to watch me follow him in, the look of confusion still on his face. "Weren't you leaving?"

"No. Not if there's something you know that can help."

He raises an eyebrow. "Wait. Did you say your name was Lavender?"

"Yeah. Lavender Reese. Why?"

"And Juniper was your twin?"

"Juniper *is* my twin. And yes. Our mom had a thing with names."

He nods like that's all he needs to know, and I say nothing else.

Jasper, I think, following him back through the hallway leading to the office. *Jasper is an interesting name.*

.::.

Dan doesn't look happy to see us when we find him in the office, talking with Tracey. He squeezes his lips together and looks at her as if he's trying to find a way to escape. Dan glances at me before rolling his eyes and turning his attention to Jasper. I study the two men, noticing a vibration of energy that rolls between them. There's a familiarity here I don't understand. Both men are avoiding the other's gaze with laser-like precision.

"Dan."

"Jasper."

The look that passes between them is nothing short of tension and veiled masculinity. I roll my eyes. Yeah. They obviously know each other. But I don't have time for a pissing contest.

"Something tells me I'm going to miss this meeting." Dan's eyes catch mine and I hold his gaze before he sighs and motions for us to walk into a small huddle room.

"We ran into each other as she was walking out," Jasper explains. "I thought she was Juniper and–"

Dan interrupts. "I hate to be short but the district attorney doesn't appreciate being stood up." He takes a look at his watch. I want to ask him if this watch is new. If that's why he loves looking at it so much. I bite the words back. He looks bored and we haven't even said anything yet. Jasper tenses and I clear my throat.

I flick a finger toward Jasper. "He had something he wanted to share. I wanted to be here when he told you."

He sighs and looks at Jasper.

"What."

"I heard you were talking with teachers and you hadn't

reached out to me yet. I wanted to share something that might be useful."

"I hardly think you would know anything I haven't already heard, Jasper. We questioned a lot of her coworkers, but I didn't leave you out intentionally. I started talking with people this morning. Nothing came up. In fact, no one really knew her. She stayed to herself, never got involved, left early on occasion...."

I shook my head. "Left early?"

"...that's not entirely true." It's Jasper's turn to interrupt. "If by *left early* you mean the times she didn't go to happy hour with the team? Yes." He looks down and takes a breath before making sure he has Dan's attention.

"Look. I knew her. We were - *are* - friends. This isn't like her to just disappear." He pauses. "She was quiet because was new — and you know the teachers at the school. They're tight. They're not the easiest group to get acclimated with once you join staff. It took your wife how long once she got a position? I remember conversations we had where she struggled to feel as though she belonged."

Wait a minute.

"Your wife works at Sacred Heart?"

Dan sniffs and stands, putting his hands in his pockets and glancing out the window. He doesn't even acknowledge my question. He's so done with this conversation. With this investigation. Any second now he's going to walk around his desk and open the door, inviting us to leave. He looks at Jasper.

"Wait." I hold out my hand, demanding attention. Something isn't adding up for me.

Dan notices my confusion and rolls his eyes.

"Tracey is my wife."

"Well that's convenient," I mutter. But then I bite my tongue. Because if Tracey's married....my eyes widen and I look at Dan.

Oh. Oh he has no idea his wife was (is?) sleeping with someone else....

Dan, obvious to my reaction, continues.

"We focused our attention on those who might have been in contact with her the most." He waves his hand dismissively. "But I didn't get much more out of the them." He studies Jasper. "Unless you have something relevant."

"Did you speak with Principal Stahl?"

There it is.

Dan turns and looks at Jasper, his expression hard.

"No. Why. Should I?"

The tension in the room just elevated about 20 degrees.

Jasper shrugs.

"Maybe."

Dan squints his eyes and the vein in his neck juts out for a moment before he bites at the corner of his lip, twisting his jaw.

"Dan, listen...."

"Don't, Jasper."

I wrinkle my nose, "don't what?"

Jasper looks at me and then turns his attention to Dan again.

"You're doing it again. You're focusing your suspicions on everyone except Tracey."

"Jasper, I'm warning you."

"And I'm aware. But — what you're doing is only refusing to see the reality of the situation, which makes me wonder how well you're handling current cases. If you can't see the pattern of your own wife cheating, what makes me think you can connect dots for your clients?"

Oh.

I raise my hand and both men look at me.

"I mean, not to add fuel to the fire, but I know of rumors and I don't even live here?"

Dan's face darkens and he shakes his head, as if he doesn't

want to talk about it. Jasper gets the hint and leans back in his chair.

"Do you have anything *else* for me, Jasper?"

Jasper rests his elbows on his knees and studies Dan for a moment before continuing. "I overheard a conversation a few weeks ago. It was between Juniper and a student."

Dan leans against the back of his chair and crosses his arms. "I would assume teachers speak with their students all the time. What was different about this conversation?"

"They were talking about the capstone project due next week — him asking for an extension and Juniper refusing. They've had the entire year to work on this and we always get the stragglers at the end who want an exception. But then he said something I thought was strange. I walked in on the tail end of his comment so I don't have the full context, but I wanted to share just in case." He goes quiet for a second and turns to look at me. "He told her she couldn't ignore him forever."

I frown. "That could mean anything. She constantly deleted emails from students asking for extensions because she was explicit in her policy that due dates were final. No questions asked. Why was this different?"

"I don't know. She ended the conversation pretty quickly after that because she saw me walk in the door."

Dan sighs and waves his hand in our direction, effectively dismissing us. "Thanks for letting me know. I'll keep in touch if I have any other questions."

Jasper slaps his thighs and leans back into his chair like he's just getting settled in rather than preparing to leave.

"There's more. Before Juniper ended the conversation and walked away, I saw him slip a note into a pile of papers he gave her." He pulls something out of his pocket and drops it on Dan's desk. It's a folded piece of paper. I jump from my seat and grab it before Dan can get his hands on it.

I LIKED THE BLUE SWEATER BETTER.

My blood runs cold before I can even understand the implications. Dan reaches for it and I move my hand away from his. "No. You don't get this."

He holds out his hand. "If it's evidence, yes, I do."

I take a deep breath and hesitantly pass it over, watching Dan's reaction. He's so stoic and I feel my face heat up with anger. I need him to react. To show an element of surprise or something — anything that lets me know he is actually invested in this case.

I look at Jasper.

"Did you take this?"

He shakes his head. "She found it. We were at a coffee shop later that night working on some stuff for the gala and she pulled it out and read it — freaked out — and ran to the bathroom. The note fell when she got up, and I found it. When she came back to the table she wasn't wearing her sweater anymore. It was just the button up underneath."

"Was it blue?" I ask.

"No. It was red," Jasper says. "I asked her about it. She brushed it off as nothing, but she couldn't finish the meeting. Her hands were shaking the entire time, she was distracted, kept looking around like she was expecting someone. She left early."

Dan looked at him. "Did you tell anyone about this exchange?"

Jasper frowned and shook his head. "I mean, it was pretty recent and even though she was really shaken up about it, it slipped my mind. She was pretty adamant that it was nothing and I took her word for it."

He sighs and starts picking at the lint on his pants, lost in thought. I turn to Dan.

"This note has the same handwriting. This student was writing my sister notes. Why would he do that?"

Dan rubs his temple. "Jasper, do you know this student?"

He shakes his head.

"I would know him if I saw him, but when I say I walked in on the tail end of the conversation, I mean I wasn't really paying attention to who she was talking with — it was only after everything happened that I thought it might be important."

"If we could found others it might show a reasonable trace that points to a relationship or something between the two..."

I bristle.

"My sister wasn't involved with a student."

"I didn't say that."

"Well get it out of your head. Think of other possibilities. This is the second time you've jumped to conclusions about my sister. Juniper is a lot of things, but not someone who would get romantically involved with a minor."

"I can vouch for her too," Jasper says. "The conversation might have been awkward and weird, but it was not romantic. Looking back on it, Juniper was obviously uncomfortable and relieved when I walked through her door."

Dan studies him.

Jasper shrugs. "I just don't think we're looking at a sordid relationship here. She has a boyfriend."

"Had," I correct. Jasper looks at me in surprise. I offer a small smile. "They broke up again right before she disappeared."

He nods in understanding.

"Oh," I whisper, something else clicking into place.

I stand up and reach for my bag resting against the chair. Dan takes another look at the two notes side by side and places both back in the file on his desk. He looks up when I stand up suddenly and widens his eyes, expectant.

"I think I know the first place to look," I say.

Jasper folds his hands in front of him and leans back in his chair to see me.

"It's 11am. Juniper has a planning period now. And my sister has a whiteboard full of notes. If the mystery student left her another note, it would be there." I start walking out the door. "You can come if you want, but I'm headed to her classroom. There's about 100 notes to look through and I'm betting this kid left something."

.::.

They both decide to come. Dan reschedules his meeting with the district attorney. I try to refrain from making any jokes about him being the sponsor for a game of strategy.

It doesn't take long to find what we're looking for - within minutes I hear Dan mutter under his breath, trying to get to a note in behind two others sprayed with some kind of pink glitter.

"This is going to be all over me by the time we leave, isn't it?" he asks, wiping his hands on his jacket.

I laugh and mimic an explosion with my hands. "You look like a glitter bomb exploded all over you." I scan my finger up and down, pointing at his suit now covered in sparkling remnants of glitter. "You definitely look like you've had a hell of a night."

He scowls and reaches again for the gloves waiting for him on the desk, and then the note that caught his attention. Jasper and I lean in, trying to get a good look at what it says.

"It was the only one I saw in all caps. Made me think of the other ones." He pulls it off the wall with his plastic gloves and lowers it for us to see.

IF ONLY THEY KNEW.

I suck in a breath.

"Damn," Jasper whispers.

Dan slaps the note against his hand a few times, thinking. He's obviously concerned, and this makes me relieved.

Finally.

"Maybe she felt threatened and left without a trace to get away from whoever is pursuing her. Maybe she just needed to get away temporarily and with the stress, forgot to tell someone."

He pauses and looks at the notes again.

"I'll get my guys to look into this as soon as possible. I'll let you know if I need anything else." He dismisses us. Turns away and walks out the door, already on the phone, the note in a plastic evidence bag he brought in case we found anything.

I close my eyes in relief. Something substantial. I don't even know if it's worth anything, if it's truly a lead, but it's *something.* I open my eyes and look at the clock on the wall. It's almost 12:15. Nothing makes sense. My brain tries to grasp at the clues that we do have and nothing happens — just a blank space where the answers should be. I feel an exhaustion settle in my bones and find myself collapsing into one of the desks, resting my head on my arm.

No one warns you about the crazy-making urgency of looking for a loved one who has disappeared. It's only been a few days and still I am convinced Juniper will walk around the corner any moment, frustrated that we're in her space and questioning why we're freaking out about her brief vacation.

"I told you I was leaving." She would look at me in that way of hers, where suddenly I wonder if we really did share the same space — the same everything — for nearly 22 years.

"Oh." I would remember a conversation with clarity and then flush with embarrassment. "You're right. I forgot." I'd wave my hand, a *can you believe me?* type of gesture, and laugh it off.

That's just a twisted sort of fantasy though, a way my heart is handling this separation that feels more like an amputation. A make-believe world filled with stories of pretend. I don't know how to exist in this world without my sister taking up space next to me, and so I am creating one where she is still here. Still present. Still bossing the hell out of everyone around her and making me feel less like her identical twin and more like the forgotten and annoying little sister.

I rest my hands on my hips and roll my shoulders, feeling the knots constrict and separate. My stomach growls, a low murmur that grows exponentially. I grimace, realizing I haven't had anything to eat since the banana I grabbed from my kitchen yesterday afternoon.

I open my eyes and notice Jasper watching me from his perch against one of the desks.

"You okay?"

I blush a little, embarrassed by his concern.

"I'm fine. Don't you have classes or something?"

"I took a long weekend to prep for the gala. It was an agreement between Juniper and me. I would take today off and then she would take next Monday off to wrap everything up."

"Oh. Is it really that big of a deal?"

He laughs and rolls his eyes. "Like you wouldn't believe. Think prom times ten."

"Wow."

"Yeah." He rubs his face. "There's way too much money floating around here."

He pushes off the desk and stretches his arms above his

head, his shirt lifting just enough for me to get a peek of his stomach. I bounce my eyes away quickly.

"I'm starving."

"I don't think I've eaten in over 24 hours," I respond. I'm running my fingernail against a notch in the desk, avoiding looking in his direction. The air seems to have shifted in the last few minutes, and I can't place it. It's not attraction. I don't even know this person. Maybe it's just chemistry. But whatever it is, I'm not doing it. I shut down, waiting for him to leave.

"I was planning on grabbing some Mediterranean for lunch if you want to join. There's a decent place off Thayer St." He shrugs and keeps his face nonchalant.

I think for a moment.

"Yeah. Yeah food sounds amazing, actually. Do you mind driving?"

We make our way down the hall, and I tell myself it's just lunch — it's nothing — it doesn't have to be *something* because he's a guy and I'm a girl and we're going somewhere. I twirl my keys, trying to find something casual to talk about, when I feel like someone is watching us. I turn around suddenly, expecting to see someone following behind, but I only catch a brief shadow disappear around the corner by Juniper's door. I frown, craning my neck to see if I can catch any other movement.

Nothing.

"Everything okay?" Jasper's voice cuts through the silence and I can feel his breath on the back of my neck. I didn't realize he was so close and I jump.

So much for casual.

"Sorry," he says, stepping back.

"No. It's fine. I'm just...I thought I saw something. It's nothing."

But it's not nothing. I know it like I know the hairs still standing at attention on my neck and the way my insides bounce against each other, threatening a gag reflex. I try to stay calm and keep my hands from shaking, but it doesn't work. My nails leave indentations against the palms of my hands and I can feel a sheen of sweat gathering on my upper lip. I glance behind me again as we walk through the door outside, but there's nothing to prove what I know.

Someone is watching us.

I just wish I knew who.

4

I watch as they rummage through your things, my curiosity growing by the minute. What do they see? Has your smell lingered? The mix of cinnamon and mint that intoxicated me from the moment we met?

The detective picks something up from your desk and I bristle. He's going to ruin everything. I lean in closer, just a bit, so I can get a better view. I wish I could see what they were doing from my perch. One of them looks like that man who followed you around like a puppy — Jasper? I roll my eyes. I know you have something about names. I'm surprised his didn't turn you off in a millisecond. I half imagine his emotions to be just as porcelain as the stone from which his name comes from. And then there's this woman. Her frame feels familiar. I haven't been able to see her face though — but it feels as if I know her.

Do we know her?

They weren't supposed to know so quickly, but I guess it's a good thing they will understand soon just how much you and I belong together. How necessary it was for me to take you into safe keeping.

Keeping.

There's a strange word.

It's an action word meaning to own, maintain, or protect. I'd like to think that's what's happening with you and me.

Me, keeping you.

Me, owning you.

Me, protecting you.

Like a pet.

They leave your classroom and I fall back into the darkness so they won't see me, and that's when I see *her.*

My breath stops and the atmosphere turns opaque. For a moment, I forget to breathe. For a moment, I forget where I am and I begin walking toward her, thinking I must have seen an apparition. It can't be. I left you behind — safe, warm, sleeping in your new bed.

Beads of sweat pop up on my upper lip and I lick them gently, imagining, just for a moment, they are your tears.

Her tears.

She stops for a moment and turns around, looking right at me. I swear she sees me. I hold my breath, watching her expression for any indication that she can spot me in the shadows. Jasper asks her a question and her brows touch in confusion and she shakes her head slightly. She steps back and runs into him and her face blanches.

I smile. She knows. She sees what you didn't.

"No. It's fine. I'm just...I thought I saw something. It's nothing."

She turns around and rubs her hand against her neck before clinching her fists by her sides.

She felt me.

She knows I'm here.

My heart rate quickens and I blink back tears because *this* is what connection feels like, Juniper. I could power an entire city with the electricity coursing through my veins right now.

I can't wait to get back to you.

My entire world just expanded in a few moments and you are the only person in the world I can share this with — because your entire world is walking around Providence and I'm going to bring her to you.

I'm going to keep her. Just like you.

5

My stomach is still moving topsy turvy when we get to the restaurant, so I opt for grape leaves and pita chips instead of the falafel I was initially craving. We find a booth and I collapse against the leather backing. I don't even know if I will be able to finish this food. I'm not even hungry anymore.

I am just so. unbelievably. tired.

I finger a pita chip and dip it into the hummus, tasting the salt against my lips when I take a bite. Something ignites inside and I remember the hunger, my insides slowly settling from being spooked at the school. What remains is the constant nagging in the back of my brain.

Who was it? Who was following us?

The more I eat, the stronger I feel. The more *present* I feel. I begin to notice the heaviness of my limbs and how much it takes to simply exist in the moment. I need a break, but there is no such thing. Not now. The emotional weight I've been carrying since Juniper disappeared is finally taking its toll. The only thing I want to do is crawl into bed and fall asleep forever. Instead, I blink against the heaviness of my eyelids and try to focus on Jasper. I begin to notice him for the first time. The way his hair curls into a Q on the right side of his forehead, the muscles in his shoulders flexing and contracting when he rearranges himself in the booth, the way his tongue reaches for his food before his mouth does.

No.

I choke on some rice and take a swig of ice water.

He looks up, startled. He moves to reach for me then decides not to, his hand hanging in mid air before dropping by his plate.

"You okay?"

Not here. Not now. Focus, Lavender.

I nod and hold up a finger, motioning for him to wait while I chug down my distraction.

"Wrong pipe," I sputter before I take another sip. He nods, satisfied.

The last thing I need is to feel any sort of curiosity or attraction toward Jasper. I sigh, content that I'm not going to cough any more, and place my hands in my lap, tangling my fingers together in an attempt to make them behave because what I *really want to do* is reach for that curl against his forehead.

"So how close are you and Juniper?"

There. A safe topic. Juniper.

He takes a bite of his tabouleh. "We've definitely gotten closer since the beginning of this year. With her teaching Pre-Cal and Statistics, we see each other a lot."

"What do you teach?"

"AP Literature."

I blink. He laughs.

"I know. I don't look like your standard English teacher."

He doesn't. Although, I don't have much to measure against. I look at what he's wearing: skinny grey jeans, a black fitted turtleneck, and a jean jacket rolled with precision.

"I admit. When I think of English teachers I think of cardigans and loafers. Maybe, if they're forward-thinking, an occasional tattoo based on literature."

Jasper laughs, and I notice the way his face wrinkles around his eyes, framing the sea of green. I feel a jolt of electricity — a reminder — *you are sitting with this man because your sister is gone.* And yet, I feel pulled to know more.

He twists his arm to show me the skin under his elbow. Written in type-like font is the word *timschel.*

"Thou mayest," I respond.

He nods. "One of my favorite books. I guess I fit your forward-thinking stereotype."

I manage a smile.

"At least it's not Vonnegut. Then you'd just be cliché."

He spreads his hands wide in surrender. "So it goes."

I offer a small smile.

"What made you decide to teach English?" I ask.

"What made your sister decide on math?"

I hate when people answer a question with a question, but I give him this one. I breathe for a moment before answering.

"Curiosity," I manage. "Curiosity and an insatiable desire to help."

He wipes his mouth with a napkin. "I can see that. She's always finding ways to get the students move involved with the content. Senior year is hard — especially spring semester. All signs point to graduation and the malaise sets in deep." He tilts his head dismissively. "But we were the same, right? At least I was — I couldn't wait to graduate and get the hell out of town."

I shrug. "I definitely had my moments of fear, but yeah, I was ready to move on for sure. Did you study English in college?"

"Literature and Creative Writing," he answers. "If I could do anything, I would be writing screenplays. And I dabble in it a little on the side. My grading stacks multiply like bunnies though, so I don't get as much time as I would hope. Especially being the sponsor of the chess club."

I almost spit out an olive.

"The *chess club*?!"

He frowns.

"Prime example of the newbie being dropped into clubs no one wants to take responsibility over — your sister found herself a sponsor for Pokemon loyalists. Did she tell you that? It nearly drove her insane before another teacher decided to step in because he was legitimately interested. I thought for sure she would take Steve or Scott or whatever his name was up on his offer to join his company."

I laugh and then pause.

"Simon asked her to join his company?"

He stops mid chew. "She didn't tell you? I think it's why they ended up breaking it off initially. He never got over her unwillingness to leave the school. Said teaching was wasting her brilliance." He rolls his eyes.

I look out the window. Juniper had mentioned nothing about Simon offering her a role at his company, but she had said plenty about how proud he was of the capital gained for his tiny start up — within six months he would be the CEO of a cloud-based security company that went from ten employees to over 200.

"She's one of those people who wouldn't be able to take what she's good at and make a fortune, like working in finance or something for a massive corporate company. Even a smaller company, like Simon's, would be like pushing an ice pick into her brain. She wouldn't last." I take a strand of my hair and wrap it around my finger, remembering conversations I had with Juniper about her decision to go into teaching.

"Her teaching math was more about the students than it was about the subject matter, really. She could have taught anything. She chose this because she's one of the few people who find it intriguing." My lips turn upward and a small laugh escapes me and I think about her sitting on the couch, watching *Stand and Deliver* wrapped in a blanket with tears running down her cheeks.

"She wanted to be her very own version of Jaime Escalante."

"Wanted?" Jasper asks, tentatively.

My heart stops.

"Wants," I whisper. "She *wants* to be her own version of Jaime Escalante." My fingers hover above my lips, afraid of what might come out if I'm not careful. "I need sleep."

Jasper turns around and grabs a to-go box from the table of supplies behind our booth. Grabbing my unused fork, he begins taking my food and packing it up.

"What are you doing?" I look at him in shock.

He points at me with the fork. "You're done. You're going back to Juniper's place. You're going to walk through the door, put this in the fridge, and collapse into bed." He focuses again on packing the food before taking another look at me. "You're exhausted. I've known you for like two hours and I can see it plain as day."

I gape. Literally. Gape. My mouth flies open and I have no words. I watch as he pulls a pen out of his pocket and writes something on the box before handing it to me.

When I look down, I see his number and a note.

"In case you need anything," he mumbles, his ears turning red around the edges.

"Thanks," I croak. I'm blushing now. I feel the heat creep its way across my cheeks and temples and I make a quick escape, not even saying goodbye before I realize with absolute mortification that he was my ride to the restaurant and mentioned he would drive me home. I feel like a middle schooler, and I'm suddenly angry at how adorable Jasper acted when he gave me his phone number. I walk back into the restaurant to see him still sitting at our booth, glancing around awkwardly.

"Um. Are you still willing to give me a ride?"

He nods and, without saying a word, gets up from his seat and motions me to his car. I throw my bag and the box of food in the back seat, nearly knocking both over onto the floorboard. My phone pings and I see it's a Calendar invite for something at work. I don't even care. I decline quickly, reminding myself to send a follow-up email later.

Who am I kidding? It's already 3pm. *Later* means tomorrow, most likely. Any anger I felt has dissipated into a shaky exhaustion and I'm fighting to stay awake as we drive the route back to Juniper's cottage by the sea in silence, hoping against all logic that she'll be waiting for me when I get there.

.::.

I wake up to the sound of my phone. I nearly fall off the bed trying to disconnect it from the charger. I have that heart-racing-from-being-woken-up-suddenly feeling and I take a shaky breath before answering.

"Juniper?"

The line goes silent.

"Hello?"

"Um. Hi. Sorry, Lavender. It's Jack."

I move the phone away from my ear for a moment so I can tap it against my forehead in frustration. Of all the calls I had to answer. It's Jack. My ex.

"Oh. Hi."

"...did I wake you?"

"Yeah. I uh...I thought you might be someone else."

Translation: *I really wish I wouldn't have answered this call.*

"Sorry about waking you." I can hear the noise of the street and I know he's walking into work. I check the time on the clock hanging on the wall and raise an eyebrow.

It's 10am. I can't remember the last time I slept this late — or this long. All I remember from yesterday is collapsing into bed after Jasper dropped me off with the reminder to sleep. I rub my face, trying to shake the grogginess out of my brain.

"Well it's too late and I'm up so...what do you need?"

He pauses at my tone and I roll my head, stretching my neck and feeling the muscles waking up. I can't hold on to his feelings right now.

"Jack?"

"Yeah. Uh. Sorry. I was just checking in with the proposal for Stephanie from IronClad. I know everything is happening with your sister, but do you have it?"

"Stephanie should have the edits in her inbox. I sent the mock-up to her yesterday."

"Oh."

I roll my eyes.

He continues, slightly clearing his throat. "So uh....how is your sister? Have y'all found her?"

Translation: *I'm asking about your sister. I can't remember her name, but I'll still appear thoughtful. Also, I want to know if you're there with anyone, even though I know your sister is the only family you have left, so I will subtly include this within my questions.*

"No, Jack. *We* haven't found her yet."

It's suddenly clear that Jack calling doesn't have anything to do with Stephanie from IronClad missing her project. I lean my head against the wall behind me and massage my face with my hands. Relentless. He was *relentless.*

The worst of it? He never wanted to call me when we were together. For three years, I was the one chasing him. And then he decided he wanted to chase Chloe, and that was that. Juniper was ready to fly out and go Carrie Underwood on his ass, but Chloe ended up turning him down and since then, he's been trying to rectify his mistake.

Relentlessly.

"Oh. Babe. I'm so so-"

"Jack."

"Yeah?"

"I need you to not call me anymore."

"You're on my team, Enny. What am I gonna do? Just ignore you not being here?"

My lips curl in disgust. God I hate that nickname. It doesn't even make sense.

He lets out a small laugh like he can't believe he's even having to explain. "I just wanted to get an update to make sure we're on track and to make sure you were doing alright."

I ignore his feeble attempt at sympathy.

"Stephanie is taken care of — next time use email. Or get someone else to call and check in with the status of the proposal. Anyone but you, Jack."

"Ouch."

"Yeah, well. Apparently you didn't get the hint the last few times. You broke up with me, remember? You can't keep doing this. And please....stop calling me Enny. That's not my name."

"Whatever, *Lavender*." I heard him swipe in to the office and knew he'd be getting off the phone soon. He might be trying to fix what he did with me, but that didn't change the fact that he also wanted Chloe to know he was still interested if she ever changed her mind. And chatting with me on the phone would not fit that profile.

"I need to go."

"Yeah. Sure. Thanks for keeping me updated on the profile. I'll need you to send those edits as soon as possible. We're already running late and Stephanie isn't the most patient person to work with here."

I shake my head. Unbelievable.

"Tell Chloe hi, will you?"

I hang up on him and throw my phone across the room, waiting for the satisfying *thunk* of it hitting throw pillows agains the wall. I bury my head in one of the pillows and scream. And then, out of nowhere, Juniper's voice fills my head.

"It must be his name. It's so...ordinary."

And then I laugh.

It was always Juniper who got me through breakups in high school and college. We would turn on something breathtakingly weepy and sit on the couch, tissues and chocolate and vodka and ice cream and an assortment of junk food between us, and we'd cry and laugh and eat until we were punch drunk on both food and alcohol.

"Mourn him tonight," she would say. "Celebrate tomorrow."

And we would. We always did. And it always worked.

Thanks for the reminder, I think to myself.

When I finally convince myself to get out from under the covers, I'm surprised by how frigid the air feels. It has a sharpness to it, like when you put your hand in the freezer for ice and cut your finger on the edges. I walk to the window, grabbing my phone face down on one of the pillows below, and check for damages. The screen is still intact. Good.

I look outside and watch the seagulls dive bomb the water, looking for food. The waves are almost still. Even the ocean is still hibernating while the last tendrils of winter hang on for as long as possible and the April sun tries to push out any last remnants of frost. I stretch for a moment, allowing my body to produce its own version of sun salutation. Only then, as I'm bending down to grab my toes, do I see the folded piece of paper stuck underneath the window.

I pause, my back parallel to the floor. Snapping back up to attention, I push the curtains aside and pull the window open, grabbing the paper before it flies away with the wind. At first, I think it's Juniper's doing. Maybe her screen was uneven, maybe she put it under there on purpose to keep the window shut. Our mom would do similar things growing up in our small apartment. But this paper is too new. I can tell by the lack of crease in the fold.

By the time my fingers work to unfold the note, my hands are shaking. I stretch the paper and notice a picture of Jasper and me, taken through the window at the Mediterranean restaurant. What? How in the world...this was yesterday.

But then I know. Without a doubt, I know where this note comes from. I feel my knees weaken and I reach behind me for the bed, easing myself down on the mattress.

My eyes fall to the words written underneath and my blood turns frozen.

STOP LOOKING. YOU WON'T FIND HER.

6

My hands fly to my mouth in shock, the note falling to the floor. I trip backward, landing on the bed. My breath comes in short gasps as I reach for my phone. I keep looking around me, expecting someone to be watching me — waiting. It's a surreal feeling to have the brightness of day surrounding you and yet feel as though a darkness is permeating your vision. I growl in frustration as I try and navigate through my phone. It shouldn't be this difficult to send a text and yet I keep opening up the wrong application.

My movements are robotic. My vision begins to blur at the edges, making it hard for me to focus. I keep trying to blink it away, but it only makes it worse. I finally give up, the tears threatening again. My hands are shaking too much. I hold the phone close to my chest, breathing deep. I can't help Juniper if I hyperventilate. I close my eyes for half a second, trying to collect myself. I remember what's true: I need help. I can't be here alone. Someone is clearly watching me.

My pulse jumps at that last realization. Someone *is* watching me. I think about yesterday, in the school hallway, thinking someone was watching us as we left.

He was there too.

I inch off the bed, wincing at the sun blinding me from her window as I stumble into the kitchen. I feel drunk — the initial adrenaline is beginning to dissolve and all that's left is lack of basic motor function and shaky limbs. I open the fridge and find what I'm looking for — Jasper's number is scrawled on the to-go box from the Mediterranean place. I'll text him first.

Got another note. This time for me.

I snap a picture of the note and send that along with my text. That should do it. I pull up Dan's number next, my fear and surprise slowly turning into a boiling anger. Jasper responds immediately that he's on his way and I send him the address, assuming he's never been here.

Before I can send the message to Dan, I feel my phone buzz. It startles me. I grimace automatically, thinking it's Jack calling me back. He's known for waiting five or ten minutes and calling me again, thinking that is ample time to "calm me down" and "get me into a rational state of mind."

"What."

My voice comes out short and angry. I'm still trembling. I don't have time for this.

"Lavender?"

It's Dan.

"Oh thank God. I was just about to text you. I —"

"Hey, listen," he interrupts me.

Something in his voice makes me pause. I forget about the note and place my hand on my chest.

"What. What did you find."

"There's a body, Lavender. They found a body. Can you— can you come identify whether it's Juniper or not?"

The world splits in two.

Air rushes out of me and I can't speak. The phone drops out

of my hand and I'm frozen in place, the breathing becoming more and more labored as I wait for the fracture to hit. When it doesn't, I look around to try and figure out this new landscape I've found myself in without my sister.

She's gone.

She's not gone.

She's gone.

She's. Not. Gone.

I swallow the scream threatening and shake my head. I refuse to believe this. Even though it feels as if I'm walking through a tunnel, I manage to reach down and grab my phone, my hands shaking so bad I can hear the way it scratches my cheek as I try to find words.

"It can't-it can't be her."

"Juniper's ID was found on the body."

I couldn't swallow. The lump in my throat pressed in on all sides and I let out a choked sob.

"That's impossible," I whisper.

He sighs.

"Lavender, I know this is hard. I'm sorry this is happening over the phone, too. I get it. Frankly, it's not what I want to be doing either. I wish all of my cases ended in a clear cut happen ending. But in order to move forward, can you please come in and take a look at these pictures? If necessary, we'll head to the morgue for final identification." He grows silent and then clears his throat. "I know you're not from here, but is there anyone you can bring with you? Make it easier?"

I can't believe this is happening.

"Jasper is on his way," I manage.

"Good. Have him bring you."

I barely get out an agreement before he hangs up the phone, clearly done talking with me. I groan in frustration and toss the phone on the couch.

"Fuck you very much, detective," I mutter under my

breath as I nervously throw my hair up into a bun. I pace back and forth from the kitchen to the living room. At any other moment, I would be admiring the interior design of the architecture and the way Juniper's style has permeated every single space. A massive leather couch is the centerpiece of the room, resting on top of two stacked rugs thrown criss-cross on top of each other. The walls are filled with large-print photographs and wall hangings, and if you look close enough, you can see the rhythm Juniper used to create the flow of the gallery.

I wouldn't be surprised if she had a mental x/y slope to complete the look, making sure the spacing was perfectly even. I pause for a moment in front of a picture of us two back in San Jose. I remember this. We'd just graduated Brown and were on our way to Stanford. She went for Education — Learning Design and Technology specifically, and I got in for International Policy Studies.

She finished the program. I...did not. Mostly because of Jack. I feel a sting of something akin to *regret* and *wonder* and swallow it down before I make myself start questioning every single moment of my recent history. The years after this photo were not the greatest for me.

But this photo — this photo brings back good memories.

We're on the beach, arms draped over each other. We're at a bonfire, our legs resting on the sand, our skin glistening from a day in the sun. Our mouths are hanging open and we're looking at each other laughing. After this photo was caught, Juniper leaned in and rested her head on my shoulder. I feel the space next to me quiver from her absence and I close my eyes.

Juniper. Help me out here. Where are you?

I snap my eyes open and look toward the window in the living room. I think I hear a car driving, but I see them pass the house and know it isn't Jasper or Dan. I grip my phone and begin tapping the bottom against my open palm. I start pacing again and think about what I know.

1. The person sending the notes knows where Juniper lives.
2. The person could possibly be a student, given what Jasper saw.
3. The person wrote a note after she disappeared, leaving it for her (us?) on her whiteboard.
4. They also know we're looking for her.
5. They're following me.
6. There's a body with her ID.

I STAND THERE FOR A MOMENT, frozen. If I'm not careful, I can forget every molecular connection I have with Juniper. If I'm not careful, I can immediately assume that she's gone forever — that based on historical evidence of my life, it would only make sense that this body they found would be her. I suck in a quick breath.

I know this isn't true. I know it like my own breath.

Growing up, Mom used to always tell us, "be still and know, girls. Cause you will always know. Your gut is golden and you get your intuition from your mama. Trust it above all else. She'll always tell you the truth."

For a few moments, I let myself grow still. I listen for that knowing I've come to rely on — the same knowing that sent Juniper to Providence without her even realizing it was what was propelling her to go. The hairs on my neck stand at attention and I allow a small smile. She's alive.

I still feel her, somewhere, inside of me.

I hear something behind me and it breaks me from my

trance. Turning, I see Jasper pull into the driveway and run to the front door. I move to open it for him and motion him inside. He takes one look at me and furrows his brow.

"What is it?"

"We need to meet Dan at the station."

.::.

I FILL Jasper in on the way, and like me, he refuses to believe we're actually about to identify Juniper.

"There's no way."

"I know."

"So they just found a body and assume it's her?"

I clear my throat, still trying to figure out this next piece of information.

"Apparently she uh...she had Juniper's ID on her."

Jasper makes a face and shrugs. "Police plant shit on people all the time. That tells me nothing outside of wondering how the hell they got her ID in the first place."

I nod in agreement, staring out the window at coastal scenery I would normally enjoy.

"Another thing — he called you? What if this was actually Juniper? How is this even remotely caring for the people you're supposed to be guiding through traumatic events? Does he just expect family members to hop in a car and be okay with driving themselves to identify a body? Jesus. This is so messed up. All of it."

"From what I've read, usually family members are not surprised when they get this call."

Jasper rolls his neck and blinks through a twitch in his left eye. I've gotten to know this look in the last 24 hours. He's worried.

I pinch the skin on my throat, fighting the way it's pushing against me — threatening tears at any moment. I do not want to cry. I catch Jasper's fingers tapping on his knee, a forced rhythm, and wonder just how much this is impacting him. I drop my hands, inspecting my nails, and wish for the thousandth time I could wake up from this nightmare.

"Let's just get this over with," I whisper to no one in particular.

Jasper doesn't even respond.

We drive the rest of the way in complete silence, each of us in our own world of worst-case scenarios, regardless of what truth we know. It's the nature of the beast we're currently fighting, and right now, it's kicking our ass.

When we get to the station, Jasper pauses for a moment before turning off the car. He looks at me and we communicate without a sound.

I set my jaw with determination.

It's not her. It's not her.

Walking in, he grabs the hand that's shaking at my side and I squeeze his fingers briefly before letting go. Dan meets us in the lobby and glances around us instead of at us. This irritates me. I twist my lips and fight whatever sarcastic comment is threatening to escape. The *least* he can do is provide some eye contact. I can't even think straight right now and he's refusing to connect with us in any way.

He takes us to a room in the back and invites us to sit down. I look around, surprised I don't see one of those two-way mirrors somewhere. It's just as stale as you expect though, and when another officer quietly asks if we would like some coffee, I consider the sludge most likely percolating somewhere. I shake my head.

"Water's fine."

They leave us in the room for a few moments, and Jasper places his head in his hands.

"Fuck," he whispers.

I rest my hand on his back for a second before lifting it, realizing it might be too much or too awkward.

"I hate small rooms like this. No air." He leans back in his chair and fans himself with his shirt. "Never thought I would feel as if I were the one being questioned here," he says quietly. I laugh under my breath, hearing the sarcasm in his tone. Before we can say anything else, the door opens and Dan walks in with my water bottle. When he hands it to me, I see the envelope under his arm. My skin turns to ice.

Regardless of what I think about Juniper, there is a body. Somebody's body. Somebody's daughter. Possibly mom. Someone loves them and would feel the hole from their absence for the rest of their life. The water soothes the nails suddenly in my throat and I swallow to keep the bile down.

I do not want to look at this body.

Dan sits across from us and for the first time, looks us in the eye.

"First of all, I know this isn't easy."

The heat rushes to my chest and I can feel my breath quicken.

"It's more than just *not easy,* detective. It's excruciating. It's terrifying. It's exhausting. It's devastating. You can't just sum this up with a simple adjective like everything will suddenly make sense. Nothing makes sense right now. My sister is missing and you're about to show me the body of someone I fully believe belongs to someone else."

Dan rubs at his chin and nods. "I know. You're right. I did minimize the impact there and I'm sorry. It was an awkward way of opening up this process. It's not like you see on television. I'm not going to take you to some back room where our forensics team works and you're able to pull back a sheet and say yes or no. That's not taking care of you as an individual. This body has had some significant violence done to it, and so these pictures are taken specifically of markers that you would recognize if she were your sister."

Jasper grabs my hand.

"I can't just look at the face?"

Dan pauses, "....not for this case, no."

His words land heavily and I hold back a sob, realizing it's because the face is unrecognizable. I place my free hand over my mouth and nod. I can do this. I have to do this. I have no choice. It's the only way we're going to be able to move forward and actually find Juniper. I watch as he pulls the pictures out and lays them on the table in front of us, face down. There are five of them. My innate curiosity immediately begins to wonder what could possibly be identifying on these photos? How can you break down an entire life into five snapshots?

"I want you to take your time here. You do not need to turn these over immediately. I'm going to give y'all some space to look through them — at your discretion — and will wait for you outside in the hallway."

He waits for us to acknowledge him and then offers a small smile before getting up and walking toward the door. Right before he opens it, he stops and looks back at us.

"Oh and, we have grief counselors ready to talk if you need anything."

With that, he opens the door and disappears into the dimly lit hallway.

Jasper and I are in silence again, the pictures mocking us from the table.

"I feel like we're about to play Memory with someone else's life," Jasper whispers.

"We just have no idea who the matching tile belongs to, huh?" I counter as he fingers the edge of one of the photos.

I know, intrinsically, this is going to need to be like a

bandaid. Rip it all off quickly, turn the photos over and figure out what I'm actually looking at here. I take a deep breath and before I can second guess myself or talk myself out of it, I reach for the squares and flip them right side up. My breath catches without warning. Jasper gasps in shock and I feel him tense next to me.

The photos are indirect.

A finger.

A thigh.

Some hair.

A foot.

Immediately, I know it's not Juniper. The finger has a huge diamond on it — an engagement ring it looks like. The thigh has a massive tattoo of a diamond full of wildflowers. The hair is curly — curlier than Juniper or I have ever been able to manage to keep ours. And aside from the scratches from what look like a run on asphalt due to the debris and dirt left behind, there's a birthmark shaped like a checkmark on the foot.

None of it belongs to Juniper. We both exhale in relief simultaneously, collapsing in on ourselves with the weight of this.

"It's not her," I whisper.

Jasper shakes his head and tries to talk but can't at first. He takes a moment and clears his throat.

"It's not."

Both of us grow silent though as we notice the last photo. I turned it over so quickly it slid away from the others so we didn't notice it at first.

"Holy shit," Jasper chokes out.

I can't say anything. My hands grab at my elbows and I pull them in toward my middle, protecting me from some unforeseen monster. There on the last square, Juniper stares back at me. Whoever this is, they really did have her ID.

7

"It's not her."

I haven't even opened the door all of the way before the words escape from my mouth. I couldn't get out of the room quick enough once Jasper and I realized the body didn't belong to Juniper.

Dan looks up at me in confusion and then shock.

"It's not? Are you sure?"

"She wasn't engaged, she hates tattoos, on a good day her hair is wavy at best and her birth mark is not on her foot. It's on her cheek." I point to my own clear skin. "It's how people are able to tell us apart," I add.

"This isn't good."

I scoff. "I don't know captain, I think it's pretty damn good news myself, but who am I shitting? It's only my sister." My voice is dripping with sarcasm, but I can't help it. I'm so done with his inability to hold an emotionally intelligent conversation.

"Lavender, of course it's a good thing this isn't Juniper. But now I have even more of a shit show on my hands because if this isn't your sister, then how the *fuck* did she get her ID? That's why this isn't good."

I stand there, silent, and feel Jasper walk up behind me. Without thinking, I find myself easing my way back to rest against his chest. It's comforting. And he doesn't stop me, so I stay, feeling only slightly guilty for jumping at Dan before getting more information.

"What this tells me is that someone must have planted her ID on the body, which begs the question how this person *knew* there would be a body to deflect our attention."

He dropped his face in his hands and groaned.

"Meaning, Lavender, your sister's disappearance is most likely not an isolated incident."

Chills race across my skin.

"What do you mean? Do you mean this person could have been kidnapped and killed by the same person who has Juniper?"

Dan lifted his head and looked at me.

"Yes. That's what I mean."

I drop my hands to my knees then, suddenly finding it hard to breathe. How do people survive these moments over and over and over again? How do you continue to keep moving when the walls keep pressing in? I feel Jasper's hand on my back and it steadies my breathing some. His voice cracks against the silence.

"Did anyone happen to find notes on this victim by chance?"

I startle.

Notes.

I had completely forgotten about the note I found this morning. I straighten and look at Dan.

"That reminds me. We need to talk. I got a note."

His eyes widen.

"You were going to tell me this when?"

"When you called and told me there was a probability Juniper's body was found. I was texting you when I got your call."

"Fuck, Lavender. You still coulda told me."

"If I recall, you hung up on me pretty quickly after finding out I agreed to come identify the body."

He blinks a few times before leaning back in the chair, resting his head against the wall.

"Where is it?"

"At the house."

He slaps his knees and stands.

"Guess we're going back home."

I throw my hands up in the air in frustration and follow Dan who is already walking down the hallway toward the exit. "Fine," I call out behind him. "But we're stopping for food on the way. I'm starving."

.::.

Dan texts me on our way back to Juniper's house.

I'll be there soon. Need to stop at the house to help the wife with something. DON'T DO ANYTHING STUPID.

I roll my eyes and show Jasper, who laughs.

We decide on a local crab-shack for lunch and call ahead of time. Jasper drops me off at the house on his way to pick up the food and I walk through the front door, an odd mix of relief and foreboding filling my senses.

I'm relieved because my intuition yet again proved on target. Juniper is still alive.

And yet, the implications of who is behind this grow by the

minute and leaves me speechless with the severity. Who would be capable of something like this? I felt like I was a character in the episode of *Criminal Minds* and half expected Derek Morgan to walk around the corner any minute. I raise an eyebrow.

Not that I would mind.

An idea begins to form in my head and before I can talk myself out of it, I grab a sheet of paper and start writing. I step back for a moment, reading over what I wrote.

Where is she?

I fold it identical to the first note and walk back to the window, putting it on the opposite side. I step back and bite my thumb. I know this is stupid. I know it in my marrow. This is exactly what Dan was talking about in his text and to give him credit, he must know me better than I originally thought.

But.

If this person is following me as closely as I think they are, I might as well say hello. Right? Start a dialogue? Force their hand, so to speak?

"Where's Spencer Reid when you need him," I mutter under my breath before sealing my fate and leaving the note on the windowsill.

What's done is done.

I hear someone at the door and peek my head around the corner to see Jasper's head in the window. He sees me and waves. I wave back and make my way to the front door, letting him in and noticing Dan pulling up right behind him. He gets out of his car and throws Jasper a look as he buttons his jacket.

"You didn't happen to get enough for all of us, did you?"

Jasper opens his mouth and looks at me for help.

"Actually Dan," I offer, "we only got two poboys, but I would never be able to finish this so I'll give you some of mine."

He grunts and walks past us, scoping out the living room.

Jasper catches my eyes and we twist our lips to keep from laughing.

"Where's the note?" Dan asks, looking around and oblivious to my conversation with Jasper. Every once in a while he'll pick something up randomly, looking underneath it.

"Well. Not under the flower vase." I laugh, walking to the folded piece of paper on the counter. I hand it to him and he looks at it.

"If he's following you," Dan says, "then he more than likely has this place bugged in some way."

I feel stupid for laughing, for thinking he was looking for another note in random places. Bugged? Juniper's house?

"For real?" I choke, suddenly uneasy. It's not that I've had conversations I wouldn't want others to know about; I haven't really had any time to do anything other than collapse into bed after searching for Juniper all day. But the thought of someone tapping into this space to watch or hear what was going on at all times has me....spooked. Spooked and angry all over again. "Shouldn't you have told me this before y'all left me alone just now?"

Dan turns and looks at us.

"I knew nothing about you being left alone."

Jasper sits on the couch, crossing his legs and spreading his arms across the backend of the cushion. Now that we're past the initial drama of today, it's like I'm noticing him for the first time. He's wearing cut-off jeans today that hit right above his knee. His t-shirt has the moon phases stacked on top of each other. When he spreads his arms, the muscles flex and I see that tattoo on his forearm take on a life of its own.

"She was alone for maybe five minutes and I was a cell phone call away," he says. "How would someone have access to this place anyway? And if it's bugged, how long do you think it's been going on?"

He looks at Dan and waits for an answer. I force my eyes to bounce from his legs back to Dan.

"Well. I'm not saying it's a definite." He looks at both of us while putting the note in a plastic bag he brought inside with him. "If we do find anything here, we'll need to probably come back and do a more thorough search." He looks directly at me and I nod my agreement. "Then we're talking about someone with a lot more maturity and depth than we initially thought. This is someone with intent and habit."

I lean against the counter, frustrated. My head falls into my hands and I try to breathe but am unsuccessful. I end up massaging my temples, my eyes roaming to a thread of something hanging out of the trashcan in the pantry. I walk over to get a better look and find a sweater in the trash.

A blue one.

I pull it out, the fabric barely between my finger and thumb. I feel my heart drum in my ears.

I know this sweater.

A few months before she moved, Juniper splurged on these sweaters. It was the first time she'd been even remotely spontaneous with her money. Always cautious, always logical — she had almost a full year's salary saved. We'd gotten into a huge fight about it because it was so shocking to me. A few weeks later, she told me she was moving.

I take a deep breath. For her to have thrown this away, after everything, she had to have been spooked. My gut drops with fear.

I will not fall apart here. I won't.

I sniff, wiping my cheeks and motioning for Jasper to look at me, my hand shaking.

"The note."

Jasper looks from me to the sweater and his eyes go wide.

"Oh, shit."

I nod and look at Dan, studying the sweater still in my hands.

"Do you remember? The note Juniper got from the student before her meeting with Jasper? It mentioned something about liking her in the blue sweater." I lift my hand, holding the fabric. "This one."

I start pacing the living room, looking under the cushions and underneath vases and inside lamps.

"Lavender," Dan says. "What are you doing?"

"He was watching her."

I don't know what I'm looking for — blinking red lights? A rogue wire hanging from its hiding place? I walk past him, unable to slow down — I feel the kinetic pulse in my veins and I have to do something.

Dan's mouth twists and he avoids my gaze.

"It's possible. But not conclusive." He turns away from me before I can protest and walks to the bedroom. I roll my eyes in frustration.

I might kill him before we even find you, Juniper.

He walks back out of the room, holding my note in his hands. His lips are a thin line and a vein sticks out of his neck. He might actually be really pissed at me.

"Do you want to explain yourself?"

I'm still angry with him. I don't have patience for platitudes or *inconclusive* evidence. I stare at him.

"Am I going to get in trouble for passing notes?"

Dan sucks in his cheek and I know I've hit a nerve.

"I thought I might try and make contact with whomever is doing this — it might not do anything, or we might actually get something." I shrug. "I could be reaching, but at least I'm trying." I raise an eyebrow.

He gets the message and shakes his head slightly before throwing the note on the table. "Lavender. This isn't a joke. Or a game. We now have reason to believe this person has killed at least one person."

My head pops up to face Dan and I look him square in the eyes, all of the fire and frustration of the past week built into my gaze. He blinks and looks away.

"I know this isn't a fucking joke, Dan. This is my *sister*. And you need to trust and believe that I will do whatever's necessary to find her."

He takes his phone out of his pocket. "Let's not make that disrupting an investigation, okay?" He punches in some numbers and grabs the necessary bags, making his way to the door.

"I'm calling in our forensics team. They'll be out here later today to look deeper into what we might have missed the first time around." He pauses for a moment as he's walking out and calls back over his shoulder, "Hey, Jasper? Can you not leave her alone this time?"

Jasper nods and throws up a peace sign and I groan in frustration, stuffing the note in my back pocket. My pulse is racing. Jasper catches my eye and then looks the other way, pretending to be engaged with the fray of fabric on his shorts.

I watch Dan until he gets into his car and pulls out of the driveway. He's still on the phone when he sees me watching. He nods briefly and then sighs deeply, continuing to talk with the forensics team. I know I'm exhausting him. I know this probably isn't how he's wanting to spend his day. But whatever. I would also prefer to not have my sister kidnapped by a potential serial killer. I glance at my watch. Based on what Dan said before he left, forensics will be here within a few hours and they'll probably want me present. Which is basically the opposite of perfect since right now I want to run.

Away from this mess.

Away from the fear.

Away from this persistent thought that Juniper is in real danger, and I can do nothing to stop it. To save her.

My thoughts are racing. I walk back to the bedroom, placing the note back underneath the seal, behind the curtain. I let my fingers linger for a moment, imagining this person watching me right now.

Are you watching me?

I focus my gaze outside and only see sand dunes, nearby cliffs, crashing waves, and seagulls. If he is, he knows there's something waiting for him. And if I understand his thought process like I think I do, he won't be able to stop himself from coming to check what it is.

"He doesn't have the greatest bedside manner." I pivot and see Jasper leaning against the doorframe. For a moment, I forgot he was still here. He scratches his chin, the stubble having grown considerably since yesterday.

I fight from rolling my eyes and instead, roll my neck — hoping to work some of the tightness out of the muscles.

"When he mentioned not to leave me alone I wasn't expecting this attentive of a babysitter."

Jasper chuckled and shrugged, "I'm not babysitting you. You know exactly why he said that too."

I sigh and shake my head slightly despite the fact that I know he's right. I know, even though I really don't want to admit it, that Dan is legitimately concerned about my safety.

"I can't keep up with everything. It's like emotional whiplash." I cover my face with my hands and collapse on a nearby chair.

"Want to go for a walk?"

I look up.

He sticks his hands in his pockets and juts his chin toward the window. "There's a trail right around the corner that curves the shoreline."

"Yeah," I say, remembering Juniper's walks along that trail

when we would talk on the phone. I'm pretty sure I could find my way around it just by memories of our conversations. I pull at my ear, a nervous tic, and roll my shoulders again.

"I could use a distraction." And then I blush as Jasper stretches and my gaze lands on the small glimpse of skin. I'm realizing too late this distraction has nothing to do with the views of nature.

8

The first time you told me you had a twin, I didn't believe you. There's no way, I told you. You showed me a picture of her then, proving your point (you always love to be right), and I couldn't speak anymore because there she was — another you.

Lavender.

And now here we are, full circle. When she showed up at your house the other day, I couldn't believe my luck. It's destiny — you know that, right? I've been waiting since the black of dawn for her to find the note. I ask you how long you think it's going to take and you groan, still groggy from the night before. I watch you for a moment, waiting for you to wake. You turn your head and your breathing steadies again and I sigh. I miss you, Juniper. I walk over to where you're sleeping and run my finger along your arm, raising an eyebrow when I see the goosebumps rise on your skin.

Even in your sleep, you want me.

I just want you to *talk* to me. You fought me most of yesterday, screaming until your voice was gone. I flex my fingers and feel the scratches stretch against the skin. They sting, but it reminds me of your strength. I smile. I know the fight in you is simply a ruse. It's what you think you should be doing right now.

But I know what you want.

I look down at my watch, realizing it's nearly 10am. My smile shifts into a worried line and I glance back toward the windows. Will she ever wake up?

And then she does, and so does my heart.

I lean forward, watching her open the curtain and start a stretch that looks like a variation of yoga. I suck in a breath because she looks so much like you. I want to run and grab her, have her join us, but it's not time. Not yet.

So I just sit there, mesmerized. She stretches her arms above her head, a small smile on her lips, and her shirt lifts just above the hem of the shorts that barely cover the lacy underwear I know is underneath.

I know because you wear them, Juniper.

God. You – her — both of you — are so beautiful.

How is it possible I've managed to stumble across perfection twice?

She finds the note and my heart rate triples. I lean so far forward I almost tumble over, but I break into a grin when I see her hand fly up to her mouth. She loves it. I knew she would. She walks away for just a moment and I lose sight of her. I think about checking the other views on the monitors in the other room. Something keeps me focused though, and I'm so glad I'm paying attention because she comes back and this time?

Oh my god.

This time she places something under the window. Juniper, you never did this! Is that a note? For me? Tears threaten to fall. I knew she'd be different. I knew she'd understand. She wasn't deterred by the small distraction I sent their way with the body. She knows we're out here, love. She craves connection.

My fingers itch for the note and I stand up as if I'm about to walk right over there and grab it but something stops me in my tracks.

That fucking detective.

He walks into the room and finds it before I can get it.

I hiss. That's mine! I shove my fist in my mouth to keep from screaming. The anger pulses underneath my skin and I claw at a scab on my wrist until it turns bloody again. She should have known. She should have known not to let him follow her back home. I close my eyes and shake my head violently. If he's there, I'm almost positive Jasper is, too.

They'll ruin everything.

Jasper, the prick with those pansy looking shorts, almost ruined my chance with you. It's like he's obsessed — he always appeared at the most inopportune moments, looking at your hands as if he wanted to reach out and grab them. And I knew, because he lacks the courage necessary, nothing would ever happen.

Like I said. He's a pansy. Definitely not right for you — quoting poetry and waxing philosophical about the screenplay he's working on at night. He bored you. He didn't even know you.

But I do. I know you better than anyone.

You get mad when people don't listen to you.

You dream of a life that is yours — separate from Lavender. You always told me, "you have to find yourself in order to know what you're meant to do with this life."

You never knew that every time you said that, I became more and more aware that what I'm meant to do in this life has everything to do with you. You're not like the others. You never had any idea that the reason my heart beats is because I imagine the moment I will feel your heart beat against mine. I smile to myself and glance back at you, eyes droopy with confusion. Yesterday, you fought me when I tried to feed you —

biting my shoulder and screaming until you were hoarse. Naturally, I had to calm you down, so I gave you some Valium with a vodka chaser. You went right to sleep and are just now starting to wake up.

I sniff at the memory, feeling the excitement of the chase rise all over again. I look back toward the window, and notice the detective is leaving. I lean forward as he shakes the gravel pulling out of the driveway. A motion in the bedroom catches my attention and I see you put the note back under the window.

That's right. Fight for me.

Lavender and Juniper, sugar and spice.

Soon I will have everything nice.

A curious obsession indeed.

9

I follow Jasper down the trail, or I guess I should say up — the trail leads to the cliffs nearby, winding up and down along the coast. The sun creates a warmth that counters the wind that brushes cool against my skin. I take a deep inhale, noticing the difference of how the Atlantic caresses the shore. I'm used to the break and tumble of the Pacific, a different kind of grace that crashes against cliffs and creates new landscapes from its existence. I can see why Juniper chose this place. A small grin escapes the weariness of my expression and I let the muscles in my shoulders relax. It helps to see and feel my sister in and around her normal surroundings. I feel, for the moment, centered. Mom always told me the ocean rooted you to the core of who you are: "it's the rhythm and strength and beauty of those waves, baby,' she'd whisper in my ear as we'd all watched the sunrise crest over the horizon. When we would look at her, her red hair forming a halo in the growing light, she could tell us anything and we'd believe her.

"The Reese women have ocean in our veins, girls. We need her to breathe. Don't ever stray far from her or you'll most likely get lost." All we ever knew was her eccentricity, so we've only ever lived as if this were true.

I take a deep breath and allow the oceanic crashes to sync with my own internal rhythm. Right here — right now — I am okay. I am doing what I know to do, what Juniper would be doing for me if roles were reversed. She always lectures me about not taking breaks. I run too hard, she says — and I know it's true. I can't run from my ghosts forever. The hard part? I'm really good at doing it. And she was really good at seeing.

Dammit. Is. She *is* really good at seeing.

"Come see me," she always tells me. "You have vacation stored up. I know you do."

I always say no. I'm too busy, too focused, too distracted with filling my schedule to run from the hurt. A parent's death for anyone would be difficult to navigate, but for me it felt like a wound I couldn't escape no matter how hard I tried. And now no matter what I do, my mother's ghost seems to haunt me with memories so intense they feel like a constant weight around my middle section, taking me under.

And then there was Jack. For the past ten years, I've run from one trauma to another. And now Juniper. Forget Mercury. It feels like my entire life is in permanent retrograde.

I let out a frustrated sigh and shake my arms loose.

I don't want to admit it, but I really needed to get out and breathe the fresh air. I watch Jasper out of the side of my eye, only slightly annoyed by his self-appointed role as my babysitter. I'm grateful he wants to help find Juniper, but if they are so close how come I never heard about him? My eyes narrow at the realization that it's one more thing my sister never really told me, one more thing I'm adding to the list for her to explain when we finally reunite. For now though, he's all I have connecting me to her.

"I need to ask you something," I say. "It might be awkward."

Jasper reaches for a stone in front of him and throws it off the side of the cliff, watching it bounce until it disappears.

"I'm a native in the country of Awkward. Give it your best shot."

A laugh escapes from my lips and my hands reach up to gather the hair on my neck in a pile on the top of my head. With one finger, I grip the rubber band around my wrist, pull it off, and wrap it around my untamed hair.

I'm delaying the inevitable. I have no idea how to jump into this conversation.

Help me out here, Juniper.

I close my eyes, fighting the impending embarrassment. "I'm trying to figure out why you're here. Why you haven't left yet and seem to be so invested. Were you guys like a thing?"

Jasper falters and widens his eyes for a brief moment before creating a rhythm with his steps all over again. His lips curve down briefly before nodding.

"I mean," I put my hand up and brush against his sleeve in embarrassment. "I know *why* you're here now — you were commissioned as my guardian or whatever." I'm starting to stumble over my words and my hands start fluttering in front of me, a tell I'm getting frantic.

"Don't get me wrong. I'm grateful you're here. It helps having someone who knows Juniper and can provide some context to this gut feeling I had before showed up. I just...I don't know you." I shrug. "And I'm wondering why you care."

"I guess that makes sense."

I keep walking, avoiding his gaze and hoping he's still within earshot. My eyes stay on the path in front of me. I think I feel him behind me, but I'm not sure.

"Juniper never mentioned you." I stumble through my words. "I mean, no offense. I'm not saying you don't mean anything to her. She doesn't tell me everything — clearly — because I didn't know she was getting notes or being harassed?

Stalked? by a student. Or I guess we don't know if it's a student, huh? Anyways..."

I'm rambling.

I take a breath to stop me from talking. I pause for a moment, chancing a glimpse at him and hoping he hasn't tuned me out. I'm surprised by how close he is — my breath hitches as he nearly runs into me. Jasper wipes his forehead with the back of his hand and smiles as he side steps me, preventing a collision.

"Lavender. It's fine." He places his hand briefly on my shoulder and I hide my surprise at the heat he leaves behind.

"Juniper and I were close. She helped me through a really tough break up right around the time she and Simon were beginning to have difficulties."

He sniffs.

"I guess you can say we were each other's lifeboat." He squints and looks ahead, continuing to walk. He pauses more to accommodate for the steeper incline. "But no. We weren't romantically involved, if that's what you're asking."

I blush again and suck in my lip, unsure of how to respond. I settle for "oh," suddenly wanting to disappear from the awkwardness I'm feeling. Yep. Wasn't prepared for this conversation.

"But," Jasper raises his hand and separates his fingers in a frustrated push against the air around him. "She really is one of my closest friends here." He looks out past the cliff. "She's family to me. That probably sounds ridiculous." He laughs and hangs his thumbs on the loops of his shorts. "She told me about your mom. How it happened."

I breathe sharply and blink away the tears suddenly threatening the surface. Nope. Not ready for this. Not even a little bit. I study his profile and how the words fall off his lips. He turns to look me in the eye and runs his fingers through his hair, trying to find the words. We've both stopped on the trail and we're facing each other, the sun beginning to make its descent on the horizon. I can see the gold around us taking over.

"I don't...."

He puts his hand up, interrupting me. "It's fine. You don't have to say anything and I won't say any more. I just wanted you to know. Thought it might help you understand how close we were."

He glances at me.

I feel the edges of hurt scrape against me and I wince. Juniper telling Jasper about Mom's death could mean anything. It's been ten years and it still feels like those first few moments after it happened — struggling to breathe, the rush of adrenaline, the horror of seeing her broken body on the side of the road.

My fault. My fault. My fault.

"I know y'all don't talk about her a lot."

"Ever." My tone is sharp and biting. I clear my throat and use the back of my wrist to dig into the corner of my eyes, drying what tears have made their way despite my attempt at pushing them back. He nods and looks away, choosing to keep walking, getting the hint.

I am clearly done with this part of our conversation. My body language turns rigid and I'm standing as far away from Jasper as I can possibly get without falling off the edge of the cliff. He's a few steps ahead of me when he looks behind his shoulder and offers a smile.

"Juniper was there for me at my lowest point. So to me, she's like the sister I never had. And if you're family..." Jasper says, his voice dropping an octave. I pretend I don't hear the emotion behind the shift. "I'm going to do whatever I need. If you're family, I'm going to fight for you until I find a reason not to — so...."

He leaves his thought hanging and I turn away from him, embarrassed by the way his voice cracked. Embarrassed by my own reaction. I wrap my arms around me, my fingers reaching for familiar territory. I'm fighting my own thoughts creating a thunderstorm of emotions. My phone vibrates and I pull it out of my pocket, my heart shaking again. Maybe this time...maybe it's Juniper. I see Jasper rush over to me and hover, trying to see who's calling.

My heart slams against my chest and I feel the disappointment scrape against my insides like a razor.

It's not her.

Will I ever stop wondering if it's you?

I choke out a hello.

"What's wrong?" It's Detective Dan. He immediately launches into suspicion. He must hear the hidden emotions in my voice.

"I-I'm fine." I shake my head quickly and dig one of my fingernails into the meaty part of my flesh. I should probably stop lying about how I'm doing, but I also can't find it in me to care.

Dan makes a noncommittal grunt and says something under his breath that I can't hear. It's probably for the best.

"Okay. Well. The forensics team is on their way, and they'll need you there in case they have any questions." He waits a beat. "Are you still home?"

I look at Jasper and motion for us to walk back toward the house and he nods in understanding.

"Yeah. Yeah, we're here. We'll be here."

And I hang up, not knowing what else to say. Strangers are about to comb through my sister's things. Will they find anything? I tap my phone against the palm of my hand, a tattoo of emotional angst and nervous energy.

We're silent the rest of the way home, the sounds of the ocean becoming the soundtrack to each of our thoughts, lost in the never-ending question of how someone could just cease to exist, and how her disappearance continually pushes us together, whether we're ready for it or not.

.∷.

THE TEAM IS at the house when we get back from our walk. One of the men walks up to introduce himself to me and I recognize him from the hallways of the police station. His name is — honest to God — Morty. On a sliding scale, my confidence in this investigation is dwindling by the second.

"What are the chances of finding something?"

He crosses his arms and rocks back on his feet. He's clearly unaffected by the pomp and circumstance of this search. "We know what to look for, so I'm sure we'll turn up something."

I catch Jasper's eye and watch the frown flash across his face.

"Listen. I'm sure this is an unnecessary reminder, but can you show a bit of empathy here?" He steps closer to me and juts his chest out a fraction of an inch. I suck in my tongue to keep from laughing at the bravado. As if it's needed.

Morty lifts his chin and raises an eyebrow in an overt attempt at challenging Jasper's size. I give up. I wave the men off and turn around to walk up the porch, waiting on the swing while I hear the chaos of the search inside.

It takes the team less than an hour to pick apart every square inch of Juniper's house before they find something. Her house doesn't even look like her house anymore. Cushions are upended, the large ottoman in the corner with the pile of blankets has been turned on its side and is resting against the wall. Light fixtures are torn apart and hanging loosely from the ceilings, even her mattress has been pulled and tossed aside so they could take apart the bed frame and look inside the metal pieces. They aren't even done. I can't believe the absolute disaster her home has become.

Sorry, J. This is going to take forever to clean up.

From the corner, I hear a small gasp and nervous energy.

"It looks like a camera of some sort," the guy says when he finds it. I feel dizzy.

A small ball, barely recognizable, hidden in plain sight within her diffuser. Whenever the diffuser turned on, so did the camera. Even more terrifying: it had range of the entire home: her bedroom. The living room. The kitchen. If he was capable of rigging a diffuser to look like a camera, he was capable of a lot of things, the team tells me. I might be sick.

I can't speak. When did he put that in there? How did he get access to her home?

"You should probably stay somewhere else — maybe find a hotel until we can be certain there isn't anything else lingering here."

I stare ahead, unable to process. My brain is going a mile a minute. If he was watching Juniper, does that mean he is watching me? I take a deep breath, trying to focus on the specialist in front of me.

"You think...you think there's more?"

The guy drops the diffuser into a container and looks back at me with an empty gaze.

"If there's one, there's always more."

I fall into the couch behind me and feel Jasper's hand rest on my back.

"I have an extra room if you..."

"No." My response is shorter than I mean it to be but let's be real. My hands are the shape of a prayer between my legs. I can still feel them shaking. Or maybe that's my entire body. I can't even tell anymore. I push my tongue up against my teeth and breathe. Stay at his house? *Please.* I'm shaken, but not desperate.

"Sorry. I just…" I look at him, barely able to hold his gaze. "I need my space I think. I'll just get a hotel."

Jasper has his lower lip in between his forefinger and thumb and I've spent enough time with him these past 36 hours I already know it means he's thinking about how to try and word something.

"Are you sure?"

I reach for my phone on table in front of me, trying to steady myself.

"I'm positive." I look down at my phone again and punch in our location and get more than a few options for hotels. "You can help me find a decent place to stay though," I offer an olive branch — albeit a weak one. "I've seen Psycho. Last thing I need is a sketchy hotel where the owner has his dead mom stashed somewhere."

He swallows a reply and nods.

"Okay. Check out Hotel Providence. They're decent. But it might be difficult to find a room right now — Waterfire starts tomorrow."

"Waterfire?"

"A local festival. Basically, we put bonfires on the river — about 80 total — and there are fire tenders who show up and make sure they stay lit. Everyone shows up, there's music and the scent of the wood burning is unlike anything I've ever experienced."

I tilt my head.

"Sounds ritualistic."

He smiles. "It's something, that's for sure. The crowds get bigger every year."

I punch in the information for the hotel in my phone and find they have availability, but it's limited. A timer starts ticking at the top of the browser and I realize I only have two minutes to book this room that now, according to their built in countdown, is their only vacancy.

Shit.

I point toward my bag resting on the chair across from the coffee table.

"Could you hand me my bag? I need to reserve this room before it disappears out from under me and I'm left bunking with a stranger."

He looks offended for a few seconds before reaching for the strap and handing it to me.

"I'm not a stranger," he mutters under his breath.

"I wasn't talking about you," I respond, giving him a smile as I take my bag from his hand and reach for my wallet. I'm not paying attention to what I'm throwing out of the bag in order to get my card, and within minutes I have the room secured. I breathe a sigh of relief and glance up at Jasper triumphantly. My victory is short lived. He's apparently no longer thinking about my slight jab of staying with a stranger over him or whether or not I'll get the room. He's looking at a piece of paper, his face white. His lips shrink into a thin line and he shakes his head slightly, his eyes wrinkling at the corners in concern.

"Jasper."

He looks at me and hands over the note. It doesn't take long for me to recognize the handwriting. My fingers start shaking as I read.

YOU KNOW I can't tell you where Juniper is — but she's safe and sound. I bet you can't find her.

"HE WAS HERE." I twist my head around the living room, expecting something to give me some type of clue. I look at

Jasper, already up and rummaging through the mess left behind by the forensics team.

"He was here," I repeat, looking at the note and then back at my bag. "He put this in my bag. He was..." the tears start falling then and Jasper turns back toward me and is by my side in an instant. He gathers me in his arms and places his hand behind me head, pulling me close.

"I know," he whispers. "I know."

This whole time, I didn't understand. I knew Juniper was alive because I felt her like I always do right beneath my ribcage. And then the notes started showing up and I thought maybe it was just some stupid prank her students were pulling or that there would be some type of logical explanation for why they kept showing up but now I'm not so sure.

Now I'm beginning to see the severity of her not being here next to me.

Now I know that I have to find my sister.

If I don't find her, now I know he'll kill her.

10

I'm frozen on the couch. I can't think, can't move — I lose track of who is coming and going. I can't grasp anything. It's like I'm in a tunnel with images that blur into fading light. I've never been this terrified before — this shaken. From the time I left the cottage with Jasper to take a walk until the time we came back for the forensics team, it couldn't have been more than an hour. Which tells me two things: he was watching me, and he's efficient at what he does. This is what stops me in my tracks. Juniper is the most vigilant person I know. Her efficiency is rooted in preparedness. For him to have caught her off guard means she knows him. I close my eyes against the nightmare and pray that somehow, I'll wake up in my loft sweaty and shaky and laughing at the horror of this dream.

Jasper gives Morty the note and they inspect my purse, just in case. I watch them inspect the stitching and turn the purse inside out, cringing a bit when they pull at a loose thread.

That's a 500-dollar purse, I think to myself.

I might be in the middle of a nightmare, but I have my limits.

Dan returns to the house and looks at me for an extended

amount of time before sitting in front of me on the coffee table. He's reading me. He's trying to find a way to start the conversation.

"I don't bite," I say.

He nods and looks at his hands.

"I'm sorry I wasn't listening to you before."

I glance up at him and then back down to my thumb circling my fingerprints, one by one. Mom used to grab my hands when I did this, telling me it was a nervous twitch. I breathe in tight and swallow.

"I can't lose her too."

I don't bother with the apology. As difficult as it is for guys like Dan to apologize, I also know he'll probably be an ass again in about 30 minutes.

He sucks in his lips and looks out the window. The buzz of the forensics team is starting to slow down, and Jasper has come to sit next to me. I close my eyes and soak in his presence, a neutral energy.

"So, it seems we were right. We have someone who is in it for the hunt."

I look up at him and pray he can't see the way my heart rate just doubled.

"What does that mean?" My voice struggles to find purchase — it lands softly against my tongue and I clear my throat. My pulse turns staccato.

I hate this feeling.

"We have no reason to believe Juniper has been harmed. But due to the pattern of notes we found written to her before her disappearance, we think he might have his sights set on you now."

"Okay, so we trap him. Right? Doesn't that seem obvious?"

Dan tilts his head, a compassionate gesture that I want to punch. His change in demeanor is unnerving.

As if everything I was feeling about Juniper's disappearance is actually true.

The drumbeat turns louder in my veins.

"Naturally, that would be the thing to do. You would think he would be easy to read." Dan leans back and rests his hands on the wood. "The problem, though, is this person is calculating. He's probably watching us right now and more than likely, is three steps ahead of what you are thinking."

"So what do we do?"

"We wait."

My spine straightens in protest and I inadvertently grab Jasper's knee with my fingernails. He gasps and shoots forward and I let go quickly.

Oops.

"We...wait?" I repeat, in disbelief.

"It's the only thing we can do. We still move forward with the investigation, but we need you to act as normal as possible. The threats, although serious with potential, are still pretty tame compared to what they can be — there hasn't been any promise of physical harm."

I watch him, unmoving. I am once again in disbelief.

Ah. Here's the asshole I know and loathe, I think to myself.

"And we'll never be more than a few minutes away, just in case."

Jasper chuckles at this and I look to him for support. He's still rubbing his knee where I left four indentions from my nails, but he's shaking his head in disbelief.

"So detective," I say, feeling every ounce of sarcasm and fear in my words. "What does *normal* look like?"

He looks at me and glances toward the forensics team packing up. When he finds my gaze again, I can almost see the hesitancy in his expression.

"Well first, we're going to organize a search party."

"A search party."

He nods, massaging the space between his thumb and pointer finger. "What we know now is Juniper is missing. He knows we know that. As far as we know, he doesn't necessarily know anything else of what we've discovered....and it's important that we keep it that way."

"You don't think him dropping my sister's ID on the other woman's body is a particular tell we should be concerned about?"

"Oh we're concerned about it. We just can't play our hand yet."

"But a search party is okay? How?"

"Because you would expect someone to look for a missing loved one. You've asked around, but we haven't really done any extensive searching for Juniper." He pauses. "Right?"

I nod. I showed up and immediately called him. I hadn't really done any searching on my own.

"So we'll host a search party. See if we can get a bunch of people to show. Pay attention to anyone acting remotely suspicious or particularly bought into the ordeal."

He studies me and Jasper. "Whatever you do, though — don't say anything about this case yet. Not to anyone. We have no idea who we're looking at here....okay?"

He waits a beat before dropping his eyes to meet my gaze. "Okay?"

I roll my eyes. "Yeah. Whatever. I get it."

"I also need her ex's number. What's his name? Sam?"

"Simon?"

He points at me. "Yes. Him. We need to chat with him about their relationship and make sure there isn't anything there we should be concerned about...."

I stifle a laugh.

"Simon is *not* the guy you're looking for, Dan."

He twists his lip and stares out the window.

"That's what they said about Ted Bundy."

.:::.

BY THE TIME we leave the house, there is nothing that hasn't been touched by the forensics team. I'm only allowed to bring my purse because it passed an initial inspection of *good enough*.

And, bonus for me! I now have a security detail. Apparently I'm a *risk*.

I roll my eyes when I see the tinted windows of the car trailing us in the rearview mirror.

"That's not discreet," I mumble.

Jasper mimics my glance in the rearview mirror and frowns. "If he's watching you, and we think he is, there's no way he doesn't see them trailing us." He glances at me and then returns to focus on the street in front of him.

"The offer stands, Lavender. If you need —"

"I don't need."

He nods, purses his lips, and I glance out my window. I'm done talking for the night and I'm *definitely* done interacting with people I've barely met.

He breathes in, as if he's about to say something else, and I close my eyes, willing him to stay quiet. I don't begrudge him the hospitality, I'm just...spent.

He doesn't catch my cues. He continues his thought.

"I'm not comfortable with leaving you alone tonight."

I sigh.

"I'm a grown woman, Jasper."

"Yeah, and so is Juniper and she's not here right now, is she?"

I watch as his knuckles turn white from gripping the steering wheel.

"No..." I whisper. "She's not. But I'll be fine. You're dropping me off at the hotel. You can walk me to my room if you want." I roll my eyes and motion behind us. "And these guys aren't going anywhere any time soon, unfortunately."

His facial expression tells me he's not convinced, but there's no changing my mind.

I need space. I need to think.

And besides, there's not much more I can do at this point. I've never felt so powerless before. Well, yes I have — but that memory lingers just below the surface and I refuse to let it lift.

I clench my fists so tight that tiny crescents form on my palms. I watch as we move from Newport to Providence, the view turning from coastal to collegiate. By the time we reach the hotel, I'm exhausted. We get into the room without any issues. Jasper immediately moves to the window and shuts the blinds and curtain.

"Who's the discreet one now?" I ask, the sarcasm oozing from my tone.

His lips are a permanent line of stress, and he says nothing as he prowls across the room, checking the shower and the closet. He catches my eye during one of his pass-throughs, and I raise an eyebrow while collapsing into the chair. He checks the lamps, the sheets, the chest of drawers. He checks to make sure the phone is connected. He checks behind pictures.

Behind pictures?

"Jasper. This isn't Cabin in the Woods. You're not going to find a double-sided mirror there. Can you just...it's fine. You can stop. Seriously."

Satisfied, he stops in the middle of the room in with his hands on his hips.

"Are you sure you're okay?"

"I'm sure."

I'm not.

"Do you promise to call me if anything happens?"

"I will."

Not likely.

He nods to himself for a few moments before puffing his cheeks.

"Okay then."

I get up from the chair and walk toward the door.

"Okay."

I open it. He walks past me and out into the hall, stopping for a quick wave before turning around again. I wave back, but it's too late. He's already around the corner. Breathing deep, I close the door and press my forehead against the wooden frame.

What the fuck have I gotten myself into?

I see the tears dripping off my chin before I realize I'm crying. I push away from the door, wiping the stray tears, and wish for something to throw against the wall that would shatter into pieces. I don't want to *cry* right now. I want to thrash and fight. I want to see things break the way it feels as if I'm breaking internally.

Instead, I opt for one of the pillows on the bed. One by one, I throw them against the wall with everything I have, my chest heaving with sobs. With each quiet thud, my frustration grows. I pick one off the floor and scream into the fabric, feeling my insides crack into a million shards.

I cannot handle this grief anymore. No wonder I pushed Jasper away. It's too much loss for one person to handle. I collapse onto the floor and curl up into a ball, letting the sobs move through my body. I think of my mom, broken beyond repair. I think of Jack and his promises of forever. I think of Juniper and the man who made her vanish into thin air.

And when I can't sob anymore, I think of myself and my tendency to run and I let out a guttural wail.

This is pain I cannot get away from no matter how hard I

try. I close my eyes against the memories, but they're too vivid. They take me under.

.::.

THE DAY MY MOTHER DIED, I was at a guy's house. Thad was five years older than me, and I thought I was tough shit catching his eye. We met, of all places, at the movie theatre. I had gone to see a show with my friends and he was there, checking tickets and directing us to the correct theater.

When he handed me my ticket torn in two, his fingers grazed my own and he winked. Never in my life had I felt the level of electricity that coursed through my veins when he touched me.

I was a goner.

During the movie, I acted like I had to use the restroom and walked out to find him standing right where I left him. I completely forgot about my friends, spending the rest of the movie talking.

"Aren't you with friends?" he said.

I shrugged. "This conversation is a lot more interesting than the blood and guts they wanted to watch."

"Oh yeah? Are you a rom-com girl?" He smirked and I wanted to lick the smile off his face.

"Indie." I looked him in the eye. "Rom-coms are fake."

He didn't need to know he actually read me pretty well: my friends and I argued for hours before I finally gave in because at least I wouldn't have to be in the house pretending to do homework.

"So...what's a guy gotta do to get your number?"

I smiled, and with confidence I didn't realize I had, I reached for his pocket.

"Give me your phone and you'll find out."

We spent all night texting. I never considered it odd that a man in his 20s would want to hang out with a teenage girl. Juniper, ever the wise one, told me it would only lead to heartbreak, but I refused to listen.

"Really, Lavender. It's so predictable, it's pathetic. He only wants you for one thing."

Of course, that infuriated me, and so I stopped talking with her for the first time in our lives.

She got concerned by my silence. When my mom picked up on the ice between us, she cornered Juniper — the one who could never tell a lie. She told my mom, which resulted in me being grounded from everything for the rest of my teenage life, so said mother.

"Really, Lavender? A *Thad?!* Out of all the boys you fall for — you fall for someone named Thad?!" She grimaced as I rolled my eyes. "Do I need to spell it out for you why this is a bad idea? I didn't even have to know his age to know this would be catastrophic."

Juniper was horrified that she was pressured to tell my secret, and was determined to make it up to me despite her disapproval of my relationship with Thad. So like any redblooded teenager, I rebelled against the punishment handed to me and snuck out one night to meet him at his house. I turned to Juniper, in our room studying for a test.

"He has a surprise for me, Juniper. Can you cover for me? Please?" I crawled into bed with her and snuggled close, desperate.

She sighed. "Seriously, if you can't figure out what *surprise* he has for you then maybe y'all deserve each other." Her eyes widened. "Just this once, Lav. Promise."

I kissed my index and middle fingers and held them toward

her so she could do the same, our secret handshake since we were five.

"I'll be back before you know it," I whispered as I crawled out of our window.

"That's what I'm afraid of," she called after me.

He was waiting for me in his car when I got to the street. I still remember that feeling of dropping into the passenger seat and driving down the highway toward his place with the windows down and the heat of spring washing over us. I felt alive. Free. It lasted only a moment.

When we got to his place, I knew immediately I was in over my head. It was a secluded area of town and he was the only one home.

"Where are your roommates?" I asked, suddenly nervous.

"Oh, they knew we needed some time so they left for a few hours." His voice was melodic — I realized too late he'd been drinking and was silently thankful we didn't get into an accident on the way there.

When he kissed me and I tasted something foreign on his lips, I knew I was dealing with more than alcohol.

"Come on," he said and I fought from making a face at the smell. "Let's go inside."

His house only had one bedroom where both of his roommates stayed. He stayed on a pull-out couch in the living room.

"It's just for now though," he said as he caught my gaze lingering on the sheets haphazardly fit around the cushions. "I'm on the waitlist for an apartment in another part of town."

He walked into the kitchen and grabbed spritzers from the fridge. I took one from him and pretended to drink, knowing full well the way my stomach was flipping on its side I would regret drinking anything other than water.

He looked at me for a few seconds before taking his hand and grazing my cheek with his finger.

"You're beautiful."

I blushed.

His hand moved down my arm and thumbed the space in between my crop top and skirt. I felt the skin prickle despite my uncertainty. He gave me that smirk of his that at one time won me over and pressed his hips into my own so I could feel him. I swallowed as he started kissing my neck, making noises as he pulled me closer to him and pushed us up against the wall.

I pushed him away, trying to act coy by running my fingers along the zipper of his hoodie.

"So what's my surprise?"

He pulled me close.

"You haven't figured it out? It's me, baby. I'm your surprise."

I giggled and turned my head away, suddenly disgusted by his insistent pursuit of my touch.

Dammit, Juniper. You were right. Again.

I started running through how I would explain this to her — how I could twist it so it didn't sound *all that bad,* considering. I knew she would read between the lines, though — she would know. I was desperate to be wrong about him — about *this.* Surely I could get out of this one.

"Thad, I–"

"Shhhh...." he placed his hand over my mouth and pushed me down on the couch.

He didn't hear me say no.

He didn't even see me cry.

When he was done, he kissed my forehead and whispered, "you should probably leave before everyone shows up."

He pulled up his jeans and walked away from me into the bathroom where he turned on the shower. I was frozen. Did I say no? Did I...did he hear me? What just happened?

I rearranged my clothing and wiped the tears off my cheeks and ran outside into the damp midnight air. Only when I was a few blocks away did I manage to pull out my cell phone and call my mom sobbing.

"Oh baby," was all she said. "Oh, baby. I'll be there soon. Don't you worry."

She was on her way to get me when she was t-boned by a drunk driver running a red light.

I never heard from Thad again, proving Juniper right, and now our mom was gone forever.

To this day Juniper and I refuse to talk about the real reason we're orphans.

We both know it's me.

11

From my perch, I can see everything. You walk with that waste of breath down the path and the anger pulses beneath my skin. It should be me walking with you. He has nothing to offer, and I'm sure you're only placating him because he's latched on to you like a parasite since you've come into town.

As you walk, your jean shorts begin to ride up your legs and chills race up my arms. You have a dancer's physique: toned, smooth, supple. I place my hand against the window and caress your skin with my finger. You put your hands in your back pockets, and I glimpse a small sliver of your lower back. I bite my lip so hard the taste of copper fills my mouth.

I can't help but wonder how you would taste.

I've been watching you constantly, daydreaming about what it will feel like to have both you and Juniper safe with me. It's the only logical next step. I glance behind me to make sure she's still sleeping off the drugs and turn around once more toward the window.

You have no idea how close you are to me right now and the thought thrills me, like a secret begging to be released. I can almost feel you, pressed up against me, your head thrown back in ecstasy.

One day.

For only a moment, you disappear from view. My feet start tapping an impatient rhythm, wondering where you've gone and why you feel it necessary to be with Jasper in the first place. I breathe in sharp. I don't trust him. But I can't worry about that right now; I don't have much time. I take one last look at Juniper, making sure she's secure, before running over my own surprise. It doesn't take long — a twist of the lock and I'm in.

I find your purse quickly, and I drop the note where I know you'll find it. My hands shake with anticipation. I finish what I need and then leave. By the time I'm back with Juniper, it's only been seven minutes.

It doesn't take long for you to appear over the crest of the cliff again, but this time, I can tell something has changed. My eyes dart to the house and my skin grows cold. Roaches. All of them. Invading Juniper's space and looking for traces of me they'll never find. My anticipation grows and I gnaw at the skin by my thumbnail, waiting.

I can tell it's bothering you, the way they rip into everything and look for clues. They're idiots. They'll never find it. You continue to pace the living room and I wish I could hold you as the nerves take over. Jasper sits on his ass and does nothing, but what else is new.

Soon enough, the roaches fall right into my trap, finding the device I left for them in the diffuser. A simple contraption, it would be noticeable to anyone looking. But what is this? You appear...shaken. What about our game? Aren't you happy that I'm watching out for you?

You glance out the window and I press my hand against the glass again when I realize we bite our thumbs the same way.

We are meant to be, you and me.

When you hand Jasper your wallet and he finds my note, I hit the wall with my fist.

It's not for him, Lavender. It's for *you*. Why do you let him in so easily? My breath catches when I see the detective start to talk to you. What is happening? Why is Jasper leading you to his car?

Where are you going, Lavender?

"You bastard."

I blink, caught off guard. Turning, I see Juniper staring at me. I smile and move to walk over to her but her eyes widen as she turns into a wild thing, bucking and fighting against the constraints. I relax for a moment, enjoying the show.

Your sister is so feisty when she's upset, but I'm sure you know this already.

"Youbastardyoufuckingdidthisyouwillpayyoumotherfuckerletmego."

I tsk, shaking my head.

Such a mouth on this one. I had no idea just how feisty she was until I had her all to myself. I take my finger and lightly trace a vein that pulses beneath her skin. A quiet tear escapes from one of her eyes and I smile as I wipe it from dripping down her cheek.

I know it's because she's overwhelmed with love for me.

"Juniper," I whisper. "You have to trust me. You know this is for the best. Can't you see what I've done for you?"

"You've done *nothing* for me." Her words come out in a hiss, and I breathe deep to keep from reacting. I reach for her again, and she jolts away, snarling against my touch when I try to move the hair that sleep and struggle have plastered against her forehead..

I sigh.

"Would you have such disdain for me if you knew I was watching over your sister?"

She goes still.

"What."

I just stand there, watching her, smiling. Her entire face collapses and I know the relief that is coursing through her right now.

"Lavender — ohmygod. No. *No*. What did you do?! Where is she?" Her eyes grow wild again and I can see her breath come out in spasms. I lift my hand to calm her.

"She's fine....*because I'm watching her.*" I smile. "Perhaps she should join us?"

She starts shaking her head slowly at first, and then vehemently, the tears falling freely now. "Please no. Please leave her alone. Please. What do you want...what....I don't...." her sobs come out in gut-wrenching waves, and I reach for the sedative again. As I push the needle into her skin, I kiss her cheek.

"Don't you get it, Juniper?" I answer her in soft whispers against the crest of her lips. She tries to turn her head away from me but is already too drugged. I lick a tear that has found its way down her cheek and she whimpers. I close my eyes against the taste and force myself to fight the urge to take her now.

"Don't you get it?" I repeat to no one in particular as I trace the kisses down her neck and where the line of her t-shirt grazes her breast.

"I want all of you. Even her."

I kiss her softly as she fades into oblivion. As her breath evens out, I turn my mind back to you. I walk over to the monitors in the corner and press a few keys.

They should have done a better job of checking your purse, Lavender. In between the threads of the designer leather, I dropped a camera. No one would have ever known.

I smile as you step away from the hotel door and wipe the tears from your eyes. I have my eyes on you all over again.

12

I startle awake to a vibration under my hip. My hands grope my strange surroundings until I find my phone haphazardly pushed to the side. Waking up has so far been the absolute worst. For a few blissful moments, I remember nothing — and then everything comes roaring back.

Like why I'm lying on the floor in a hotel room, my cheeks still wet from crying myself to sleep. I groan and pull my phone up to see who in the world would be trying to reach me.

My eyes are stiff and, for a moment, it stings when I look at the bright screen of my phone. I rub my eyes, yawning.

I can see the midnight blue of the sky outside and know it's late. Finally looking at my phone, I realize I've been asleep for a few hours. It's just after 2:30am.

I blink a few times, trying to focus on the messages filling my screen.

One is from Stephanie: *The edits look great. I know you're out of town, but can we move the date up at all? I'm thinking next week? I can talk to Jack if I need to...*

I shake my head, refusing to lose a project at work to *him*. I respond quickly — who cares about the time stamp that will show up when she wakes tomorrow. If she's even asleep. She's as much of a night owl as I am.

Next week is fine. Just give me specifics and I'll push the design to our team.

The other messages are from coworkers checking in and shipment notifications. I set up a voice reminder to call tomorrow when I'm more aware. As for my coworkers, I shoot them variations of the same message: *hey. I'm fine. Thanks for checking in. Talk soon.*

When I'm done, I drop my hands by my sides and stare at the ceiling. It never ceases to amaze me how life continues to move when you feel absolutely frozen solid with grief.

I sit up slowly and stretch the tightness out of my muscles, yawning as I make my way into the bathroom to finish unpacking my toiletries. This is the first time I'm really taking notice of my surroundings and I raise an eyebrow at the clawfoot tub. Out of the corner of my eye I notice full-size skin care products from a popular luxury brand — including three bath bombs. I grab one and unwrap it, setting it on the corner of the sink. It smells like lavender and almond. I close my eyes and breathe in the scent.

A noise in the hallway makes my pulse quicken to double time, but the giggles and sounds of bodies running into the wall remind me of drunken college nights and I slow my breath.

Despite knowing I'm alone in this room, it still feels as though someone is watching me. I glance toward the thin window lining the ceiling of the bathroom and realistically know there's no way anyone can peep into that window and see what I'm doing.

Even still.....

I know Dan has some guys watching out for me, but they're not....*watching* me are they? They can't be...I thought it was just like, scouting or whatever. Sitting in their car and trying not to fall asleep and watching the door of the hotel for things that go bump in the night.... I laugh. What do I know. My extent of law knowledge comes from *Brooklyn 99* episodes and the entire episodic library of *CSI* and *Criminal Minds*.

It doesn't matter. I'm not going to risk it. For reasons I can't explain, I turn and shut the bathroom door before peeling off my clothes and dipping into the water, letting the bath bomb fizzle into foam and coat my skin. It feels luxurious. I take a few breaths, allowing my muscles to slowly melt with the heat and water, before reaching for my phone.

There's one thing I haven't done.

I adjust my neck against the edge of the tub and keep a towel close by to dry off my hands when needed. Once my set up is complete, I pull up Google and type in Juniper's name.

The results are vague. I tap on the search bar and edit my search to *Juniper Reese, Providence RI* and hit enter.

This limits the results considerably. A few articles about the school are the top hits, along with her virtual yearbook photo from last year. Apparently her *mathletes* won a competition last year. I laugh at the picture — her wrapped around the students, absolutely glowing. It was clear she'd found her calling.

Her forgotten Twitter account also rests at the top of the list, and I remember a conversation we had before she moved to Providence.

"How are we going to keep in touch?"

She rolled her eyes at me. "I don't know, Lavender. Maybe phone calls? Texts?"

I wrinkled my nose.

"Can you at least create a private Instagram account so I can spy on your life and live vicariously through your decision to completely jump ship and abandon me?"

She grabbed my hands.

"First off, I'm not abandoning you. You know why I'm moving. Secondly, can you imagine my students finding *any* social media account of mine and thinking they can follow me or worse...be my friend?!" Her face had a look of unmistakable horror and disgust.

She shook her head. "No. No. I'm not doing it. I can't."

I run the edge of my fingers against the water and I think. If I were writing about my sister online, how would I describe her?

A thought hits me and I pull at my bun in frustration because *of course.*

I edit the search bar one more time.

Ms.. Reese Sacred Heart Providence RI

I GLANCE THROUGH A FEW WEBSITES, scrolling as quickly as I can while trying to capture key phrases. I'm just about to give up when something catches my eye. It's a blog with a pretty innocuous title — *The Spotless Sunshine of a Teenage Mind* — but it's the excerpt with my sister's name that stops me cold.

OUR FIRST DAY of class was today and I found out I have Ms.. Reese for Pre-Cal. At first, it was just another class. I mean, I've seen her in the hallway and everything but didn't really think anything of it. Until today.

She is, by far, the most beautiful person I've ever seen in my entire life. Her eyes pierce into your soul and you know she's seeing you for who you really are. She smiled at me today and I could read between the lines: she feels it too.

Senior year just got interesting.

·   ·   ·

I sit upright in the tub, the water splashing over the sides.

What the fuck?

I click into the site, scrolling through post after post about my sister — dated as far back as August. One, in October, had me shaking my head in confusion.

Ms.. Reese held me after class today to talk about my progress. I've been in her class for months and she's never held me after, but I've seen her look at me a few times and it's clear she feels what I feel. When we spoke, I could literally feel the electric current running between us. I can only imagine how it would feel if we actually got to touch.

This student, whoever they are, catalogued every single interaction they had with Juniper. Even when they found out she was dating Simon.

*I walked into Ms. Reese's classroom today and there was a man waiting for her. At first, I thought nothing of it. Teachers get visitors all the time. I asked him if he needed anything and he smiled and told me he was surprising HIS GIRLFRIEND and taking her to lunch. His girlfriend?! Does he even know who she is?! He doesn't **own** her. He doesn't even love her. Not like I do.*

Surely this wasn't a coincidence. Looking into posts from previous years, it seems innocent. But since the beginning of the year, the purpose has largely become a diary outlining the mental gymnastics of a teenager in love with my sister.

Some of these posts were detailed in their misrepresentation of how my sister would interact with her students. One even misconstrued her calling on someone else to help with a project as a direct snub and meant to cause jealousy. There's no way I could send this to Dan yet, not without more context on who this could be — the last thing I need is for him to think Juniper was having some type of relationship with her student. We've already been down that road.

I don't want him getting the wrong idea.

However, Simon and Jasper might be able to shed some light on who might be obsessed with my sister. I hesitate for just a moment before sending Simon a text. I haven't even reached out to him since landing in Providence, and it's for no other reason than it would just feel...awkward....talking to my sister's ex. And maybe it's not the best way to let him know I'm in town and surprise! my sister is missing, but it seems as good a time as any.

I copy the website and pull up Simon's number before I can second guess myself.

HEY, Simon. I know it's late and we haven't spoken in a while. I'm not sure if you know or not, but Juniper's missing. I'm currently in town trying to figure out where she might be. I found this blog by one of her students and I'm wondering if any of it rings a bell? Did she mention anything about a student who was, for lack of a better word, obsessed? I guess I should probably ask this, too: do you know where she is?

I SEND Jasper a text as well.

LOOK WHAT I FOUND. Who is writing this about my sister? Can you figure it out by process of elimination? I don't know the students like you do.

. . .

I HIT send and then tap the phone against my chin before opening up my messages again.

ALSO, sorry about tonight. I know I was more than a little cold. I'm just...dealing with a lot. This is all so surreal. I know you understand.

I SET my phone on the rug next to the tub and pull the hair tie out of my lion mane, massaging my scalp. And then I do my favorite thing in the world since I was a little girl: lying prostrate in the tub with only my face above the water. Here, completely immersed, the sound of water fills my ears and I can let go — if only for a moment — what's happening outside. It's always been this way. I close my eyes and let my mind empty for a moment. Water has always been my chosen element, which is why I could never live anywhere landlocked. In the water is where I feel most held. After a few moments of breathing and steadying my pulse, I fully submerge myself — a baptism of sorts. I'm still exhausted, but possess a little more mental clarity than before. I'm definitely still reeling from finding the blog online. I pull the drain and watch the water spin down as I towel dry. Before I can even get dressed, I notice my phone ringing.

It's Jasper.

"Hello?"

"Hey, Lavender. It's me."

I pull the phone away from my ear just long enough to check the time and frown.

"I know. Why are you awake? It's 4:00 in the morning."

He laughs, a throaty sound heavy with sleep.

"I uh...I had a lot on my mind too. Tonight was not a night for sleeping, I suppose. Plus I got back-to-back messages that definitely made me forget about allowing myself to forget about what a nightmare this week has been."

I put him on speaker so I can get dressed. With the hotel robe wrapped around me, I dry my hair enough to throw it back into a top knot. Putting it up like this while it's still wet basically requires that I'll be wearing it piled on top of my head until I can actually wash my hair tomorrow, but I could care less about actual styling right now.

"Did you check out the blog?"

"Yeah. I did."

"And?"

I hear shuffling on the other end of the line and it sounds like he's readjusting himself in bed. I swallow and push back images of him tangled in sheets and pull out my pajamas and a pair of underwear. I take one look at the window in the room and there's still a sliver of sky that I can see through the break between the two pieces of fabric curtains and I grab my phone and walk back into the bathroom.

I'm ready for this feeling of someone watching me to just go away.

"I'll be honest and say I couldn't help but think of that kid I saw talking with your sister — the one I told Dan about?"

I put the phone down on the counter so I can throw on my clothes and rub overnight serum on my face. Once I'm done, I pick up my phone and walk back into the main area. I collapse onto the bed, wiggling under the covers. I sigh in satisfaction.

Jasper chuckles.

"Lavender? You okay?"

I blush, and am immediately grateful he can't see me. "Uh yeah. Sorry. I just crawled into bed and the sheets felt divine. I'm listening."

He makes a clucking noise with his tongue and I'm left to

wonder what he's thinking, because he continues talking about the blog. My mind can't help but make up stories. At the mention of me in bed, did he have to focus his thoughts on the conversation too? Is what I'm feeling sleep deprivation or trauma bonding or legitimate chemistry?

Or all of the above?

I blink and focus back on what he's saying.

"I just wish I knew who the kid was, because I didn't get a good look at him. Outside of a few students, we don't have a lot of overlap between our classes. He didn't feel familiar to me."

"It just seems like such a stretch."

"What does?"

"All of it. It seems like everything connects, but....it just doesn't seem possible."

I twist my lips, thinking.

"It just seems like someone would have found this already, you know? With all of the cases out there of teachers falling in love with students, a blog like this would have to gain attention, right?"

"What if he didn't want anyone to find it until he was ready? It doesn't take much to set one of these blogs to private. Maybe he didn't meant for anyone to find it until now."

"Why would he do that?"

Jasper stifles a yawn. "Why does anyone do anything? Don't we just need a motive? If you read these posts, you see his obsession growing over the course of the year. It makes sense that maybe he's also wanting that notoriety, too. He wants to be known as the person who thought of this — who managed to take your sister. In his mind, they're meant to be together."

I frown. "You think so? If we take a step back and think about this logically, we're talking about a high schooler here. They're not capable of something like this....right?"

Jasper's quiet for a moment.

"You mean like could a teenage boy take your sister and be

smart enough to rig her house with surveillance equipment so he could start watching you?"

I stare at the ceiling, a chill running down my spine.

"Yeah."

"Wasn't there a TV show once where a high school girl did some pretty crazy shit to her friends? Hacked into phones and sent random text messages?"

I laugh, despite the situation.

"If we're thinking of the same show, you have a point."

"Basically, I think anyone is capable of anything given the right situation."

I rub at the space in between my eyebrows and then stop for a moment, remembering. My mom always told me when I did this it was my third eye trying to get my attention. I always told her it was because I was stressed.

I still don't know which one it is, but I can't help but continue worry at it, my fingers pressing indentations into my skin. I close my eyes against the fear that's rooting at me.

He hears my silence and recognizes the uncertainty.

"Did you talk to Dan about this?"

I snort, the derision evident.

He catches my hesitancy.

"Don't you think this is something we should share?"

"The last thing I want is him having eyes on this and thinking my sister had anything to do with one of her students. His mind already went there, Jasper."

"I know. I just wanted to be sure."

"It's only you and Simon who know."

"Have you heard from him?"

"No."

I hear his sheets rub together as he adjusts himself again. I bite my lip against the mental image and squeeze my eyes shut. Worst timing ever for any type of attraction.

He clears his throat.

"Listen. I don't know if this will work, but I know someone who might be able to help. He's a friend from college who's involved in cyber-security. I can see if he can figure out if there's any tracing or badges that point us to who could be writing these posts."

I drop my hand.

"That would be amazing, Jasper. Thank you."

"Of course. I'll uh...I'll text him tomorrow though." He pauses. "Or today. Later today. I'm so exhausted I don't even know what day it is...."

"It's Thursday," I respond.

"Ah. Yes. I remember now. This week has...completely disappeared."

"Along with Juniper?" I respond.

He grows silent, realizing his choice of words, and I reach over to turn off the lamp on the nightstand. I can't even keep my eyes open, and I know he's exhausted, but my brain *just won't shut off.*

"I think what freaks me out about this whole thing is that we just have no idea." I struggle for breath, "I have no idea what really happened to Juniper and who could be writing these notes. It's maddening. I've never felt so unhinged."

Jasper sighs. "It can be terrifying when your enemy is faceless."

I don't even have the bandwidth to think about the truth of this statement. Despite the thoughts scrambling around inside, I feel my eyes grow heavy with sleep.

"It's late. You're talking like an English teacher now."

"What does that even mean?"

"Riddles," I respond, my voice barely above a whisper.

"You need sleep," he whispers back.

And that's the last thing I hear before falling all the way down.

13

I'm in the shower when Simon calls me back. It scares the shit out of me. The steam is so dense that I stumble and nearly crack my skull open on the corner of the marble sink.

Despite me nearly pulling every muscle in my body reaching for my phone, I still miss his call. I tap the corner of the phone on my forehead and wait for my heart to slow down. I think some small part of me still believes that Juniper is just going to up and call me out of the blue.

"Hey, sis. Sorry I've been out of pocket. It's actually a crazy story...."

If only.

I stand dripping on the lone rug listening to his voicemail. It takes less than three seconds to remember all over again why I never liked him.

His message is short. Basically, no he didn't know Juniper was missing, why didn't I call him before, *whinewhinewhine* can I just call him back *whinewhinewhine*.

I curl my lip and make a face in the mirror. Yikes. Juniper

told me a lot of things about Simon, but she never mentioned how deep his need for validation went. Never mind that we have no idea where she is right now. She *clearly* dodged a bullet with this guy.

I know I need to call him back, but it can wait. Instead, I return to the shower, enjoying the way the water feels cascading down my back. I'm exhausted. I got maybe three hours of sleep? I vaguely remember getting off the phone with Jasper around 5am. It was early enough that the first light of morning was starting to peek through the curtains. So even though I spent a good bit in a bath last night, I made the decision to tame the atrocity that was my hair and attempt to wake myself up with a shower.

I reach for the shampoo and massage it into my scalp, allowing the sensation to ease the tension I feel — the exhaustion rooting itself in my bones. I know I need to rest. I know this type of living isn't sustainable, but I haven't rested in years. Why start now? Every time I close my eyes I see Juniper being stalked by some lone figure in the darkness.

How did I not know something was wrong? How did I miss it?

I shake my head, refusing to let myself follow that train of thought. Instead, I run through everything I know so far. Everything is running together now: the drive to Juniper's, meeting Jasper, seeing her school for the first time...

...finding out someone was watching me, too.

Chills erupt on my skin. This week has been one big nightmare. Everything has been one big shit show. Well. Maybe not everything. My mind moves to Jasper. Something flutters at the bottom of my ribcage and I roll my neck in embarrassment.

This can't be happening.

The thing is, it is happening. I know this like I know the all of the true and right things in the world. As much as I fought those first inklings of attraction, they only came back stronger the more I saw him. And well, we've seen each other a lot these past few days.

Our conversation this morning was the most natural conversation I've had in a while. Even though we were fighting lack of sleep and talking about Juniper and trying to parse language on a website written by a high schooler, we bounced off each other organically — the awkwardness and frustration from the car ride earlier in the night vanishing.

I rest my forehead against the wall and let the steam billow around me. This is ridiculous. It's so easy to blame all of the nervous tension on finding Juniper. But that wasn't the entire reason I was nervous, though. If I was being honest with myself, and I'd been trying to do more of that here lately, I would admit that a huge chunk of that nervousness and terror was that I was somehow falling for one of my sister's closest friends.

What the fuck, Lavender.

I push back from the wall and push my fists into my eyes. No amount of denial was going to stop me from seeing what was right in front of me: there was chemistry between Jasper and me. And I had no idea what to do about it.

I lean over and turn off the water and stand there for a moment before grabbing the towel and wrapping it around my hair. Lifting the robe off its hook, I sink into the thick cotton and appreciate the lushness of fabric and how it feels against my skin. I open the bathroom door, tendrils of steam flowing into the main room as a rush of cool air moves its way through the heat of my makeshift sauna. I grab the towel soaking up excess water in my hair and slowly unwrap it, watching my curls cascade around my face.

Looking at my reflection in the mirror, I pause. It's amazing how stress reads itself on your body. My face is blotchy, most likely from the heat of the shower but also probably because

I've drank maybe 12 ounces of water in the last 48 hours. I have to physically work to relax my shoulders so they're not inches from my ears. My eyes are still swollen from all of the crying last night.

I sigh. I know it doesn't matter, not really, but I need to at least *feel* a little more put together. I decide to go with a hair spray promising beachy waves, moisturizer, and mascara. I use the complimentary full-size samples and think about another moment in time where this would feel luxurious and not like I was delaying the inevitable or wasting time thinking about a man I wasn't entirely sure mattered.

The truth is this: I know grief. I know how it plays tricks on your memory or what you feel is important. How suddenly, you can't remember exactly how the person laughed — was it a quiet melody with the face scrunched in glee? Or was it full-eyed, open-mouthed joy? Everything about them fades except for the dull ache of their absence and I would be lying if I didn't acknowledge my mind was already trying to do this with Juniper.

Despite me knowing she was still alive, the only thing I've been able to focus on was the constant refrain of *she's gone. She's gone. She's gone.*

Which makes me feel very much alone.

I breathe deeply, pushing the thought away as I purse my lips and lean into the mirror for one last look before walking out to the bedroom. I tighten my robe and glance at my suitcase. Do I want to get dressed now?

I haphazardly pilfer through what I tossed into the bag before settling on a peach crop top and jeans. I feel my throat tighten and I collapse onto the bed. Wiping my nose, I wonder how anyone can manage to do anything after experiencing something traumatic. I'm useless. I stare at my clothes in a pile next to me and finally curl back under the covers, opting for comfort rather than efficiency. It doesn't last long. My phone vibrates and I look at the screen. It's Dan.

"Hello?"

"Lavender, please tell me you didn't go to the media about your sister."

"I'm sorry?"

He clears his throat, frustrated.

"I'm watching a report right now about your sister. Please tell me you didn't say something."

I turn on the TV and startle when I see Juniper's picture staring back at me.

He's right. Her disappearance is on the local news.

I feel my insides turn topsy-turvy because while this is good, and while it means that movement is happening, it also means it's real.

"Dan, I had nothing to do with this."

The other end of the line grows quiet and I twist my lips, suddenly nervous.

"Hello?"

"Would Jasper?"

I blink in surprise.

"I honestly have no fucking idea but I wouldn't see what he would have to gain in breaking a story. This isn't TMZ, Dan. It's the local news."

He sighs.

"Yeah but if it wasn't you — and it wasn't Jasper — then it's either someone else wanting to be a makeshift vigilante on missing persons or it's him. And if it's him, he's moved to another stage of wanting notoriety."

It's my turn to be speechless.

"He'd scoop his own crime?"

"They do it all the time. Proof they're operating on a failed sense of justice and a severe need of validation."

"Unbelievable," I whisper.

"Just do me a favor," he says, his voice strained. "Stay close. Don't travel too far. And definitely don't go anywhere alone. He did this for a reason, and he's most likely got a plan for his next steps."

A chill runs over me and I nod before realizing he can't hear me. Without thinking, I start telling him about the website.

"Hey, Dan. I - I found something last night."

He's quiet for a moment and I can't tell if he's frustrated about me digging into Juniper's disappearance or waiting for me to continue.

"It's a website. Um. A blog? It's by a student of Juniper's and honestly, it's creepy as hell."

"Tell me more."

"Can I send you the link? I think it would be better if you just read it for yourself."

He sniffs and I can hear a wrapper in the background — as if he is juggling talking to me and breakfast.

"Send it over."

"Sure. Of course. Just...keep me updated."

He hangs up without saying goodbye and I'm left watching the end of the segment, curious at the details they chose to include. I see her picture pop on to the screen again before b-roll footage of the front of Sacred Heart. That's when it hits me all over again.

Juniper is really gone.

I shake my head, forcing the mantra out of its loop, and focus on something else - like the fact that I'm still in my robe. I reach for my clothes, deciding that comfort will obviously have to wait. I unravel my robe and shiver against the cool morning air. I dress quickly and then sit on the edge of the bed, waiting.

I don't know what I'm waiting for, though.

My throat clenches again and I push my fists into my eyes.

I will not cry, I think, threatening my tear ducts with

violence and runny mascara. I blink rapidly, pushing back the tears, and grab my phone.

Desperate times call for desperate measures. I bump my to-do list and hesitate for just a second before pulling up my contacts list.

Calling Simon should help. He never did anything except bore me.

As predicted, he answers on the first ring.

"Were you...were you holding the phone waiting for my call?" I ask as a greeting.

"Well hello to you too, Lavender. Long time no talk." Simon's voice is clipped. I've never gotten used to his accent: a mixture of Long Island and old money. Right now, though, he's just annoyed. It's clear my lack of communication has struck a nerve. I yawn and wave my hand in front of me in a dismissive gesture even though he can't see.

"The pleasure is all yours, Simon." I pause for a beat before launching into the whole reason I was voluntarily talking to him.

"Listen. I know in your message you mentioned you didn't know Juniper was missing. When was the last time y'all spoke?"

Simon clears his throat. "That would uh....that would be when she broke up with me. It was a few days ago, actually. I hadn't tried contacting her or anything since then. I was....trying to give her space."

The change in his usually confident timber startles me silent for a moment. Everything I've ever heard about Simon is that he loved being in control. His insistence on taking care of Juniper in his own way was a muzzle. She would consistently complain about how he would order for her at restaurants before she got there if she were running late or would assume she didn't know how to handle an oil change on her car and would swap vehicles in the middle of the day so he could get it done. I always thought his bravado came from veins of arrogance. Talking to him now? It seemed as if it came from somewhere else.

Knowing my sister, it would still be a deal breaker. Especially if the fragility came at the expense of someone else's freedom and autonomy. I choose to bypass his feelings and move forward.

"I'm honestly not sure if I should even be talking with you about this, but once I found that blog last night, I couldn't help but think you might remember something — anything — that could help us figure out who might have her. Whoever it is has been leaving her notes everywhere. And this blog was written by a student. Is that even a possibility? Could a student be responsible? I don't remember her talking about anyone in particular who gave her a hard time..." I took a breath to pause my own rambling.

Simon was silent.

"Hello?"

"Hey, listen Lavender. I can't talk about this over this line. Can I call you in two minutes?"

"Um...sure?"

The hair on the back of my neck stands at attention as I hear a click. I lower my phone to look at the screen and sure enough, he hung up on me. Even though I know he's supposed to call back, I still jump at the way my phone begins to vibrate in my hand when it starts to ring again. Unavailable flashes across the screen. I answer it, annoyed.

"A private line? Really?"

"Lavender-"

"An odd way to flex you owning a security company, but okay."

"It's not —," he begins but then pauses. "Never mind. Not important. Lavender, your sister and I didn't break up. Not really."

I shake my head.

"Yes - *yes* you did. She called me."

"She lied."

I drop down on the bed, in shock.

"Why would she lie?"

He sighs.

"How much time do you have?"

14

I have no words. I close my eyes, wanting to block out everything he's told me even though I know I can't go back. I'm just about to end our conversation when a knock on the door startles me. I drop my phone and it lands on my pinky toe. The pain is immediate and intense.

"Motherfucker!" I scream. The corner landed right in the meatiest section and already there's a bruise forming. I know Jasper is on the other side of the door, because he is now hollering my name, asking if I am okay. Firecrackers go off inside my veins.

I pick up my phone and catch the tail end of Simon's concern.

"...der? You okay?"

I limp toward the door. "Hi. Yeah. I'm fine. Sorry. I dropped my phone. Hold on a sec." I open the door to see Jasper leaning into it, his muscles taut and his face stressed. My eyes go wide.

"Hi. Sorry. I'm fine. I dropped my phone on my toe." I repeat for Jasper and glance down at the offending limb, now red and throbbing. So much for wearing my converse today.

Jasper runs his hands over his face and breathes a sigh of

relief. "I swear to God, Lavender. If you hadn't answered that door in two more seconds I was going to break it down."

I offer him a half smile and pinch my thumb and pointer finger together.

"Break down the door? That's a bit much. I'm fine. Dial down the machismo, Jasper. You're at like a 10. I need you at a two."

A blush crawls up his neck and once I know he's calm, I return to Simon still waiting on the phone.

"Hey, I'm sorry. Someone just got here —"

"Yeah I heard. It's Jasper. I'll uh...I'll let you go."

"Oh, you know him!" I exclaim, turning a surprised face to Jasper. He looks at me, confused. I mouth *Simon* and his smirk is so large his eyebrows raise. I point my finger at him, threatening him a serious face.

"Oh I know Jasper, alright. Juniper couldn't stop talking about how much he was helping her...how great he was with the students...if she didn't talk about how much she wanted you to meet him I would have thought she wanted him for herself." He laughs quietly. "She uh...she talked about him *all of the time,* Lavender. She really wanted y'all together."

My eyes widen and I catch Jasper's questioning glance before turning away. I can't even be bothered by him saying Juniper was planning on hooking me and Jasper up — but I'm still shook by everything he told me.

"Bye, Simon. Stay safe."

"Bye, Lavender. Don't forget."

I nod, even though Simon can't see me.

"I won't."

I hang up and look at Jasper, who is now sitting at the desk and toying with the on/off switch of the lamp. He's wearing khaki high waters today with a fitted button down Oxford shirt that's a mixture of floral patterns. It's so tight I can see his muscles strain against the fabric. I want to reach out and run

my hands down his back. I blink and look away, confused by
the tingling in my fingers.

"That was Simon," I explain, glancing at him out of the
corner of my eye.

"So you said," he grins.

Oh, god. When I'm nervous I repeat myself.

I can't be nervous right now.

"You told him to stay safe?"

I suck in my teeth.

"Yeah. Yeah he told me some things. Apparently him and
my sister *didn't* break up like everyone thought."

I watch him look around the hotel room and wait until I
have his attention.

"Wait what?"

I nodded. "Yep. That was my reaction too." I pointed at the
chair.

"You're gonna need to sit down."

He crosses his ankle over his knee and rests his chin in his
hand. "Are you as tired as I am?"

I laugh, and some of the nervousness dissipates. "I am in a
perpetual state of exhaustion."

His lips form a thin line and then crack open with a yawn.
He leans back in the chair and stretches, his shirt coming up
just above his pants. I blink and turn away, hoping to alleviate
the blush that just radiated across my skin. He rubs his face
with his hands and then lets them fall in his lap.

"I should have brought coffee over."

"There's some downstairs in the lobby."

"That's peasant juice."

I laugh again.

"Touché."

His eyes crinkle at the edges when he smiles and a playful
look escapes before he can stop it.

"So, speaking of Simon...." He begins.

"Yes. Um. He is looking for her as we speak."

"They didn't break up."

I shake my head. "Quite the opposite. They tried to play the game and played right into his hand."

I bounce my phone against the side of my leg, knowing I could tell him more, but also wanting to protect him. I err on the side of caution and tell him the most important piece.

"He's also gotten notes."

Jasper freezes.

"Notes?"

"Well....*a* note. The morning after they faked their break up he had a note waiting for him on his windshield. Said he didn't deserve her anyways or something like that...."

His eyebrows rise and he drops his leg so both feet are on the floor and he's resting his elbows on his knees. He looks at me.

"That's disturbing. He was watching them. He knew."

I nod in agreement and walk toward him, sitting on the bed. "That's exactly what I told him. He said he's pretty sure he knows who it is and is contacting Dan about it. He left me something downstairs, too. I need to go get it as soon as I can."

Anxious, I pick at the skin on my thumb. I can't talk about this anymore. The anxiety of Simon believing he knows who took my sister, but not filling me in on his identity, is beyond frustrating. As if I don't deserve to know who did this to her.

"So...did you just come by to check on me or...."

He sits back in the chair. "A little bit of everything, really. I wanted to check on you, but I also wanted to make sure you were eating. So I was going to take you to grab some lunch." He looks down where his hands are clasped in front of him.

"And then I saw the news report this morning on Juniper's disappearance." He pauses. "Did you see it?"

"I did."

"At first I thought for sure it was Dan's doing, but then they didn't talk to any law enforcement at all. It was almost a human interest piece."

"He called me thinking we did it."

"Dan?"

"Yeah."

"I'm assuming you told him no."

I start pulling at a strand of hair, still wet from the shower.

"Well, yes. Of course. And then that almost freaked him out more. Made him think this guy is responsible for it now. That he's changing tactics or whatever. Wants more notoriety or something."

Jasper grimaced.

"I've seen this episode on any crime show. It's never a good sign when they change their approach."

I shiver, this time the chills an all-together different sensation than attraction. I move to open the curtains. I need more light.

"On the way over here, my buddy called me. The one who I talked about last night?"

I nod.

"I gave him all of the information he would need to track the website and see if there was any way we could determine who created it. He found something."

Picking at my cuticles wasn't enough; my thumb is now in my mouth and I'm gnawing at the edges of my nail. My heart is racing. I can't say anything. I'm too focused and yet, I feel as if I am in a nightmare all over again. I don't know if I want Jasper to tell me what his friend found. I don't know if I want to be reminded for the second time this morning that I am not dreaming; that this is very real.

Juniper is gone, and someone took her.

I know though that Jasper won't tell me anything unless I ask. Not because he's being facetious and holding on to infor-

mation, but because he's wanting to make sure I'm ready —
that I can handle it.

"What did he find?" I ask, my voice barely above a whisper.

Jasper studies me for a bit longer before continuing.

"He was able to track the IP address to a location in
Newport. When he gave me the area, it's really close to your
sister's house. Like...really close, Lavender. This person could
be a neighbor. Someone she sees all the time."

I frown. "So it's not a student?"

Jasper shakes his head. "I didn't say that — remember,
Sacred Heart is a private school. We don't have districts.
Students simply choose to attend and their parents, guardians,
family — whomever — pay for tuition. It's likely that more
than a few students live in Newport."

"She was so concerned about having a life outside of
Sacred Heart," I say. "Not that her students weren't everything
to her, but she was so adamant about having that boundary."
My lower lip twists in on itself and Jasper wrinkles his
forehead.

"You uh...you just said Juniper *was* adamant."

"What?"

"*Was.* It's past tense. You were talking about Juniper in past
tense."

I freeze, the tears immediately piling on top of each other
and cascading down my cheeks. "You know what I meant," I
sniff. Not willing to look at him. Not willing to admit that internally, my hope is shrinking.

"So all we know is that this person lives near my sister?
That's it?" I can feel the hysteria rising in my chest and I start
pacing again to avoid eye contact. How is this okay. How are we
possibly *here* — within spitting distance of someone who is
actively hurting my sister and out to get me — and basically
have our hands tied.

"Well, there's more."

I stop in my tracks and look at him. My face contorts into a grimace.

"More?"

"There's a name."

I blink a few times, disbelieving. "Your friend was able to track down the person's *name*?! The person who's been leaving us notes and putting in tracking devices to stalk us? Suddenly we have a name?!" My voice is getting louder by the second and I can feel myself hyperventilating. First Simon, now Jasper. "Way to bury the fucking lead, Jasper."

I start clawing at my neck, hoping for some breath to come, but nothing happens. Jasper notices and hesitates for just a moment before standing up and walking over to me in one motion, pulling me close. I hold on tightly, clenching the fabric of his shirt in my fists while the emotion escapes. I can't stop crying. I can't stop thinking of Juniper. Somewhere, somehow, I let her down. Again. It's all I've ever done.

And now here we are, and she's so close yet so far. I practically feel her breathing next to me and yet I can't touch her.

"Let me clarify. We have a name, but we don't necessarily know if it's the person who targeted Juniper. We just know this was who wrote the blog. It's one step closer. My buddy is sending everything to Dan as we speak." I can feel his chest vibrate as he speaks and it's oddly comforting. My breath slows as I take in this information. I have no idea why *this* — an actual tangible piece of evidence, is the one thing that set me off. I step away from Jasper, suddenly embarrassed.

"I'm sorry," I sniff. I swat at the tears on my cheeks, frustrated.

Jasper stands still, watching me. "Lavender, you don't have to apologize. This is a lot. What you're dealing with is a lot. There's no rhyme or reason for when emotion drops like this."

I blink away some tears and try and gain some footing.

"I know. I just....it's not useful."

"It's incredibly useful," he counters. "Feeling your emotions — whatever they are — is healing. You're getting out the pain and terror that you've been holding inside since this began."

"I know that, I do. It's just...have you ever felt like someone threw a grenade in the middle of your life only to run away? That's what this feels like. The grenade just blew up everything and I'm left picking up the pieces."

He lets me sit in the silence for a moment, and then slowly and methodically he grabs the tendril of hair I was playing with earlier and brushes it behind my ear. I feel the skin rise up to meet him and I catch my breath. It's only a moment, though. He drops his hand and my skin craves the heat of his touch.

It's too much. Too fast. My breath catches with the weight of wanting and he steps away, noticing my hesitancy and seeing it as a rebuttal. He has no idea how much I want to push him toward the bed right now.

"You don't have to pick up the pieces alone, Lavender. But you'll need to let others help you."

I stare at him, willing myself to talk — to say something.

"The thing is, Jasper, every time I do that I only end up hurting people more by letting them into the middle of my chaos."

He shakes his head. "That is not true, Lavender. And I think deep down you know it. I think you use this assumption as a way to protect *yourself* from getting too close — and I can prove it to you."

His words are touching a tender spot I've held closely and I walk as far away as I can without actually leaving the room. I'm at the window, once again looking outside, when he goes further than anyone has ever attempted, outside of Juniper.

"It's the reason you haven't been to Providence to see Juniper," he says, his voice dropping an octave. He's gotten so quiet I have to strain to hear him. I turn around quickly, daring him to go further. He does.

"You think that if you stay in San Francisco and build a life without your sister — your twin — up until a few years ago your closest friend — she'll forget about you because you're too much trouble."

"That's not it at all, Jas-" I gasp out the words because the air around us is combustible. I can't breathe because I'm afraid any movement will turn this into something entirely different.

"...And if this happens, you'll be alone." He's not stopping anytime soon. His eyes spark with an intensity that sets me off. My entire body is plugged in, ready to be detonated. I swallow and look away. There's nowhere I can go without hearing what he has to say.

"And you won't have to worry about hurting anyone else. Because the grenade can't go off if there's no one to pull the trig—."

I stop him the only way I know how. I close the distance between us and pull his face toward my own. He startles at first, but doesn't resist. The sound of his words is replaced with the truth of our lips colliding and immediately begging for more. I punish him with my tongue, earnest and heartbroken. He latches on to my waist, his hands digging into the skin. And then just as soon as it starts, I feel his grip loosen and he gently pushes me away. I stand there with my eyes closed for a half second before opening them. The humiliation is overwhelming.

"Lavender....no."

"I-I'm sorry. I just..."

His hands are still on my waist and he moves them to grab my hands and hold them between us.

"No. Not *no never,* just...no. Not like this." He bends over to make sure we are looking eye-to-eye. "Trust me. Pulling away was the hardest thing I've had to do in years."

I fight the urge to look away.

"I was trying to shut you up."

"I know exactly what you were doing. That's why I stopped. You can't use sex as a means to avoid the intimacy of someone really knowing you, Lavender."

His words hit me all over again and I take a shuddering breath, trying to hold back sobs.

He kisses me on the forehead.

"Here's what I'm going to do. I'm going to go get us some food. You stay here. When I come back, we can talk about how we need to fill Dan in on what we've found."

I nod, stepping aside as he walks by me and heads for the door.

"I have my phone if you need me," he says. And I offer a half smile, waving goodbye before he shuts the door behind him.

After he leaves, I stand there for five minutes, frozen. I have no idea how to handle the fact that for a moment, I had forgotten that Juniper was missing. When his lips were on mine, I had forgotten about everything else entirely.

I groan and fall back on the bed, my hands covering my face.

Boom goes the dynamite, I think.

15

You know, I thought we had this psychic connection, you and I.

I thought you understood me.

When you found the blog, I thought you'd see. (How clever of you. My audience never amounted to much of anything outside of Reddit threads for that sort of thing and yet, here you were.) But then you read it — all of it. You dove deep into my words and I never felt so seen. I thought you'd understand the depths of my love and how I can take care of you. I thought you imagined it as I did. Sure, those words weren't for you, but they were for your mirror — they are part of who you are, and so they belong to you too.

But I guess I was wrong.

I sit at my desk and watch as you and Jasper pace around each other in the hotel room, the pheromones so potent I can smell them from here. I snarl.

Fuck the words. Don't you know you belong to me?

When you kiss him, I bite my knuckle so hard I can feel the sharpness break skin. The blood trickles down over my wrist and it feels good, seeing this red while watching you make a fool of yourself with a man who doesn't deserve you.

He even pushes you away and if I was in my right mind, I would probably do the same.

But you have me under your spell and it's all I can do to stay seated and not run to you as soon as he leaves.

All in due time.

I hear a thrashing behind me and know Juniper has woken up. I smile again, anticipation thrumming in my fingers to touch her — feel her — own her.

She catches my eye, the wildness in her gaze a beckoning. I stand up, rolling my neck as I walk over to her.

She waits until I get close enough to taste her before she opens her mouth.

"Asshole."

I blink. Well that was unexpected.

"Juniper. I understand you're confused. I really wish you would—"

"Don't. Call. Me. Juniper." She hisses — hisses! A tingle of excitement brushes across my limbs. Who knew I captured a snake. I hide a smile and rake my fingers through her hair. She jerks away, as if my touch burns her.

As if I'm too hot for her.

"You are an asshole. A degenerate. A —"

I sigh.

"I thought we'd be able to finally have a conversation. Don't you know what I did for you? What I saved you from?"

I open my arms wide, "you have me! Forever."

Her eyes widen and a laugh escapes me.

"I know. It's a lot to take in — breathe for a moment. I know how excited you are."

"You are *sick,*" she whispers under her breath. She catches the feed behind me and starts crying. "Why....Lavender — why do you? What are you going to do?"

"Shhh." I place my finger on her mouth and she wrinkles her nose, turning her head from me. I drop my finger and wrap them lightly around the back of her neck, grabbing a scarf with my other hand. I tie it around her, just tight enough she gets the idea.

"Don't worry about Lavender. She's in good hands. If you're good, we'll try tying this around other body parts. Give ourselves a little fun."

I hear her breath release and relax. Maybe she's finally beginning to see. I close my eyes for a split second, inhaling her scent. She rears back her head and hits me in the forehead and I stumble back, the pain is intense.

"You *whore,*" I say without thinking. I turn to punch the wall before I retaliate and ruin her.

My knuckles throb with the impact and she blinks in pain, a red spot forming on her forehead from where she hit me.

Good.

"You ungrateful bitch," I wrap a chunk of her hair around my fist and begin to pull lightly. Her head shakes slightly, trying to free herself from my grasp.

I laugh. "Don't know you know you won't ever escape me?"

I look her in the eyes, my thumb caressing the skin from her ear to her chin.

"You're lucky I still love you."

A tear leaks from her eye and I smile, lean forward, and catch the waterfall on my tongue. I feel her tense beneath me and a thrill pulses in my veins. She still wants me.

And that's when I realize what you've been trying to tell me this entire time.

You don't want Jasper. You can't stand him. What you're after is *me.*

I kiss her on the forehead and make sure her restraints are tight enough. I gather my things and turn off the feed showing you lying on the bed with your head in your hands.

I won't need that anymore.
You're humiliated, and you should be.
But don't worry.
I'm coming.

16

My whole body hurts. It's probably from how I am curled up in a tight knot, every muscle taut. I ran downstairs after him, thinking that I could do something? I don't know. It was all instinct. Primal. A desperation for connection. I didn't catch him, but I was able to pick up Simon's package while I was downstairs.

I shove my knuckles into my eyes, the exhaustion taking over. I make a concerted effort to stretch, a yawn escaping out of habit. I rub my face with my hands and run over my interaction with Jasper. Again.

I can't believe I kissed him.

I can't believe I kissed him.

It felt like the only option in that moment, like the magnetic force was too strong for our opposing forces. But still. There has to be some circle of hell for those people who fall for someone else while their family member is *missing after being kidnapped.* The shame is visceral. I squeeze my eyes shut, begging for the images of us together to disappear entirely.

I can't believe I kissed him.

I can't believe he pushed me away.

I groan and hide my head under one of the pillows, feeling as humiliated as I did when Jeffrey Sanders stood me up for the middle school dance. Except that time, Juniper decided to stay home with me in favor of eating our weight in Ben and Jerry's and watching *Dirty Dancing* over and over and over again. It might not have been the time of my life, but I wasn't alone and I didn't have to face that heartbreak on my own.

This time I am definitely on my own.

What I would give to hear your voice, Juniper.

I reach for the remote, wanting to see if the news happens to say anything else about Juniper, when my phone vibrates. I look down and see it's Jasper asking what I want to eat. It almost makes me feel worse: knowing he came over to take me to lunch only to run out of the hotel room so quickly after I kissed him that he changed his plans completely *and* forgot to clarify what we were eating.

A flash of embarrassment rakes across my neck and I scratch at the skin, desperate for the heat to go away. I send him a quick text letting him know it doesn't matter. His choice. I've made enough mistakes for the day.

I hit send before I can think better and then throw my phone across the bed. It starts to ring and I roll my eyes. I almost think about ignoring the call, knowing it's Jasper trying to mitigate whatever humiliation he's feeling in the moment, but at the last second I reach across the comforter and hit the green phone signaling connection.

"Jasper, I told you. I don't care. It's fine."

There's silence on the other end of the line.

"Hello?"

I pull the phone away from my ear and check to see if we're still connected. Only then do I realize I'm talking to Dan at the same time he starts to speak.

"Lavender, it's me."

"Oh. Hi."

"Listen. I just spoke with Simon. I also got quite the dossier from Jasper's friend. I think we have a lead."

I hide my curiosity, allowing him to fill in the gaps as he needs.

"Your sister's behavior those last few weeks is concerning and shows a potential pattern. She definitely felt as if she was being watched. We're sensing a familiar countdown that wasn't there before — almost as if we're racing the clock for his next move. There's nothing for you to be worried about....at least not yet. We still have reason to believe your sister is alive. But we're going to move with more urgency."

"Okay. What does that mean, exactly?"

"We've been talking over here and we think we're going to do the search party sooner rather than later. Like...right now. With the news breaking about your sister, we can ride the media wave and hopefully find something. It might be chaotic with Waterfire happening tonight, but that might actually make our search easier."

I blink a few times, trying to get my bearings.

"Wait. Like right now, right now?" I hear sounds in the background that I'm not familiar with — voices talking about framing a shot and specific messaging for the public. Someone shouts a two-minute warning.

"Yep. And uh...we need you to stay put for the time being."

"I'm staying put," I respond.

"I'm serious, Lavender. Part of the escalation we're seeing with this guy leads us to believe Juniper wasn't his first, and she won't be his last."

"You think I'm in danger."

"It's not a supposition at this point, unfortunately. It's pretty definite."

I stumble backwards and land on the bed, my hand flying up to my mouth. I try and control my breathing. My limbs grow cold and I fight the fear from taking root. I glance at the window.

You are as safe as you can be right now. They have people watching — people waiting. He's no match for them. Just...just breathe.

Breathe, Lavender.

I take a breath and clear my throat, but I can't control the shakiness.

"Are there still people watching me?"

"Turn on your TV."

I reach for the remote and flip on the television and turn it to the local station, letting out a squeak of surprise when I see Dan staring back at me in the corner of my screen.

"That-that's you. You're on television."

"Yeah. I don't have much time. You can see they're already taking the stage. Pretty much our entire detail is waiting for the official word to start looking, but we do have one or two guys still keeping an eye out for you. Just...be careful. Please. I know you left your room when Jasper left and stopped by the front desk, but no more of that — we need you stationary. Safe. We've scrambled together a press release where we will discuss a little about the case and focus on the search party. I wanted to fill you in just in case you stumbled into it."

"Stumbled into it?"

"The press conference. It will be on all major networks locally. I figured you might see it."

"Thanks? I guess?"

He makes a noise I can only assume is a grunt of approval. I bring a shaky hand to my forehead and try to rub some of the tension away.

There's a knock on the door.

"Hey, Dan? Jasper's here."

"Sounds good, Lavender. Stay safe."

I hang up without saying goodbye, keeping my eyes on the

television screen as I walk to the door and unhitch the lock. I hesitate before opening the door, wanting to delay any embarrassment or awkwardness for as long as possible. But before I can even swing it open, I see a foot wedge into the space between the frame and the door. Confused, I only have a second to wonder why Simon would force the door open with his shoe when I hear a voice snake across my consciousness.

"Hello, Lavender."

17

What is your weakness, Lavender?

Are you like Juniper, unwilling to let anyone love you?

I don't think so. I think you are a lot like me. You like the chase. It's why you're so frustrated that Juniper's missing. Why you left me notes. This will surprise no one: I *know* you. Like anything I lack an education on, I have studied you extensively.

You love it when people love you. You just have a hard time returning the favor.

Is that why you left Jack?

Why you let Juniper leave California?

I'm in the car now, eyes on your hotel window, amazed at how easy it was to track you down. But then again, it's the hunt that always thrills me.

Juniper figured that out quickly. Just yesterday she asked me how many times I'd done this before, and I quickly kept her mind off the others before her by telling her she needn't worry. You two are all I need.

Something catches my gaze and I see Jasper walk out of the lobby. I look down at my watch, making note of the time. I shift in my seat when I realize just how close I am to you. How close you are to being in my arms. My blood runs electric, knowing it's time. I take a deep breath, steadying myself as I open the car door.

The thing about the hunt — about predators — is that we intrinsically know our prey's weakness. For Juniper, I knew it was only a matter of time before she let go of Simon and found herself more vulnerable.

For you, I knew it would be the exact moment you decide to grab hold of Jasper. A smile crosses my lips as I step out of the car, eyes on the woman struggling with carrying her luggage and newborn. Unable to tame it, her hair flies with the wind and I know she'll be perfect. With two large steps I'm next to her, reaching out my hand.

"Oh my goodness," I whisper, pointing my eyes at the sleeping newborn. "Let me help you, please. My wife and I have a little one at home and I know how exhausting this can be."

She laughs under her breath, gladly handing over a few bags.

"Thank you. So much." She adjusts herself, pulling the baby close to her chest, and I step into a cadence beside her right as the man who has casually concealed himself behind the tree less than five feet away looks up and gives me a brief head nod.

I know it like I know the strands of hair on your head, Lavender: I'm so close to you I can almost taste you and you have no idea.

Love has always been your downfall.

.:::.

WHEN YOU OPEN the door to the room, my heart stops.

God, you're beautiful. Everything about you.

You stumble back, surprised, and I take that opportunity to walk in and close the door.

"Hello, Lavender."

You open her mouth to scream but can't —your fight or flight has kicked in and your entire body shakes, trying to find an exit. Your iPhone drops on the carpet and I reach down to pick it up, putting it in my pocket. I swallow to keep from laughing.

This is going to be so much fun.

"How did you—how—"

"Did I know where you were? How to find you? That you've been waiting for me?"

I walk closer and watch as your eyes dilate with fear. I take my hand and touch your face, snaking my hand down your cheek and to your collarbone. Your eyes close when I grab a piece of your hair and rake it through my fingers.

"You should have known I was watching. You sent me those signs."

You shake your head, confused. When you flinch because my hands tighten around your hair, my breath hitches. Everything about you is art.

"I didn't - signs?"

"The notes, Lavender. Breadcrumbs straight to your heart."

Your eyes turn dark and you pierce me with them. You look so much like Juniper right now and my heart swells. I can't believe how lucky I am to have both of you.

"You're sick," you whisper.

"No, love." I lean into your ear. "I've never felt better."

You try and fight me, but it's no use. You struggle against my weight and *ohmigod* if you feel this good against me now? I can't imagine what your skin will feel like against my own.

"Jasper's coming — and Simon — they're coming and

they'll —" you let out a gasp and I pull you against my chest to feel the whimpers echo against my shirt.

"Shhhhh...." I whisper, reaching behind and grabbing your neck. Your pulse is going crazy and it's driving me mad.

"Here's what we're going to do. We're going to walk out to my car. You're not going to do anything stupid because you know Juniper is still with me and I can do whatever I fucking want to her if you're not around."

You nod against me and I take a deep breath, relishing your movement against my body.

"I've waited so long for this, Lavender."

You let out a sob and I know you have as well. And when the needle pierces your skin, you look at me once more, and I swear my entire world shakes beneath the power of your gaze.

Finally, you are all mine.

JUNIPER

18

No one knows why I moved to Providence. Lavender thinks it's because I had this undying need to get away from her and become my own person. And part of this is true — we've done nothing but be together and do everything together for as long as I can remember. There were times when I wasn't even sure I could breathe without her reminding me to exhale.

But it's not the real reason.

The real reason is that, for once, I wanted to be the one who ran away from the truth. For so long, I tried to power through it. I did counseling and learned all of the tricks; I joined book clubs and support groups and hired a life coach. None of these worked. On the outside, I looked strong. Healed. Resilient. But on the inside, I was as stormy as the ocean in front of me. Grief crashed against every rocky abyss and took me out constantly.

I sigh, staring out into the Atlantic. I miss the warmth of the Pacific. I miss laughing with Lavender and how easy it is to exist next to someone who just....*gets* you. I hear footsteps behind me and my skin grows cold. I fight from looking to see who it is, because I have a feeling I know and I'm wishing — hoping —

it's not him. When I feel hands on my arms I stiffen, only to relax half a beat later. I'd know that touch anywhere.

Simon.

I catch his eyes and smile. "Hey, babe." I lean forward and kiss his cheek, the stubble tickling my lips. He slides back a little and inspects my gaze. Frowning, he roots himself in the sand to really study me.

"What's wrong?"

I swallow and look out to the horizon, avoiding his gaze.

"It's nothing. Just stress about work."

Not a lie, I think.

"Are you and Jasper still up in arms about funding for that formal?" His annoyance is apparent and I hide a smirk. So easily, I could send him on a spiral of jealousy. It's almost cute.

"No. We got that covered. Although we still have a lot left in planning." I take a step to lean into him, letting his scent even out my own breathing.

"You know the offer still stands. I have a spot for you—"

"Simon," I interrupt in warning. "Not tonight. Please."

What he will never know is how tempting this offer to come work with him is for someone like me. I feel out of my element in every way and logically know that my skillset would be needed at a startup like Simon's. But in another quiet, but more unrelenting way, I know quitting my job as a teacher would really be an acquiescence. And I refuse — regardless of what's happening — I refuse to send that message.

We stand there in silence for a moment, watching the colors across the sky shift into indigo and violet.

"You know my mom almost named me Violet?" I ask.

Simon laughs and I can feel him shake his head.

"She told me she loved the imagery of Violet — how it seems to leak into everything. Like ink splatters. She wanted me to be expansive and noticeable."

"Well I think she got her wish even without the name."

I twist my lip to keep from grinning.

"She opted for Juniper because of the same reason — except in her eyes, Juniper held more bite than a color." A laugh escapes me and I look into his eyes.

"My parents named me Simon after Simon and Garfunkel."

My laugh turns into a wheeze and I feel myself being led back to the pier where our dinner reservations are waiting for us. Still laughing, I glance behind me at the waves crashing against the shore, trying to ignore the lone figure that appeared a few minutes ago in the shadows.

I know you're watching me, I think.

I feel Simon's eyes on me and I turn to him and give him my best smile. I know this trick like the back of my hand.

Swallow the storm and exude the sun — no one will ever know the depths of fear and grief and heartache collide beneath the surface.

.::.

I DIDN'T NOTICE it at first. Who would? I think about those moments often — the beginning — how innocuous it all felt. I wanted to make a difference and at first, I thought that's what was happening. I had no idea what was coming — no idea the terror waiting for me. I questioned myself constantly, thinking I was making something out of nothing.

Until it was too late.

Until I knew with unshakeable clarity that in the middle of finding my dream job, I had stumbled into a nightmare.

The worst part? I knew no one would believe me.

.:::.

THE FIRST DAY of school always brings with it a certain chaos: you have the high-pitched reunions of friends who have been separated during their summer break, the whispered earnestness of groups trying to find their place, and the raucous confidence of those who own the halls.

And then there's me: the new teacher.

Or as the group of senior boys I just passed said loud enough for me to hear — "hey look bro, fresh meat."

You would think, after all of the horribly cheesy and addictive teenage rom-coms we suffered through in the late 90s and early aughts, they would know better. I roll my eyes and continue walking, choosing instead to let the freshmen girls walking by me at the same time believe they were talking about them.

Judge your mom.

They blush and giggle, but one of them has the audacity to turn and give the group of guys the finger, biting back, "Horrible idea. Wrong bitch, fuckface. I'm gay."

I hide a smile behind my coffee cup.

I like her.

I'm still smiling when I run into a formidable presence with an arm full of papers.

"Oh!" I exclaim, immediately checking my blouse for coffee. I breathe a sigh of relief when I see that it's still clean. Looking up though, I feel a deep sense of dread. Now that my senses are catching up to me, I realize that coupled with the *formidable presence* is a distinct floral scent spiking the inside of my nose with its musk.

Dammit, I think to myself. There's no way to escape this now.

It's Tracey.

"Oh gosh, I'm so sorry — I was —"

"clearly not paying attention," she interrupts, her lips a solid line of anger. She side steps me and barely turns her head before saying, "I get on to the students for having their gaze focused on cell phones all the time, *Juniper*. It might help if you model the proper behavior, don't you think?"

I squeeze the mug in my hands and take a deep breath before closing my eyes and choosing to ignore her. I survived middle school and graduate school politics — I can certainly survive a petty secretary bitter about her life circumstance.

When I got here this morning, she was already setting up the registration station in the foyer for the students who missed their deadlines over the summer. Folded schedules lined the linoleum-capped tables and I had a brief memory of Lavender and I comparing our small print-outs to see which teachers we'd be able to try and trick over the year.

"Good morning, Mrs. Reese," she clipped, focused on adjusting the sign hanging haphazardly against on of the chairs.

"It's Ms.., actually — or you can just call me Juniper," I said, noting her refusal to listen to the three other times I've asked her to just use my first name. She raised an eyebrow and shrugged a shoulder, mentioning something about having a *blessed first day.*

Now, walking into my classroom, I can't help but notice her distinct choice in using my name when in the hallway full of students — a decidedly pointed power play. I walk to my desk, my heels clicking on the floor and echoing across my empty classroom. I glance at the whiteboard with the date and day's agenda scrawled across it with my handwriting and smile all over again as my gaze lands on my graduate degree nailed into the wall.

If she wants power play, I can give her power play. But Tracey has no idea the kind of bitch I can be when pressed.

.::.

FIRST DAYS of school always turn into second and third and fourth, until before you realize it, you're walking down the halls in late October having developed a rhythm to your days. I know now to get here early — like dark-thirty early — in order to avoid the mad rush of our cafeteria and hallways once students arrive. The silence is grounding, allowing me a moment of zen before the craziness of hundreds of teenagers asking you invasive questions like "do you want to go to the beach party tonight?" And "it's technically not against the law for me to have an empty beer can in the back of my truck is it?"

I roll my neck and mentally prepare for the checklist waiting for me today:

- Grade last week's exams
- Plan next quarter's curriculum
- Call Lavender

I HAVEN'T SPOKEN to her in days and it's weird. I shoot her a quick text, knowing she won't get up for another few hours. I glance at the time on my phone and smile. If it's dark-thirty here, it's still the dead of night in her world.

"Hi, Ms. Reese."

I drop my phone and gasp, grabbing at my chest and in the process dropping everything on the ground. Once I'm able to see through the blotched vision of terror, I fight from rolling my eyes.

"Silas. What are you — it's not even seven in the morning yet...." My heart rate is still going a mile a minute and I'm having to actively train my expression to not show annoyance or anger.

"Did you get my note?"

"Your....your note? What?" I blink and look around, trying to figure out how to get away from this awkward conversation and simultaneously realizing with a sinking stomach that we are the only ones here.

Alone.

"Silas — seriously. What are you doing here? My open office hours aren't until tomorrow. Shouldn't you be at home?" I look around. "Where's Steven?"

Steven is his twin. They're the odd ones out in a lot of ways here at Sacred Heart. Seniors, they fall into the category of late bloomers who possess a birthday too late into the year for their typical peers. Both of them turn 19 next month, and only one of them shows the maturity to match. Where Steven holds emotional intelligence and humor, Silas possesses a strange wit and almost creepy vigilance.

He purses his lips.

"He's lazy. He's still sleeping."

"As you should be, most likely."

The corner of his lips turns into a smile and I cock my head in confusion before deciding to walk past him toward my classroom. I have no patience for this today.

"My note's on your desk."

"Okay."

"I like that sweater," he adds.

Forgetting what I threw on this morning, I glance down and notice the blue threading of the cashmere sweater I purchased simply because it reminded me of mom's acclimation toward anything sensory. When I got it, Lavender balked at the price and didn't understand my reasoning. We got into a huge fight about it.

"You're telling me the *one person* who knows how much mom loved the feel of things against her skin doesn't remember her cashmere sweaters? And doesn't understand why I would purchase this?" I had nearly screamed at her, clenching the fabric in my hands.

She pried the sweater away from me, looking at me out of the corner of her eyes.

"No. I do understand. I get it. I probably would have purchased it myself. Which is why I am shocked you allowed yourself the luxury. Usually I am the impulsive one." She reached for my hand and squeezed it.

I knew she was right. It *was* impulsive of me — so impulsive I bought two. It was that moment I decided to move away.

My hand shakes slightly as I straighten the front and look straight ahead, clearing my throat.

I will not cry here, I think to myself.

"Have a great morning, Silas," I say as I walk away, trying to ignore the footsteps behind me. In normal circumstances, I wouldn't brush off a student like this. But this isn't normal circumstances.

Why is he still following me?

I turn slightly and call over my shoulder.

"I'll see you fourth period." He follows me for a bit, and if I listen carefully enough, I can hear him whispering underneath his breath. It's just soft enough to where I can't make out what he's saying, but it's way too creepy for my taste. I wrinkle my nose and am about to turn around and ask him to leave when his footsteps just...stop. I keep from stopping too, not wanting to invite more conversation, but I can't help but chance a peek around my shoulders to see what he's doing, preparing myself for whatever he might say to trap me into conversation again.

An uneasiness creeps into my veins when I realize he's completely disappeared. I do stop then — doing a complete 360 as the uneasiness slides up my neck. There are no classrooms in this hallway. Mine is in front of me, about 30 steps away. I shake my head. This wasn't magic. There had to be some kind of explanation and I was simply too tired to care. There's no way he could just...dust himself.

It's too early for this fucking Harry Potter shit, I think to myself as I turn around toward my classroom. When I walk to my desk, I see his note peeking out from the corner of my planner, neatly folded. I frown as I pick it up and sit down in my chair. The ruled paper is reminiscent of notes Lavender and I used to pass back and forth in middle school and high school. When I open it up, the uneasiness returns. It's nothing sinister. Anyone reading it would think it a simple note. But with him suddenly appearing this morning and then just as quickly vanishing, I'm struck with a sense of wrongness. I stare at the handwriting again — carefully lined and perfectly placed in the middle of the page.

YOU AND ME? WE ARE THE SAME.

WHAT IN THE ACTUAL....

I SHAKE MY HEAD FURIOUSLY, as if my memory is an Etch-N-Sketch and just the movement will erase the words in front of me. I crumble the paper in my hand and toss it in the trash can under my desk, making a mental note to talk with Lavender about this later tonight. She's the one obsessed with podcasts and the psychology of twisted individuals. For now though, I can't focus on the way my spine feels a little tingly as if I'm still being watched. With a quick glance to my door to make sure it's closed, I pull the stack of papers out of my drawer and choose one of the colorful Sharpies out of my Mason jar-turned-pen holder.

For now, I have exams waiting to be graded.

19

I completely forget about the note until three weeks later, right before Thanksgiving, I get another. And then another when we get back from the break. They're everywhere — in my windshield when I leave for the day. In my drawer waiting for me first thing in the morning. In a sticky note on my whiteboard. One time, I even found one in my purse while fishing inside for a tampon during a two-minute restroom break between classes.

The messages are all obscure, but specific to conversations we've had or things he's told me. Some mention that he likes what I wore to work. Others have something simple about him thinking about me while he's doing his homework at night. Some are questions about my own preferences: do I like the ocean or mountains? (He asks because my eyes remind him of the sea, he writes.) Do I get notes from other students? What do I do when I'm at home by myself? Do I think about my students when I'm not at school?

Do I think about him?

The other night, after our date, Simon almost found the piece of paper before I could. Hanging precariously between the windshield wipers, I snatched it and with one swift movement, crumbled it up and tossed it in the bushes next to us.

"What are you doing?" he asked, curious.

I didn't realize he'd seen me. I looked up at him, my eyebrows raised. "Hmmm? Oh." I brushed my fingers across my skirt, flinging my hands in the same direction I did when I tossed the note. "There's just all of this static that I'm trying to get rid of — it happens every winter," I chuckled under my breath and then shrugged my shoulders like the Elmo gif. I smirked and leaned forward, far enough to where I knew he could see a good angle of my cleavage. "If you're brave you can come kiss me and see if there's a spark...."

He laughed then and rolled his eyes, keeping his attention at the way my body pulled at the fabric of the blouse. I knew I had effectively gotten his mind off anything he might have seen me do, but it took a few minutes driving home for my pulse to return to normal. Right before I threw the paper, I saw what it said and it was more blatant than others had been in the past.

WHEN YOU TWO ARE ALONE, DO YOU GET YOUR LIPSTICK ALL OVER HIS BODY?

It's getting embarrassing. No, that's not right. It's getting embarrassing because somewhere inside I'm *worried* that if others found out they would think the wrong thing. More than once, I've seen other students exchange glances when I discreetly toss a scrap of his paper he left somewhere into the trash. I remember being in high school and seeing things teachers didn't think I noticed. I know they see, and I know they're talking. This is terrifying. I'm thinking about the oddity and just how to handle it when I hear movement in my doorway. I glance up, and fight from sighing.

"Silas."

He enters then, as if he were waiting for my acknowledgment before moving forward.

"I brought you a Christmas present."

"Silas—"

He puts his hand up and smiles in a way that's condescending. This shocks my joints in a way that's difficult to describe, given his age. How these kids are able to literally stop me mid-sentence because of a single look I will never understand. Gen-Z is a force unbeknownst to even themselves. I raise an eyebrow and fall back to rest against the back of my chair.

"Are you going to see Lavender over the break?" he asks.

I'm about to ask how he knows about my sister when I realize we had this conversation a few months ago when I dropped the fact that I had a twin in the middle of class. He stayed after to question me profusely and even mentioned at one time he had a hard time believing that the world was lucky enough to have two of me. It made me feel weird then, and it makes me feel weird that he's asking about her.

He notices the question fall over my face and he laughs and shakes his head.

"I honestly still can't believe there are two of you."

He has no way of knowing how this grates on so many of my triggers of being one and the same with Lavender. I wrinkle my nose.

"I think, being a twin yourself, it's easy for you to know there are not in fact two of me. My sister and I are very much our own people."

He shrugs and looks at me, and is just about to say something when I lean forward. The weather is getting bad outside, the hallways are getting dark with staff leaving, and I need to get out of this classroom and yet another situation where it's me and this kid by ourselves. I just decided, this moment, to talk with him about the notes. Bring the power back, so to speak.

"Actually, I'm glad you stopped by, Silas."

His gaze shifts and his entire being lights up with an energy I'm not ready for and I stall for a moment, caught off guard once again by the way he was able to fill an entire room with an obvious anticipation. This might be more difficult than I thought.

"These notes you're leaving me..."

He takes a step forward.

"Yes?"

I breathe in for a moment, searching for the right words. I know the way I say these next few sentences will make or break an entire year with this student if I'm not careful. Hell. It could impact the entire class. Word spreads. Fast. And with one false move, one careless whisper, I could undo everything I've been working on this semester. I decide on frank honesty.

"I'm going to speak candidly for a moment. These notes make me uncomfortable." I avoid his gaze while speaking, knowing just by the shift in temperature a cloud has settled on his features.

"There are boundaries that exist between a teacher and a student for a reason."

"I know," he whispers. "But—"

"...and *even if* those boundaries didn't exist for a very good reason, I have a boyfriend." I interject.

He looks at me and glances away, studying the window and the snow falling outside. I wrinkle my nose when I realize my commute home is going to be a disaster.

"I understand."

"Thank you."

"Have I ever told you about the train wreck down in Louisiana?"

I blink a few times, trying to follow his line of thought.

"The train wreck?"

"There was this train wreck down in Louisiana. No one

knows what happened. There were no passengers, just crates, and the conductor wasn't injured. I think that's why no one ever heard about it. But it's important because there is no reason why the train had to derail like it did. They had engineers, scientists, mechanics — all of these people studying the impact and the how of the crash because it was a mystery. Nothing caught in the tracks. Nothing or no one jumped out in front of them, causing a shift in direction. The train was fine, and then it simply wasn't. They were picking up pieces of the train from the field and marsh for months afterward."

He's getting into his story now, pacing a little bit in front of me. I cover my mouth with my hand to hide the frown because I legitimately have no idea where he is going with this story.

He pauses for a moment and looks at me. I hold out my hand in an expectant pause.

"And?"

"And what?"

"What did they find? Why did this train crash?"

"They still don't know. But it's an interesting story."

I'm quiet for a moment.

"I don't think I understand, Silas."

He smiles and places the gift on my desk before turning to walk away. Right before he leaves the room, he turns and places his hand on the doorframe.

"Don't you know? It's never smart to stop a moving train, Ms. Reese."

Chills run down the length of my spine and I keep my eyes forward, focused on him.

"Have a great holiday, Silas."

"You too." He smiles and turns then, and I wait until I don't hear his steps anymore before I allow my head to fall into my hands.

What. In the actual. Fuck.

"Well. Let's hope that language is reserved for when students are not in your presence, yes?"

I startle and choke back a moan. I had no idea I was speaking out loud. I refuse to look up though. I massage my temples and wonder if she'll leave if I just refuse to engage.

"Silas was here late again."

Dammit.

I look up and smile at Tracey.

"He had a gift he wanted to drop off before he left."

She clucks her tongue. "That's sweet. He couldn't do it during his class earlier in the day?"

I roll my eyes and reach for a nearby hair tie, throwing my messy curls into a bun.

"That is an excellent question, Tracey. Why don't you try and engage with him about appropriate ways to handle authority next time you see him."

Her eyes fall into slits and she sits down in a nearby desk and I let all of the four letter words I can possibly think of fill up my veins.

"I'm concerned about you, Juniper. I've heard whispers, you know."

I sigh and throw my hands down in my lap, looking at her with incredulity.

"Whispers?"

"About you and your relationship with your students."

"Oh. Rumors. Rumors that are completely unfounded, might I add."

She hums under her breath.

"What did Silas get you for Christmas? A gift card? A coffee cup? Maybe some cookie ingredients in a mason jar?" She scrunches her face in a fake smile and waits.

I glance at his gift and shrug.

"I don't know. I haven't opened it."

"Oh! Exciting. Let's see."

I know I'm not getting out of this, but I definitely don't want to open this gift in front of Tracey when I have no idea what is in it. I hesitate for half a second before reaching for the bag. Just a quick peek tells me it's a frame of some kind, but I have no idea what picture he would have put in it.

"It's a....a picture frame?"

She frowns.

"Just a frame? Well that's odd. But sweet, I guess."

I pull it out and twist it around to see the picture. At first, it looks as if it's a standard stock photo of a woman on the beach, staring at the ocean. But then I look closer, and realize I know those boots. And...that blue sweater. My hands start to shake and I swallow, trying to stay calm while mentally calculating how in the world he could have captured this without my knowing.

I look up, dreading the look on Tracey's face when she sees my reaction, but she's already gotten up out of the desk and is walking toward the door. I settle my nerves by taking a deep breath and smiling the biggest smile I can muster when she turns around.

I'm a fucking pocketful of sunshine, I think to myself as she catches my smile and offers me a half-assed one in return.

"Thank you for your concern, Tracey. I mean it," I say as I begin to gather my belongings and step toward her, my intent clear. "I hope you know though there is nothing — and never will be anything — between me and any of my students. The fact that you even consider this..." I pause.

"Oh no, dear. I know you would never —"

"—but you came to me to make sure it is being *whispered* about, as you said."

"Of course. You can't be too careful. And there are always eyes in the halls. You should know that by now — how quickly the word spreads to some wild version of the truth."

I take a deep breath and look at her once more before

walking past her and into the hall. I am desperate to leave at this point.

"Thank you, Tracey."

"Juniper—"

I keep walking, face forward.

"Have a good break, Tracey."

I keep walking until I hit the bitter wind and push through until I can get into my car and turn on the heat. Only then do I notice the scrap of paper tucked into my rearview mirror, the handwriting bone-crushingly familiar.

YOU CAN'T STOP THIS TRAIN, JUNIPER.

I RIP it off my mirror and throw it outside, the sobs coming without warning. I watch as the note disappears in the snow, and I know by the time everything melts it will be gone. The feeling of it lingers, though, and I claw at my cheeks to stop the mess of tears falling with an urgency I can't contain.

I slam my hands against the steering wheel and feel my breath in short gasps trying to return to me. I can't let this get to me — I have no idea why it's affecting me so much. I try to remind myself of the truths I know:

- He's only 19 years old.
- He can't hurt you.
- You're doing nothing wrong.
- He's crossing boundaries you have clearly set.

DESPITE ALL OF THIS, there is a glaring truth that is staring me straight in the face and causing me more and more anxiety the more I ignore it. It's the truth that I am entirely alone in this.

There is no one who would believe me if I even begin to try to explain what's going on — I have no notes anymore. I have no recordings. I have no proof outside of my own story, and given Silas' intellect and his belief that we are on a moving train headed who knows where, I wouldn't put it past him to change the narrative quick if I ever said anything.

And when it comes to relationships between students and teachers, it's always the student's word over anyone else's — for good reason, too.

And yet here I am, in the middle of a literal nightmare, without any recourse to advocate for myself in any way.

I realize then Silas is right. I am stuck on a moving train. And I have no idea how I am going to get off.

20

By the time I get home, I'm emotionally drained. Not only did I have a hell of an ending to the semester, I still haven't finished inputting grades from finals, and I just drove through a NorEaster. I stretch out my fingers and grimace from the ways my muscles protest the lengthening after over an hour of clenching them so tightly around my steering wheel they stuck themselves in that clawed position.

First thing I do is kick off my heels and change into an oversized sweatshirt and leggings. Lavender called earlier, but I can call her back later tonight. She just wanted to virtually celebrate the end of my first semester and I know she'll gather that something is wrong and I don't feel like talking about it. I can't even imagine trying to capture the conversation with Silas and the note that followed. Actually, I can — she would demand me to *call someone, anyone, most definitely his parents, so that his creepy ass wouldn't bother me anymore*. But all I care about tonight is finding some type of documentary and downing a bottle of red wine...maybe with some pho. My phone vibrates and I look down to a text from Simon.

I sigh, unable to find any of the necessary emotional

strength to engage with him right now. I turn my phone off and drop it on my sofa. He can wait too.

And so can this...problem with Silas. I make a commitment to myself to deal with it all tomorrow and roll my head, stretching the muscles in my neck. My mind naturally gravitates toward Mom and how she might handle this. I stand there, frozen, and close my eyes – letting the ache take over.

"I'm sorry," I whisper, tears threatening to spill. I refuse to let go completely though. If I let go completely it won't ever stop. The grief, the hurt, the guilt — it will envelop me. I know that much. I shudder through a few breaths and open my eyes, glancing around my living room.

That's when I remember.

I walk to my closet and push the clothes back to the chest hidden in the corner. I pause for a moment, my heart hammering.

I haven't opened this chest in years.

I pull it out, my feet sliding on the carpet. I set it at the foot of my bed and light some candles, and then open my window so I can hear the waves crashing in the distance. It's cold, and I don't know how long I will manage to keep the window open, but I can't resist the urge to get as close as possible to the ocean's pulse. I stand there for a moment, watching the snow fall sideways, blanketing the cliffs in front of my house, and find myself grateful all over again for this respite I found by simply driving by the moment they put up the available sign on the porch.

I sigh, the days' stress falling away as the ocean's rhythm fills my veins, and I turn back to the chest. I sit down in front of it, rubbing my hands on my leggings, gaining warmth and resolve. When I unhook the latch, the memories trip over each other. My mother wrapping this blanket around her on the coldest nights. I rub my hand over the fabric and let the tears fall before noticing the robe she wore every single day after her shower. I touch it, gingerly, afraid of what might happen if I grab hold of it. Beneath the clothes and keepsakes, I find what I'm looking for — her box of tarot cards.

I asked her once why she did this, and she pulled me close and kissed me on the temple.

"Magic," she whispered.

I frowned, twisting my head so I could look at her. "But how can you prove it?"

"Sometimes the only things that can be proven are internal — what we feel." She studies me some more. "You know that, Juni."

She waited for a moment, letting the silence fold in around us.

"The important thing about tarot is that it's not a fortune-telling technique. If anything, it illuminates the truth of our own power and, if we're listening, helps us see the shadows of what we're missing internally. It's about energy. Intuition. I am the one who has the privilege of holding the mirror. If I'm doing it for myself, I have the privilege of holding space for the truths inside that need to come out."

I reach for the deck inside the chest, dusty and faded. Picking it up in my hands, a spark of energy flows through me and the tears are immediate. Despite my best efforts, I cannot get away from her. It feels as if she's right here beside me.

Here is a secret I've told no one: Lavender is right. Part of what made me curious about Providence was its name. Denoting magic and illumination and destiny, my research kept coming back to the small coastal town that bore the name signaling protection. It felt like what Mom used to call *a God wink*. All my life I've relied on logic and things able to be proven, and I needed something different.

I needed my mom.

I needed her magic.

I shuffle the deck, the tears beginning to flow again. I have no idea what I'm doing, but I'm allowing myself to be moved by the rhythm. I smile for a moment, thinking what Lavender would do if she saw me now, knowing that after her initial freak out she would gather the crystals she keeps in her pockets and bra and purse — many of which she took from Mom after she died — and come sit across from me, joining me.

I feel her too.

As I shuffle, I feel the atmosphere change and my ear turns toward the window. In the distance, I hear thunder rolling across the water. Chills run up and down my arms and I clear my throat, rotating my shoulders and closing my eyes to breathe *once, twice, three times.*

Each time expanding into the space more and more.

Once I know I'm ready, the cards begin jumping out of the deck as I shuffle. I take them and place them in front of me, face down. I pull five. I stare at them for a moment and gather my hair into a bun to keep my hands from nervously flipping them over unnecessarily. Now that I've pulled them, I'm feeling the hesitancy of finding out what's on the other side. I decide to do it slowly — with my breath.

The first card: Strength.

My focus and courage are an asset, I think.

Second card: Nine of Swords.

I swallow.

The strength I possess is from the trauma I've endured.

My fingers hover above the third card, unsure. A candle flickers next to me and I breathe in quickly, the cold air rushing against my neck. The wind flips the rest of the cards over and I stare at them, begging my breathing to remain calm. The three cards remaining: The Tower, 8 of Swords, and Wheel of Fortune, reversed.

A sob escapes my mouth before I can stop it. I know the meaning of these cards because I feel it in the core of who I am — my mom was right. From my marrow I see everything illuminated: upheaval is coming. It's why I feel trapped. Regardless of what I do or how I fight it, what comes next is an inevitable piece of my fate. I can feel my pulse beginning to drum a *ratatatat* rhythm behind my ears and I know I'm headed for a panic attack. I push away from the chest, anxious to get away from the cards and silently criticizing my desperate attempt to feel connected to my mother.

You knew this would happen, I berate myself.

Now, I have the silly messages of cards attempting to throw my entire mental state off-kilter. I wipe the tears on my sleeve and am about to reach for the cards to shove them back in the box and into the chest when the electricity shudders and crashes, leaving me in complete darkness outside of the candles flickering in the wind.

I sit there for a moment, frozen. Am I waiting for footsteps? I try and swallow and can't — the panic growing by the second. I close my eyes and breathe through my nose. My hands clench at my sides and I start shaking my head involuntarily, as if I can change the outcome through simple denial.

No.

No.

"Enough," I mutter. "I'm done with this Sabrina the fucking teenage witch nonsense." The wind rushes in then, flowing my curtain sideways and blowing every last candle out so I'm really in pitch black. I choke on my sobs and laugh to keep from going absolutely mad. I stumble around on my hands and knees, trying to find the edge of the chest, when the electricity flickers back on and the curtain settles in the slight breeze left behind the hurricane-level gale.

I sit back on my feet, tucked underneath me, and blow my cheeks out in a breath.

"What the fuck," I whisper to myself.

Only then do I see another card flipped over, close to my five. I frown and reach for it, and when I see what it is, I gasp and pick it up, holding it in front of my face to make sure I'm seeing it correctly.

It's the Star.

The nickname mom used to call me, from the song she'd always sing me before bed.

Baby you're my shining star....

I hold the card close to my chest, soaking in the hope and knowing that regardless of what's coming, I know it's going to be okay.

.::.

I WAKE up on the floor, warm under one of my weighted blankets. I kick off the covering and reach for my phone to check the time only to remember it's on the couch — conveniently out of reach and powered off from those distracting me from my wild night of tarot and grief. I sit up, rubbing the sore muscles of my shoulders and arm and blink slowly, gathering my bearings.

I don't remember falling asleep.

I also don't remember grabbing my blanket and putting it on me. My eyes fall toward the clock on my wall and I note the time — a little after 8pm.

I've been asleep for maybe two hours?

I breathe a few times, and notice the Star card resting next to me. I remember that — I remember the wind and the feeling that my mother was here with me, guiding me, comforting me. I pick up the card and move to place it with the rest of the deck.

If I can find the deck?

I glance around, moving my body in a slow circle, thinking

the cards had to have ended up somewhere near me. Only when I notice the slight glow of my master bathroom casting shadows across my floor do I see the entire deck safe in the box — placed gingerly right next to the chest. I blink again, this time really confused. I distinctly remember the cards being *everywhere* because of the gust of wind and my electricity flickering — I was in complete darkness when that happened.

My heart drops.

I glance back at my bathroom and my breath hitches.

I didn't turn that light on.

Also, the window. I turn my head and look at the indigo sky crystal clear through my now *closed* window.

Fuck. Fuck fuck fuck.

The window was open and now it was shut. No wonder I was sweating underneath my blanket. I'm stiff with fear, knowing there are a lot of things that can be explained away when you're this exhausted and toying with grief, but not this. Not cards being carefully placed back in their box or the light being turned on or me suddenly having a blanket over me or *the window closing by itself.*

I'm breathing heavily then, the terror taking over. He's here. I know he's here. Or he was. I try to figure out what to do — should I act as if I'm still asleep? Get up and run out the door? Hide in the closet? — when I hear something in the kitchen. I stuff the blanket in my mouth to keep from screaming. I reach around me for anything that can be considered a weapon and spot a vase on my nightstand. As quietly as I can, I get up and walk toward it, wrapping my hand around the flowers Simon got me last week.

"Oh. You're up."

I pause mid-grab and startle and I hear Simon rush to my side, his hands on my arms.

"Babe. What? Are you okay?"

"Simon," I whisper through gritted teeth. "You scared the

shit out of me. Why are you here?" My eyes shoot toward the living room and my front door. "How'd you get in?"

He puts distance between us and studies me, his hands up in surrender.

"I — I'm so sorry. I got worried when you weren't answering your texts because I knew you drove home in this weather, so I stopped by to check on you, only to find your front door unlocked and you asleep on the floor." He motions behind him, where my blanket still rests. A small smile gathers on his face.

"I didn't know you're into tarot."

"I'm not." My voice is curt. I know it and I can't stop it. Simon blinks in shock and backs away even more.

"Juniper—"

I close my eyes and sigh, my hand flying up to my forehead to massage it. "I'm fine. It's fine. I'm sorry." I motion toward the tarot deck. "Those are — *were* — my mom's. I was just looking through them." I clear my throat and throw him a half smile.

"I'm glad you're here. I just—I don't remember falling asleep and was more than a little confused and concerned when I woke up in a completely different state. Thanks for taking care of me — shutting the window, putting the blanket on me — all that."

He nods, still studying me. He pulls something from his back pocket and passes it to me. It's an envelope — sealed.

"What's this?"

"I don't know. It was on your front door when I got here." He studies me for a moment. "Babe, who is giving you these notes? Do I need to be concerned?"

I roll my eyes as I pull the paper out of the envelope and pretend to read. "It's a student playing a joke. A horrible joke, but a joke. I'll talk to his advisor after the break." I place the envelope and note on the bed and turn my attention to Simon, summoning as much sunshine as possible.

He frowns for a beat, countering the brightness of my own

features, before his eyes gravitate toward the window. "You had the window open? In this storm?"

I breathe a sigh of relief, knowing I have avoided the inevitablity of Simon finding out the extent of what's happening for one more day.

"I did — it wasn't that bad at first. There was just a slight breeze but the waves more than made up for it. Thank you — again."

He leaves the room for a moment, and I hear him rustling around the kitchen.

"I brought pho over," he calls from the other room and I fight a smile — grateful for how he knows me. My attention turns toward the envelope and I start to open it, pulling the piece of paper out as Simon walks in with a piping bowl of broth and beef planks. I'm salivating I'm so hungry. I grab the bowl and turn to put it on my nightstand, the note placed underneath it.

I sigh, my hands coming up to my face again. He wraps his hands around my wrists and pulls them down so he can see my face, pushing the tendrils of hair that have fallen from my bun behind my ear.

"You really are exhausted, aren't you?" he whispers. I lean into him, forgetting everything for a moment. I breathe in his scent and embrace the comfort of knowing someone is here with me.

"Today was a day," I muttered.

He grunts in agreement. "I would say. You don't even remember shutting the window or putting a blanket on yourself before falling asleep?" He chuckles to himself and I stiffen. He kisses the top of my head and tries to keep the laughter from his words. "Babe. It's fine. You've seen how I get before presenting to potential angel investors — I get almost delirious with exhaustion. You just need some sleep."

I squeeze him tight, the fear permeating every cell in my

body. Only then do I glance down at the envelope and recognize the handwriting and realize I was right. My eyes move to the note and I quickly read the words.

YOU'LL NEVER KNOW *how tempting you were —*   *alone, asleep, unaware.*

   Don't worry. One day, you'll feel the warmth of my skin.

I BITE my tongue to keep from screaming and cling to Simon with a little more ferocity.

   He was here.

21

I can't stop shaking. I convince Simon it's because I'm so cold. It's not entirely a lie. The snowstorm outside has wormed its way into the tiny cottage.

"I don't doubt it! I can't believe you had that window open..." he shakes his head and I bite my lip to keep from spitting back a retort when I know he doesn't deserve it. I watch as he makes his way toward the thermostat.

"Jesus, Juniper. It's 60 degrees in here. You don't even have your heat running."

"I live off a teacher's salary, Simon."

"At a private school," he quickly reminds me. I shrug and hear the heater click into gear.

"The pho is helping — thank you for bringing this."

He nods and glances out the window.

"Do we know how long it's going to snow?"

"I don't know. I think I heard all weekend?" I follow his gaze and notice the way the drifts are getting taller by the minute. I'm still not used to this — seeing a veritable winter wonderland right outside my door. We don't get snow in San Francisco, and outside of a few trips, I've never lived where this is normal.

I'm mesmerized by the way the white crashes against the black expanse of sky.

"What are you thinking about?" I ask, casually. The way he's looking out the window has me on alert. Does he see something?

"Huh?" He turns to look at me. "Oh. Um. Nothing. Just watching the snow — it's really come down now, huh?"

"You're not planning on leaving tonight, are you?" I feel the way my voice shakes and I hope he doesn't notice. I need him to stay. On top of Silas having been in my home, there's also a real risk in him driving in this storm. I lean forward and wrap my hand around his arm.

"I have plenty of groceries. I had some delivered yesterday. Even got the last few rolls of toilet paper." I wiggle my eyebrows and he laughs.

Good. Yes. Normal. Everything is normal.

"If it's okay with you, I think I will?"

I nod and he leans toward me as well, our bodies magnets. He wraps my hair around his finger and lets it fall. I can feel the temperature in the room change, the atmosphere moving from one of playfulness to one of curiosity. Of want.

"You're beautiful. You know that?"

I flinch without thinking and he rears back, his eyes wide.

"Juni?"

My skin crawls and I take a sudden breath, not prepared for the reaction. *What...the fuck was that?* His hands move to touch my thigh and I move my leg, worried about what might happen if his fingers touch my skin.

Normally, his touch moves me. I lean into it. Tonight however, the very thought of anyone touching me leaves me feeling shaky and uneven. His words, however familiar, land with a dull thud in my gut and it's all I can do to not choke. I make an awkward face while slurping up chicken broth and mutter a thank you, side stepping the conversation by pointing to my bowl of noodles.

"Sorry. I think...I think I had a bad bite of something. It tasted sour." I point to my bowl. "This needs a bit more heat. I'm going to grab some sriracha from the cabinet. Be right back."

I walk down the hall and take a few deep breaths, forcing myself to keep walking. My legs are shaking though, and I can barely put one foot in front of the other.

What just happened there? Why is my heart pounding?

My hands start to shake again, causing my broth to spill over the bowl's edges. My vision starts to blur and I reach for the counter to steady myself. I don't know why my chest feels so tight? I can't get enough air. My arms, suddenly 30 pound weights, have me struggling to lift my bowl to the microwave. I settle on the stove — for now — and lean forward, my head in my hands, and the tears begin to fall.

The fear rises up and I start to choke. I have no idea what's happening to me. Simon calls from the room, asking if I'm okay.

"Fine!" I muster in between breaths.

Wait. I've been here before.

The familiarity slowly comes to the surface. I *do* know what's happening. There's only been one other time where I have felt this way.

My breath hitches and I bite back a sob. I am not going there today. I won't. The grief threatens to suffocate me and I shake my head.

Stop.

I can't let this win. I can't. Not now — not when I've come this far. But it's too late. The memories are here before I can push them away.

.   .   .

I'M IN OUR ROOM, cleaning.

I clean when I'm upset, and I'm pissed. I've taken every single book off the wall of shelves and am reordering them by color. I know this will freak out Lavender, and it's the only thing I can think of to shake her from being such a selfish bitch.

She's not the only one who can be impulsive.

"How's *this* for chaotic energy, Lavender fucking Reese?!" I whisper as I tear a page from one of her school books she left in my room.

I sniff, recognizing it's only the title page — the one with PROPERTY OF BELLVIEW HIGH stamped in black ink. We don't even go to Bellview, *but that's not the point.*

The point is chaotic, impulsive, spontaneous energy.

Isn't that what she told me earlier, her face bright with laughter?

"You're such a bore, Juniper. You should have some fun every once in a while."

She's gone now. Told me *Thad* wanted to hang out and do something special. I shake my head, hoping to free images of her stuck in some cellar or dirty basement. What kind of name is *Thad*. Doesn't she remember what Mom told us about men and names? This guy sounds like the worst kind of character in the cheesiest rom-com. Like that guy who was a reality show star but also had an STI. Or the one who spit in girls' Coke and was called *annoying* but really ended up being a rapist.

I let out a groan and throw a book across the room. I pause. That was *my* book. Apparently I woke up this morning and chose literary violence. I sigh and walk to pick it up, straightening out the edges bent in the display of anxiety.

I don't trust him. She left earlier, despite me telling her she shouldn't. I know Thad is bad news, and I have the texts asking if I'd be interested in a threesome to prove it. I know she won't listen though, and she asked me to cover for her tonight so I'm pissed.

But I'm not angry with her. Not really.

I'm pissed at myself for telling her I would keep Mom from knowing. I'm pissed that I can't grow a fucking backbone and tell her who Thad really is — regardless of her heart breaking.

I throw a copy of *Pretty Little Liars* in the trash. One of her favorites.

Serves her right, I think. And then I roll my eyes because of course I can't throw a book away. I walk over to the trash and pull it out, throwing it on her bed in bent disarray.

I hear a knock on the door and I groan. I know it's Mom. I know she hears me banging around in here and is wondering why I'm mad. I know she'll try her hardest to get me to talk.

"Come in," I mutter loud enough for her to hear.

She opens the door and leans against the doorframe. Her crystal blue eyes find my own and she watches me for a moment before speaking.

"Hey, Juni. It's kinda late. Whatcha doin'?"

I toss books aside on my bed and shove one with a red spine against another one that's burgundy.

ROY G BIV, I think to myself again and again. It's centering. Distracts me from Lavender and her poor life choices. For a brief moment, I wish she was here next to me, her eye for design helping me pin point the perfect rainbow ombre.

I huff, frustrated that even now — even when I am so bloody upset with her — I still recognize her absence.

I glance at my mom, still waiting by the door.

"I'm reorganizing."

She pushes herself off the frame and walks in, moving some books aside so she can sit on my bed.

"I see that." She waits a beat. "Wanna talk?"

I shake my head, wiping my eyes with my forearm.

I will not break.

I may be pissed, but I'm not a rat. And I definitely am *not* going to cry over this.

"Where's Lavender?"

"Out."

"Out?"

I sigh.

"She went to the movies with some friends. I had to study for a test tomorrow, so I stayed home."

She's silent.

"So...you're reorganizing your books because...."

"...because I want to."

"Juniper."

"Mom." I can hear the frustration in my voice and I can't help it. She knows I clean when I'm mad, and she knows I'm reorganizing for some reason and that I'm not talking about it, so *why is she still in here wanting to talk about it.*

I hear her stand and a few books tumble to the ground from the movement. She walks up behind me and places her arms around my shoulders, clasping her hands in front of me. I reach up and grab her wrist out of habit. She smells like spice. Earthy. Floral. It's the scent of my childhood. She starts swaying and I follow, closing my eyes to the rhythm. I gotta hand it to her. She's got the maternal instincts of a saint.

"I was thinking tonight would be a *really* good night for ice cream sundaes and *Dirty Dancing.*" She squeezes me a bit in a hug. "What do you think?"

I let out a breath. That sounds divine.

A tiny glimmer of hope.

"Do we even have the stuff to make sundaes?"

She shrugs.

"I can go get them."

I turn around then, looking at her. I really want this. But I also don't want to be *that girl* who needs her mom to make midnight trips in order to make her feel better.

But I do want it.

"Mom. It's like 10:30."

She smiles, a coy look taking over her features.

"It is. And the grocery store is open 24 hours."

She raises an eyebrow in question.

I start laughing.

"Yeah. Okay. Yeah let's do it."

She claps her hands and does a little dance and I roll my eyes because *ohmigod* please don't dance like that, you're like 40 years old.

She really laughs then, and we walk down the stairs and into her room where she grabs her keys.

"I'll have my cell phone if you need anything."

As she passes me, she leans over and kisses me, pulling me close.

"You're my shining Star, Juni. I'll be right back."

They were the last words she ever spoke to me.

An hour and a half later, my heart rate starts picking up a staccato beat, the worry increasing by the minute. I pace around our house, shaking my arms because they feel like lead, telling myself that it's okay, she's okay, there's probably a logical reason it's taking this long.

Two hours later, I start calling her cell phone over and over and over again only to get voicemail every time.

And three hours later, when the lights start flashing in front of our house and someone knocks on the door, I already know by the way my chest refuses to let any air in my lungs that whatever is outside waiting for me is all my fault.

If I hadn't been so angry. If I would have just pretended to be okay for one fucking minute, Mom wouldn't have felt the need to leave.

She would still be with us.

It's why I stayed in my room for so long — locked away from everyone else. I couldn't bear to face Lavender knowing what I did. I didn't even know she went to Mexico until she got back, tan and pretending like everything was okay.

It took her three weeks to notice the books strewn all over my floor, the half-finished rainbow on my shelves.

Only then did she ask if I was okay.

Only then did I make a promise to myself to never ever mention what happened that night.

Lavender can't know Mom only left the house because she was trying to make me feel better.

So I stuff the memories deep and I keep the secret close so only I know just how much I fucked up our lives.

Until now.

Now, I am in full-blown freak-out mode: chest heaving, eyes closed, hands clenched in fists and half moons digging into my palms.

It can't happen this way. Simon can't see me this way. He'll ask too many questions. I can't — just stop. Stop. Fucking STOP.

It's official. A teenager is legitimately taking away my sanity, placing me back in the throes of high school hell where my own trauma exploded. Why didn't I think about this before becoming a teacher, for Christ's sake. How did I think forming the minds of these humans who are the same age as me when I experienced my deepest loss would be the way to go?

I must be losing my shit.

But I know the truth: it's not my students. Not really.

It's Silas.

He is the reason I'm bent over in my kitchen experiencing things I haven't felt in years. Nothing else has happened — my life has been perfectly vanilla until this year.

For far too long I've allowed him way too many moments of crossing boundaries because *he's just a teenager* but that's wrong. He's a grown ass man by now — a grown ass man still in high school but with the emotional bandwith of a kindergartener who is beside himself because he isn't getting what he wants.

Me.

I start sobbing then — deep, choking sobs that come from the realization that I have completely lost control of this situation. Again: who thought I should teach? Who put me in charge of these humans? Who is going to take over here? Because it really can't be this bad. I am clearly losing my fucking mind over a few notes left behind on my car and desk and inside my house.

Jesus Christ.

It's not just notes, though.

Simon walks in then, pausing in the entryway where the carpet meets the kitchen tile. I turn quickly so he can't see just how much I'm falling apart.

"Babe?"

I feel his hands on my shoulders and he turns me around, deep ridges of concern etched across his face. I lean into his chest and wipe my cheeks with my hands, inhaling his scent.

.::.

My pho cold and forgotten on the stove, we make our way back to the bedroom. I'm exhausted now that the tears have finally stopped, and I point toward the soft light filtering through the darkness.

"Can we head to bed?"

He pauses for a moment a wrinkle creasing his forehead, and then nods. He has learned in our time together that more often than not, I don't want to talk about whatever is stressing me out, so he skips over the asking me about it and moves right into reminding me of my options. Because apparently, my boyfriend is intuitive enough to know my falling apart has to do with my job.

Curling up behind me and wrapping his arms around me middle, he leans in close and kisses my ear.

"You know all you have to do is say the word and you can come work with me, right?"

I sigh and let myself collapse into his chest, my back feeling the way he rises and falls against me. His consistency — the stability — scares the shit out of me. When he talks about me working with him, I can't even begin to think about the ramifications of us falling apart and me being stuck working with him.

He wants so badly to take care of me. And I want so badly to run from any type of commitment because I know what happens when you begin to trust a sure thing. At some point, this is all going to disappear. It always does. I'm not the runner though — I've never been able to escape. Like the books. It's why Lavender freaked out so much when I decided to leave for Providence.

Instead, I freeze. I go quiet. I ghost. Emotionally or physically, at some point I make the decision to shut down in order to push the other person to leave.

So tonight, I find myself doing just that. I breathe in slowly through my nose and don't reply. I just squeeze his arm and twist my head so I'm right in the crook of his shoulder and allow myself to drift off to sleep with his breath on my neck. For now, he's here.

For now.

22

Everything is dark on my way to school. I leave early on purpose in order to get to the school before the hallways are populated: usually before 6am. This is my favorite part of the day — just me and the road, the sun peeking over the horizon and beginning to color the sky, no thoughts except for my own. More often than not, the rhythmic sound of the highway lulls me into a state of relaxation and meditative thinking and allows my creativity to take over. Which. according to Lavender, is what I need in order to stop picking apart decisions and breaking them into pieces in order to determine their worth.

"How's it in your brain these days, Juni?" she'd asked with a knowing smirk on her lips. It always infuriated me, the way she knew me and would poke me on purpose. Now I know it was her way of connecting with me. No one knows you like a twin. This is both a blessing and a curse.

I think of what she must be doing in that moment and realize that she's most likely just now falling to sleep. Outside of crazy hours at work, she prowls the night hours hunting for creativity like I waited for it during the early morning hours. Ultimately, I knew we were different sides of the same coin.

I leave early in order to get to the school with enough time to still hear my own thoughts, and she stays up late to harness the energy of the moon or what the fuck ever. All I know is that the creativity that appears during these moments is unmatched, and so I let it flow. So many people complain about the commute, but it's become my respite.

In San Francisco I relied on public transportation and didn't really think twice about having a working vehicle that could get me from one place to the other. This was great and easy and made decisions about where to go really simple. But it also took away a lot of freedom. I had a car in San Francisco, but it was fifteen-year-old Honda Accord with a questionable engine. I never thought twice about just letting it rust in storage. It's now owned by some high school senior, which is fitting because who doesn't have their own history of a dilapidated car that barely gets them to where they need to go during their formative years?

Purchasing my Subaru Crosstrek was one of the first things I did when I came to town, and I still experience a tiny thrill when it comes to being able to leave at any moment and travel the north eastern coastline.

I consider pulling my phone out to send Lavender a Marco Polo, but decide against it and continue on my way, breathing deep and enjoying watching the world wake up around me.

I see a car on the side of the road as I pass the interchange where the highway splits off in another direction. I wrinkle my nose.

"What a nightmare," I whisper to myself.

I drive for another ten minutes and see another car on the side of the road. Five minutes later, I see two more. Then five. Then with ten minutes away from the school, I notice cars lining the highway. I fight to slam on my brakes and wonder what in the world could be going on. People are out of the cars, talking to each other, pointing to their tires.

They're all flat.

"What in the —"

My whisper is cut short by a *pop* sound and I know immediately what's happening. My Subaru swerves and I narrowly miss the car next to me. I careen toward the median, embracing for impact. By the time I crash into the railing, metal is scratching and I know all of my tires are dragging against the asphalt. I barely have time to recover from the crash before I see someone walking toward my car, a smile on his face.

Silas.

I blink and try to wrap my brain around what's happening.

"Hi, Juniper. You look ravishing this morning."

I blink slowly, confused.

"Silas?"

He leans into my window, the glass crunching beneath his feet. I'm taken aback by the overwhelming scent of antiseptic. I jerk away and he reaches in, caressing my face.

"I told you, Juniper. You cannot stop this train. Do you understand now? Do you see what I will do for you?"

I slap his hand away and struggle to gain purchase in my seat. My head throbs. The seatbelt cuts into my neck. I need to get away. Why can't I get away? I glance around, and realize I'm the only car nearby. There's no one else.

"You did this?" I shake my head again, confused. "But how —?"

He opens the door and leans over to get me out of the seatbelt. I start fighting but it's no use. He's too strong, and I'm too shaken, and there's nothing I can do. I start crying then, big heaving sobs, begging for anyone to come help me. Once he loosens the seatbelt, I push against his chest in order to get away but simply pushes me back against the seat, holding a cloth in front of my face. A scent hits me like a violent fist and I gag.

The antiseptic.

"Just give in, Juniper. Just let it happen," he whispers.

As I'm going under I hear the song on the radio rise to the surface, Taylor Swift's voice cutting through the madness and ether singing about being haunted by her ex-lover's face.

I can't even wipe the tear falling down my cheek.

.::.

I AWAKE WITH A START, my heart pounding.

"Juniper?"

I stifle a cry before realizing it's Simon. I look at him in confusion, feeling his arms and chest with my hands to make sure it's really him and not an apparition.

"S-Simon?"

His face is full of concern, and I can tell he just woke up. I look at the window behind him and see that it's still dark outside. Moments from the day before circle back into my memory.

Silas in my classroom.

The tarot cards.

The snowstorm.

Silas in my house.

But now here, in my bed, next to me? It's Simon. He's leaning forward now, earnest in his worry.

"I-I think you had a bad dream. Are you okay?"

Only then do I notice that I'm sitting up, my body drenched with sweat. I swallow and straighten my back, pulling my sheet closer to my chin.

"I'm fine," I whisper.

He looks at me incredulously.

"Babe, don't get mad, because I mean it in the most loving way — but you do not look fine. You look like you saw a ghost."

I stare at him then, letting him receive the full weight of my fear and terror and anger.

"It was just a dream, *babe*. Give me a fucking minute to collect myself and I'll be okay. Just go back to bed."

He clenches his lips together then, nodding his understanding. He doesn't look happy, though. In fact, he very much looks as if he wants to dig some more and figure out what's wrong. I look away from him, hoping he gets the hint.

"Got it. Well. Sweet dreams, I guess." He snuggles back into the sheets then, back turned away from me, and is snoring within minutes. I watch his chest move back and forth as his breaths get deeper and deeper and only then do I finally let out a muffled sob.

23

I wake up with my head throbbing. I haven't had a bender in years, but this feeling rolling through my bones is like the worst rager times a million. Even worse than the morning after that rave Lavender made me go to in college. I close my eyes and squint against the sun bursting through the window and realize it's a lot brighter than usual.

Groaning, I rub my eyes and turn slowly to stretch and see the time.

11am. I blink, thinking that I must have seen it wrong. I haven't slept this late in forever. I let my head collapse back onto the pillow and watch the fan whir above me. I hear Simon in the kitchen and silently hope he's making coffee. My hand falls to his side of the bed and I realize the sheets are still warm. He must have just woken up as well.

Last night and the dream come back to me in a fog, the edges blurred from the sharp teeth of memory. It takes me a moment before the feeling drops into my belly.

The worst kind of foreboding.

I think I might be sick.

No wonder I feel hungover. Nothing like trauma and

nervous system activation to make you feel as if you've been hit by an emotional semi.

Simon walks in to the room then, a steaming cup of coffee in his hand. Despite the protest of last night's pho, I anxiously reach out to claim the liquid gold.

"Please tell me that's mine," I croak.

"I thought I heard you waking up and figured you might need this," he says with a smile, handing me the coffee. I blow on the liquid out of habit before taking a sip and allowing the caffeine to roll through my veins.

"Waking up, yes. Actually awake?" I shrug. "Debatable."

He chuckles and leans down to kiss my forehead before sitting down on the bed by my knee.

"About last night."

I take a longer swig than necessary, feeling the burn against my throat and esophagus. I fight from wincing.

"Yes?"

He pulls at a thread on the blanket and twists his lips, and I know he's trying to figure out what to say and how to say it.

"How are you feeling?"

"Fine?"

He watches me for a moment longer before nodding and looking down again.

"I feel like there's....something going on. And I don't know what it is, but it's obviously affecting you," he looks at me then and I fight to hold his gaze.

He clears his throat again and places his hand on my leg.

"What I'm trying to say is that I'm here for you." A smile peeks out and he squeezes my hand and the pressure feels good. Safe.

"I know, Simon," I whisper. I sigh. "I'm just — I'm stressed. Work is a lot right now. And there are students in my class that are bringing back all of these memories of my mom —"

He nods, a look of recognition and understanding crossing his face.

"The notes?"

I freeze for half a second before shaking my head.

"No — those are nothing. Really. They probably don't help my stress, but it's more than that — it's...." my voice trails as I try and find the words.

"Grief is a bastard," he surmises.

"Yeah," I answer.

As if you can sum up everything I'm going through with one fell swoop. As if that alone would solve everything. Even still, I'm not about to offer anything else. I let him follow that train of thought to its completion, even though it's slightly askew from what is actually happening. He doesn't need to know about Silas. Not yet, anyway.

Simon clears his throat again and I suddenly realize he looks nervous.

"I was thinking," he ventures.

I try to keep my expression open — expectant. But my heart is galloping against my ribcage.

Please don't be another conversation about coming to work with you.

"What if we move in together?"

My mouth drops open in shock.

Definitely not what I was expecting.

"Us?"

He laughs, a hint of embarrassment coloring his cheeks.

"Well...yes. That's what I was thinking." He opens his hands and gestures in front of him, "I'm already over here most nights anyway. We can make it official?"

I stare at him, disbelief battling an unmistakable sense of excitement at what this step would mean. But also, absolute terror. I think about his condo downtown.

"You want to move in here? Give up your condo?"

"I know how much this place anchors you, so it makes sense. And I can rent out my condo — there are plenty of people moving north right now."

"Oh."

It's all I can manage.

He grabs my hands and I watch them like a puzzle, hoping the answer would float up and out of our entwined fingers.

"You don't seem as excited as I would have hoped," he whispers, trying to catch my eye.

"I'm surprised," I admit. "It's not a small thing to move in together, Simon."

"I know," he says.

"And I realize I'm the one who is often asking if you want to just stay over, but I guess I just thought we had more time before we got to this stage."

He moves one of his hands and lets it rest against my cheek. I lean into him, the heat radiating from his skin a reminder of what we have — what we've built.

"I love you, Juniper Reese. And I'm committed to seeing how this relationship plays out. I want us to move to that next step — we're so good together."

"We are," I agree.

His hand falls and I breathe sharp when his finger begins to trace my collarbone and the heat transfers to his gaze. He knows I can't resist him when he touches me like this.

"Simon..." I struggle to breathe. There's so much to talk about — so much we need to get out on the table if this is going to work. So much I have yet to even mention to him.

"Let's move in together," he mutters against my lips and when I gasp as I feel his hands elsewhere, he takes that opportunity to show me just how serious he is — I almost forget about the cloud of worry hanging over my head.

.::.

A FEW WEEKS LATER, I'm in the classroom speaking with a student when I feel someone watching me. I stiffen, knowing who it's going to be before I even look up.

"Good morning, Ms. Reese."

"Silas," I intone, not offering a glance in his direction. I smile at the student in front of me and return to the conversation about the gala. "You were saying, Madeline?"

She bites her thumb and I can tell she's worried.

"I called around for sponsors and I can't find anyone. We don't have a caterer or a band or a photographer or —"

I cut her off, knowing in this state, she was only going to work herself up even more talking about it. "I'll take a look at the budget and get with Mr. Dillion about the specifics to see what we can manage. We'll figure something out."

She breathes a sigh of relief and smiles. "Thanks, Ms.. Reese. I'll see you in second period?"

I nod.

"Always."

She walks away and I turn, making my way to my desk. I feel a hand on my arm and I close my eyes for a brief second before swallowing my words.

"Were you just going to walk away from me?"

"Silas — this is enough. You're being highly inappropriate."

He glances at me then, his gaze rolling down my body.I raise my hand and throw my fingers in a peace sign, motioning from my eyes back to him.

"Seriously?" I hiss. "In my classroom? You need to leave."

He smirks.

"You're right. This conversation is probably best somewhere private. Like...your bedroom?" His eyes take on an unearthly glow and he motions in front of him, "maybe on that rug in front of your bed where—"

"—ENOUGH, Silas. I said not here."

I raise my voice enough that others look in my direction. He takes that moment to lean forward so there's only a slight space between us and whispers, "you can't ignore me forever."

Watch me.

A slight knock on the doorframe startles me back into the present. I glance up and see Jasper waiting for me, a concerned look on his face.

"Mr. Dillion." I turn my body toward his, trying to signal to Silas the conversation was over. If I had an audience before, I really did now. I could practically hear the whispers going off around me and fully anticipated another visit from Tracey because of it. Jasper was, by far, one of the best-looking humans I'd ever seen in my life, and on top of that, he legitimately loved his job as a teacher and had become my closest friend since moving to Providence. I knew a good percentage of the high school girls had a massive crush on him. I daily thought I wished Lavender lived here so she could meet him. They were the perfect match.

I turn to Silas. "We will speak later."

"Of course," he mutters. And before he walks away, he twists to pull his backpack around and lifts a stack of papers out of the side pocket. He hands them to me, his fingers brushing against my own as he does. I feel the sticky note and once more swallow the words stuck in my throat. Instead, I grip the papers in my hand tighter so I don't drop them on the floor in front of me. I stand there frozen for a moment as Jasper walks up to me.

"Are you okay? That looked intense."

I nod then, allowing myself to breathe through the waves of panic.

"I'm fine." I wave it off but inside I'm shaking. "He is, as you so eloquently put it, intense — especially when it comes to him being denied an extension on the capstone project." I roll my eyes and Jasper chuckles a bit before leaning on one of the desks next to him.

"Your lack of planning doesn't constitute an emergency on my part? Or something like that?" he says. I laugh and nod.

"Exactly!"

I suck my teeth and make a sound of agreement before turning the conversation away from Silas.

"Have you seen Madeline?"

His eyes brighten with recognition.

"Yeah! I just ran into her in the hallway. She said you needed the budget for the gala?"

I look at him and smile, "Yes. She's concerned about the budget for the gala and the fact that we haven't managed to find anyone to sponsor the event. Is this normal?"

He crosses his arms across his chest and squints to think.

"I didn't work on it last year, but I do remember hearing rumbles from students and staff about difficulty in getting the community to rally."

He glances at me and shrugs.

"It's hard to convince local businesses we need help when so many parents are rolling in cash here."

I blink.

"So can we use them?"

"Who, businesses? Well....like I said —"

"No. Not businesses. Parents. If families are so well off here, it makes sense to utilize the deep pockets, right? Colleges and universities do it all the time?"

He processes the thought for a moment before a small smile starts to play at his lips.

"Why haven't we thought of this before?! You're brilliant, you know that?"

I curtsy playfully and fake toss my hair.

"So I've been told."

He checks his watch and stands up, stretching his back before waving at a student who just walked in right before the bell.

"Let's see if we can write something up and present it to the board. It might take some adjustments on our end, but nothing we can't handle. And we still have time. Do you want to meet at our place off Wayland? With the cappuccinos?"

Our place.

I know students picked up that phrasing and will run with it, despite it being the very definition of innocent. *Our place* is the local coffee shop where we would meet weekly when he was going through a really difficult breakup in the fall. I avoid glancing at wandering eyes and give him a smile.

"That's perfect."

"Alright then. I'll see you around four — I have study hall last period of the day and can leave a little early and find us a table."

He turns to leave, high fiving one of my students on his way out. I follow behind him just so I can close the door and when I do, I hear the low hum of hormonal assumptions directed toward me. I smile at the class.

"Nate?"

The tall drummer in the corner who is leaning forward and laughing with the girl sitting in front of him falls back into his seat, jerking his head toward me.

"Yes ma'am?"

"Well if you have something funny to say to Brooklyn, don't you think the rest of us want to share in the humor?"

His eyes go wide for a moment.

"Um."

Brooklyn looks at him, sizing him up and realizing he's not as brave or bad-ass as she originally thought. She rolls her eyes and turns her attention to me, wrapping a strand of hair around her finger.

"Is Jasper, like, your boyfriend now?"

There it is.

I shake my head.

"Mr. Dillion is not — we are working together on the gala. You can rest easy — there is no salacious gossip waiting for you here."

Brooklyn looks at me and raises an eyebrow, clearly not convinced.

I return her gaze, refusing to flinch.

"If you were listening to our conversation rather than building assumptions around it you would already know that — but of course, that's entirely beside the point of why you guys are here, sitting in my classroom, waiting with *bated* breath over Thales of Miletus. There's a real controversy for you. Everyone believes Pythagorus created the Pythagorean theorem, but in actuality, it was our friend Thales."

I feel my phone vibrate in my pocket and I ignore it, walking toward the white board and grabbing a marker. I turn to look at the students and am happy to see that most of them have paused their gossip — for now.

"Veronica. Why don't you come up here and show us the steps to the Pythagorean theorem." I hold out the marker in front of me, waiting for her to get up out of her seat and take it. I'm struck by the blend of watermelon and grapefruit as she passes me and I bite back a smile. The scent of teen years. It's nice to know *some* things never change.

I give Veronica some room and find a spot in the corner where I can see the rest of the students and whether they're paying attention. Slowly, I pull my phone out of my pocket to check to see if the text was from Lavender. I sent her a message this morning and was expecting to hear from her right about now.

A number I don't recognize shows up in my Message inbox. Confused, I click on it to read the rest of the text.

WHY DON'T you ever talk to your class about Simon? Is it because you're waiting for when we can finally be together?

HOW—HOW did he get my number?

My hands start to shake and I almost drop my phone. I delete the message without thinking and drop my phone back into my pocket.

Out of sight, out of mind.

A rushing fills my ears — like the sound of ocean waves — and I know my heart rate is sky high. I can feel the pulsing in my chest. I run through all of the ways he could have gotten my personal number and none of them make sense. It was a boundary I put in place quickly when I started here. No texting, no communication, no connection outside of school.

He was crossing every personal and professional boundary I had and I was going to go crazy because of it.

I close my eyes for just a moment and try to root myself in the moment.

I'm in my classroom.

I hear Coach Bilk next door, talking about The Civil War.

Veronica is wearing the same body spray I use to wear in high school.

Jake thinks I can't see him texting his girlfriend.

He turns and look at me while reaching into his pocket — most likely for his cell phone. I shake my head and point my finger at him, letting him know I see what he's doing, and he rolls his eyes and turns around.

I take a breath.

Veronica catches my gaze and nervously mentions integers

and I nod in encouragement, all the while pushing back the feeling of nausea rising up to greet me. The last thing I need is to fall apart. She smiles and breathes more confidently, turning to continue in her explanation.

I take another breath.

Somewhere in my center, in between my gut and my ribcage, I feel a knowing burst forth. It's time. I can't keep doing this. I lift my chin and stretch my shoulders to their full width. First step: coffee with Jasper tonight, but soon? I need to see Principal Stahl. I would stop by during my planning period and see if he has any free time tomorrow. Maybe I could even stop by tomorrow morning unannounced — I know he gets here early like me, both of us in our respective offices and classrooms trying to get stuff done before the cacophony of the day took over. I take a third breath, and this time I feel sinewy and open — hopeful.

24

I walk into the small bistro later that day, slowly inhaling the scent of freshly ground coffee and baked goods. I spot Jasper across the dining room and give a small wave to the barista behind the counter as I make my way through the tables.

"Hey."

He glances up and offers a smile before motioning to the chair across from him. He snagged a window spot, and I'm grateful. I immediately start watching the people passing by and notice the way spring is starting to make its way into people's bones. We're not bundled as much as we were even a week ago. It gives me hope.

Jasper leans back in his chair, crossing his arms against his chest. A smirk crosses his lips and I once again think about just how perfect he would be for Lavender.

"So we're aiming to fleece the pockets of the parents. Did I understand our conversation correctly?"

I laugh and scratch at an itch on my cheek, looking around the dining room for the first time. I catch Jasper's gaze before putting up a finger.

"Hold on. I need caffeine for this conversation."

He points to the extra mug on the table and the French Press resting against the ledge of the window.

"I got us the bottomless French Press. Please. Take some."

My eyes widen and I whisper a thank you while reaching for the mug and filling it with piping hot coffee. The scent is amazing and I take a deep breath, letting out the stress of the day. I notice the dregs in his own mug and point to it. "Do you need a refill?"

He raises his hand and shakes his head.

"No. Absolutely not. I have officially reached the age where if I have caffeine after 5pm I will be up all night long and absolutely useless the next day."

"Sounds like the perfect cycle to me," I quip, and he laughs.

"Yeah, well. Tell that to my stomach."

I grimace in solidarity.

"So. Parents."

His brows lift and he nods.

"Yes. Parents. Our parents at Sacred Heart are not hurting. We have scholarship students, but even their families have a higher-than-average income. I think we were on the right track with seeing where we can utilize that resource."

"And maybe it's not even money," I say. "Maybe we can utilize their connections or actual resources. Like, don't Marcie's parents own their own restaurant downtown? Maybe we have built-in catering there?"

His eyes light up and he looks around the table, "I need a pen. We need to write this down."

"Aren't you an English teacher? Don't y'all have pens everywhere?"

"I'm not sixty, Juniper. I have pens, but they're where pens belong: on my desk."

I lean over to pull my purse up to grab a pen and pull some

paper out as well. "Well, luckily for you, my desk goes everywhere with me."

I hand over the paper and notice a sticky note on the back. Jasper sees it too.

"Oh. What's this?"

He pulls it off the piece of paper and I see the handwriting, my blood running cold. I snatch it out of his hand.

"Um, sorry. I just — I need that. It's important."

I manage a smile and Jasper stays frozen for a moment before turning his lips downward for a split second and offering a shrug.

"Sure."

He takes to writing down the ideas, remembering as he's writing other parents who could potentially volunteer either money or services. I try and stay engaged, but I can't stop thinking about the corners of the small square piece of paper edging into the fleshy parts of my fingers underneath the desk. I wait for Jasper to put his head down to write a quickly look at the note.

I LIKED THE BLUE SWEATER BETTER.

I look down at my sweater, a bright red cashmere I purchased on a whim because it reminded me of my mom.

"Don't be afraid to spoil yourselves, girls," she would say. "This includes reaching for the luxurious fabric rather than the most practical."

She had about ten cashmere sweaters and Lavender had taken them all because at the time, I couldn't imagine myself ever wanting to wear them. Then I found this sweater and one that was a mixture of lavender and sky blue and I had to have them both. I remember Lavender and I getting into the biggest argument because of it. She thought I had finally lost my mind, but I knew exactly why I needed these sweaters.

I must make a noise, because Jasper is staring at me when I look up.

"Are you okay?"

"Hmm? Oh. Yeah. I um...."

I have to get out of this sweater.

"I'll be right back."

I get up from the table and rush to the bathroom, locking the door behind me. I lean against the sink, trying to catch my breath, staring at my reflection in the mirror.

I remember wearing the blue sweater earlier in the year. I only wore it once to school, because the day I did, Silas commented on it in the hallway and it made me feel uncomfortable. I only wore the red one because I needed an extra layer of comfort today, and it felt as if I had Mom with me. I feel a vibration in my back pocket and reach for my phone, thinking it's Jasper checking on me.

DOES SIMON KNOW YOU'RE LAUGHING WITH ANOTHER MAN? I CAN TELL HIM. I HAVE HIS NUMBER TOO, YOU KNOW. I KNOW WHERE HE WORKS.

I THROW my phone across the bathroom and hear it crash against the wall, tumbling down to the tile. This can't be happening. I hold back a sob and rip off the sweater, grateful that I had at least thought to wear a crop t-shirt underneath. I close my eyes, willing myself to calm down, knowing I have to go back out there and pretend I am okay, that nothing is wrong, that I just got warm or something, which is why I took off my sweater and my face is red. I pick up my phone, shocked that the screen is still intact. I thought for sure it would be shattered with the force I threw it. I shoot a quick text back to the number.

.   .   .

STOP. CONTACTING. ME.
  Leave me alone.

I BREATHE DEEP AGAIN and look at myself in the mirror, my face blotchy but the tears gone. It looks like I'm just really warm.
  That's what I'll tell Jasper.
  I'm just....warm. Overheated.
  He'll understand.
  Right?

.::.

A FEW WEEKS LATER, I'm finally able to talk with Lavender. With her on a work project and me planning for the gala, we haven't talked in nearly a month. I still haven't spoken with Principal Stahl, but after sending Silas that text message things have quieted down. At first, I thought he was actually listening to my requests that he stop talking to me, but I haven't even seen him at school. According to the rumors whispered in the teacher's lounge, his family travels to China every year, pulling the twins from school for a few weeks.
  "They even hire a tutor to come, too." Another teacher told me. "They don't want lesson plans or anything — say that her instruction is more than sufficient." She lifted her hands in air quotes and rolled her eyes, laughing.
  I widened my own eyes, laughing with her, but the relief was palpable.
  A few weeks without Silas. I'll take it.

Lavender answers her phone and I can hear background noise. Her excitement immediately brings me back to the present and I laugh.

"Hey, Lavender."

"Juniper!"

"Is it a good time? Do you need to call me back?"

I can hear her walking, her heels clacking on the floor, and slowly the noise begins to fade away.

"Nope. I'm outside now. What's up? How are you?" A hint of a smile enters her voice. "Simon not staying the night tonight?"

I laugh. "Ha. He has this big project at work and will be late." I yawn. "It's why I'm still up, actually."

I'm sitting on my couch, wrapped in a blanket, my iPad screen still lit from the book I was reading. I shut the case and toss it next to me, snuggling deeper. "I'm fine though," I lie. "I just wanted to check in, see how you were doing. How are things with Jack?" I turn the interrogation toward her. She'll know I'm hiding something, but she also won't be able to resist talking about her love life.

She groans.

"That bitch ass? I don't wanna talk about it."

I grimace at her profanity, knowing the anger that simmers beneath it. Whatever happened, it was bad.

"You sure?" I probe.

She sniffs.

"He broke up with me."

I pause, waiting. I am not surprised. Jack is the douchiest guy I've heard about it in a long while. But I hear the pain in Lavender's voice and I let the silence do the work.

"What happened?"

"Everything, Juniper. Everything. He completely wrecked everything."

I trace the edges of the blanket, smiling at my sister's flare for the dramatic. I also wonder how many drinks she's already had tonight. I look at the clock — 10pm. It's 7pm on the West Coast, so she's probably two deep at this point.

"It started when we got this new woman on the team. I hate that by the way — that I can actually point to when everything started going south and it was basically new blood."

I make a noise in agreement.

"Her name is Chloe and she is actually pretty amazing. Talented — smart — can hold her own in a room full of men. Refuses to let go of her power. You know the type." She sniffs again. "Mom would have loved her."

We both grow quiet again.

"Next week is the anniversary, you know," she whispers.

I clear my throat. "Yeah. I know. So, Chloe?"

My heart starts hammering a heavier beat and I breathe a few times, reminding myself I'm safe in this moment. Even still, definitely don't want to talk about Mom's death with Lavender.

I can hear the thoughts running through her mind right now. My skin gets the familiar prickle only twins understand and I roll my eyes. She's wondering why I won't ever talk with her about Mom. Why it always ends up in a fight. There are a million reasons why this is the case, and none of them matter right now.

"Hey. I'm fine. I just want to hear the story of Jack. Did he cheat on you?"

"No. No, he didn't cheat. At least not physically." She sighs. "He broke up with me because he realized he was fascinated with Chloe and wanted to pursue what that might look like. Said they have a connection."

The derision in her voice is undeniable.

"Does Chloe like him too?" I keep my voice even. It's always a tender subject: fighting the stereotype of women being responsible for men's bad behavior. However. I won't ever understand someone falling into the trap of allowing another man to seduce you when you know he's with someone else.

She laughs then.

"Yeah, no. No. She actually pulled me aside right after it happened so she could let me know that they were under no circumstances together." Her voice changes, and I know she's channeling Chloe. "We went to grab coffee once, Lavender. And that wasn't even a date. He told me it was to talk about the WhiteWater project."

I groan.

"Yeah."

"He's a horrible person, Lavender."

"I know."

"You deserve better."

"I know."

We grow quiet then, each in our own thoughts. Finally, I hear her move — closer to the noise of the restaurant. "I should probably get back but I want to hear how school is going — we haven't talked in forever."

"Yeah! Yeah, I know." I sound too eager and she picks up on it immediately.

"What's wrong?"

"Nothing — it's nothing. I'm just in that season where everything is crazy. Students needing recommendation letters for college, planning the gala, prepping for spring finals — already — even though it's not even March yet."

"You have to plan for finals now?"

I hum an agreement. "Yeah. The tests have to be approved by our department head. Can't have them be *too* difficult." I can hear them now: "Make your tests too difficult, and students will fail. And when students fail, parents complain. When they complain, we lose their admissions."

"Eww."

"...Yeah." I stretch and yawn, giving her the out she's wanting to the conversation. "I'll be okay, though. Just need to push through and before we know it Spring Break will be here and then summer..."

"...And then you can come visit me!"

"Or you can come here," I push back.

This is where our conversation always turns awkward. Each missing the other person like crazy, feeling as if half of their own brain is missing and out roaming the world without them. And yet, we're both so stubborn. So unwilling to bend so the other can breathe.

"Maybe I will." Lavender gets quiet and I suck my lip in shock. I still have trouble believing she'd actually come to Providence to see me, but even her *maybe* is monumental.

"I would love that," I say. "Listen, I know you need to go. I don't want to keep you. I love you."

"Times a million," she answers.

"Times a million," I repeat. I drop the phone and stare at my lock screen when she finally disconnects. It's a picture of us right after college, holding hands and leaning into each other while laughing at the beach.

Lavender and Juniper.

So different, yet so alike.

Two sides of the same coin.

No wonder I feel unmoored. No matter how I look at it, the truth is that my other half is missing from the equation. I breathe quick and let it out in a rush.

My phone vibrates and I startle. Looking down, I see a message pop up on the screen.

SIMON'S WORKING LATE TONIGHT? DO YOU NEED COMPANY?

·   ·   ·

I TURN QUICKLY to the window, expecting to see a face staring at me. I see nothing except a dark expanse. I wrap the blanket closer around me and tap my phone to my lip, trying to figure out what I need to do next.

DON'T BE SCARED, JUNIPER. I CAN COMFORT YOU. HE WON'T EVER KNOW.

THE TEXT COMES in and my hands start to shake. I get up then, drawing the blinds to the window and turning out the lights. I move to the bedroom, changing my mind on drawing a bath. Instead, I walk into the closet, shutting the door behind me, and change into a sweatsuit before opening the door again and crawling into my bed.

WHY DO YOU HIDE FROM ME? IT'S NOTHING I HAVEN'T SEEN BEFORE.

I FIGHT to throw my phone across the room.

SILAS. STOP. TEXTING. ME.

MY HANDS ARE SHAKING NOW and I'm nervously glancing around, trying to figure out how in the world he is watching me. The window in my room is drawn shut, the blinds closed and the curtain tight. What this means is beyond my current ability to process — and I move my hands to my face, rubbing my cheeks in nervous tension. I see the conversation bubbles pop up again and I shake my head in disbelief. I have to talk to Principal Stahl. I probably should actually go to the police at this point — right? Is that even a thing?

I have no idea.

I do know though that whatever happens, the likelihood of someone believing me is low. Not when there are so many stories of teachers manipulating students. Just last week a teacher in a nearby district was accused. But even more than the fear of being misunderstood, there is an irrational fear of being laughed out of my position. I could hear the questions now: "She's scared? Of a high schooler?" Eye roll, laughter, *can you imagine.*

Forgetting about the teenagers who have managed to find ways to get automatic weapons and shoot up their school.

Forgetting the very real way teenage boys were targeted and groomed online for hate groups like the Proud Boys.

My cell phone vibrates again and I pick it up, the glow echoing across my face. I blink a few times, making sure I read the text correctly. My blood runs cold and I feel the flush of heat enter my cheeks — a sure sign of absolute terror.

JUNIPER, WE BOTH KNOW THAT'S NOT GOING TO HAPPEN.

YOU HAVE ME.

FOREVER.

25

I wake up the next morning in a tangle of sheets and notice that at some point Simon came home and placed my cell phone on the charger. His hand rests on my hip and I turn toward him, feeling his embrace pull me closer into his orbit. This always happens. Even in his sleep he pulls me toward him, inching me closer and closer to where he is, holding me. I've never felt as confident in someone else's love for me.

We met by chance — in downtown Providence last year at Waterfire. I had just moved here about a month before and wanted to soak in the culture. It felt so different than what I was used to on the west coast. I didn't have a car yet, so I set up an Uber, and Simon was the driver. At that point, his company hadn't really taken off yet. He had to drive in order to make ends meet. He was pleasantly surprised I wasn't a college student. I was pleasantly surprised he wasn't a creep. He found out I was new to town, offered to show me the ropes, and we just...clicked. He called in the rest of his shift and we spent the evening by the river watching the fire breathers and buskers singing on the sidewalk.

I was smitten, but after we found a karaoke bar and he sang *Starboy* by The Weeknd, I knew I was a goner. He knew every word and *performed* as if he was some hidden popstar and not a rogue Uber driver in a small-big town on the eastern coast. It was incredible. In that moment I knew how great he was — how big of a universe he dwelled in as a habit.

I smile. To this day, that is our unofficial song. He stepped off the stage that night and I ran to him, kissing him like I had never kissed anyone in my life. He looked at me then, surprise etched across his face, his lips swollen from my touch.

"You're going to ruin me, aren't you, Juniper?"

"Maybe," I had replied. "But I think we're going down together."

Neither of us ever gave it a second thought. From that point, we were in it.

We were in *this*.

I watch him as he sleeps: calm, assured, a slight smile on his face. I take my index finger and gently trace the muscle in his forearm. I feel a sharp pain in my chest and I place my hand over my heart. I love him. I love this man and yet I can't seem to find a way to commit fully. We still haven't finished the conversation about him moving in with me. I've noticed he brings more stuff over every time he stays, and I know he's trying to give me time to wrap my head around the idea.

And I love the idea. I love the thought of waking up to him every morning.

But even more than that, I have this desire to cut and run. To end everything before it all goes up in flames because *that* — the unexpected severing — would be devastating. This is a new feeling for me. Normally, I stay. I'm the one who is in it through thick and thin, despite toxicity or poor behavior. I settle. I root deep. I enmesh. But this? This feels dangerous.

It feels as if I could lose big if it all fell apart.

I don't think I could live through another loss.

I maneuver myself out of his arms and reach for my robe on the stand next to my bed. A lingering pinch in my gut has me rolling through my recent memory, trying to figure out where the unsettled feeling rests. It's more than my fear of Simon. It's deeper than that — more primal. Stretching, I glance at my phone and frown as the memory of last night's texts and apparent snooping come back to haunt me.

There it is.

I have to take care of it today — *him*. I have to end it. I have no idea how. How do you convince an obsessive individual to focus their attention elsewhere? Is it even possible? I walk to the bathroom, turning on the soft half light in order to get ready without waking Simon. I grab a brush and rake it through my hair, noticing how more and more strands are falling out these days. I wrinkle my nose at the amount tangled in my brush.

I'm stressed.

I take a deep breath and place my brush on the counter, looking at myself in the mirror.

You're better than this, Juniper. Get it together.

I watch myself — the grooves and wrinkles appearing around my eyes. The way my collarbones poke out from my robe. I stand there and witness. Wait. I know the answer will come because she always does. My mom had tarot cards. I have the cartography of my skin. The simple witnessing of myself and the stress and pain I recognize in my eyes pushes me to the answer I know I need. I do what I do in these moments — I break down the steps to the solution.

I need to pull Principal Stahl into it, but I'm not convinced this will be enough. At the very least, I need to make sure he's aware, on my side, and understands the complexities of this. I run through how the conversation might go.

It will most likely cause confusion. We're now in March, and this has been happening since the fall. He'll probably ask why I hadn't mentioned anything before and this will be easy to answer: I didn't think anyone would believe me, and I definitely thought I was making too much of a simple crush. Teenagers are growing and learning and making mistakes all of the time. This was just a bigger mistake than normal and included a teacher. Even more, I worry about the stereotype of teacher and student relationships. Technically, since Silas is 19, it's more complex than the standard grown-ass teacher going for a minor. Now it's a grown-ass adult obsessing over another grown-ass adult — different legality, same flavor.

All of this equals one big tangle of confusion that I've experienced in growing intensity along with the unmistakeable fear of the past month: I would not be believed, and I was making too much of a small thing.

I allow myself to admit as I struggle to put on eyeliner without stabbing myself in the eye: this is still a ridiculous reason. I had crushes on teachers in high school. I had crushes on professors in undergrad and in my graduate program.

I never sent them notes.

I never ignored their perceived boundaries.

I never broke into their house or spied on them.

I walk into the closet and find a simple dress with pockets and step into my heels before giving myself a quick glance in the mirror we have hanging on the door. I watch myself again: notice the way my shoulders hang low and the exhaustion that rests in my eyes. I smile. I shake my head wildly, letting my hair fly around me. I slap my cheeks a bit and then look again.

I look tired, but alive. That will do.

Satisfied, I walk over to Simon's side of the bed and give him a kiss before grabbing my things and heading toward the door. My phone buzzes, the light bouncing around our dark room, and I grimace, remembering the alarm I have set telling me to it's time to leave. I run to grab it on the nightstand, stopping the vibration in my hand. I see a few missed texts from Lavender last night and laugh at her progressive fall into an inevitable hangover this morning. It's always like this — inevitable and avoidable. She starts out hilarious and effervescent, convinced that life is beautiful and that she is the luckiest.

Her last text, about an hour ago, is completely unintelligible, but I think I notice something about wondering why people always leave her. That's the pattern. The sadness. I twist my lips and make a note to call her back later today. I'm just about to drop the phone in my pocket when another text comes through and my heart drops as I look at the window, making sure the blinds are still closed and the curtains drawn. There's no light coming in from outside at all. I turn my attention to the screen and sure enough, a text is waiting for me. Frustrated, I tap my forehead with my cell phone and breathe for a moment before making my way back to the front door and pulling up the text.

GOOD MORNING, BEAUTIFUL.
    WHAT'S IT LIKE WAKING UP TO SIMON.
    I WISH IT WERE ME.
    I CAN MAKE THAT HAPPEN, YOU KNOW.
    I CAN MAKE HIM DISAPPEAR.
    I WOULD DO IT FOR YOU.

I STOP. My veins turn into ice and I grow dizzy. I place my hand on the wall next to me for a moment before looking at the text again to make sure I read it correctly.

Is he...is he *threatening* Simon? I look around me and once again, all of the windows are closed off from the area around me. How in the hell does he know what's happening in here? How is he spying on me? I start to shake again. Does he - does he have cameras somewhere? I flinch from the thought, not willing to let it take root. I can't think about that. That would... that would be impossible, right?

His words are vague enough for me to fill in context clues and I don't have to be a rocket scientist to know he's escalating. He's following a pattern of growing intensity. This terrifies me. I look back at Simon, asleep in bed, and wonder for a brief moment if I should even go into work. Is he safe if I leave him here? Just how desperate is Silas? I decide to err on the side of Simon being a grown man and able to defend himself since I really do need to talk about this with Principal Stahl. I stand there for a little while longer, watching the man I love, and feel the splintering begin at the base of my heart.

I know what Silas was talking about now.

I'm on a fast-moving train and I can't get away.

26

I get to the school even earlier than normal. I stay in the car for a bit, watching the sunrise. Principal Stahl isn't here yet anyway, and so I know I have some time to burn. Inside the school, I see the darkness of the hallways and feel a chill running through my bones.

I'm avoiding that darkness for as long as I possibly can.

I try calling Lavender, knowing it's time I need to talk with her about this, and ask her to call me back when she can. I text her as well, letting her know I'm okay but I need to chat as soon as possible.

I also text Simon, asking him to let me know when he wakes up.

"I have a question for you," I tell him — when I don't. I just need to know he's okay. I will think of something later.

I allow my thoughts to wander and I process how everything got to the point where I am actually experiencing terror. Did I miss a clue? Did I say something that encouraged him and set him off? Did I wear something in those first few weeks that made him think I was an easy target? It made no sense.

The pink cascades across the sky and edges into yellow and

orange and I know the blue is behind it. I can see it under-neath, waiting, holding out for its time. It creates an ethereal glow and for the millionth time, I wish my mom was here with me. She was the one who taught me about sunrises and the beauty of beginnings when you're faced with an ending. And that's when I realize that was the unsettled feeling I had this morning when I woke up in Simon's arms: an ending. And not necessarily *him* or *me* or *us* but a period of time slamming shut and making way for a new one. I was inevitably careening toward the end of something.

I just wish I knew what.

I watch the sunrise for a bit longer, hoping for an answer, but all I hear is silence.

The hallways are eerily dark as I walk to my classroom. The sense of someone watching me hasn't left since last night, and I look over my shoulder more than a few times before unlocking my classroom door and walking inside. Despite everything I've experienced over the past few weeks, for a moment, I question myself. The doubts are persistent and thick, a web clouding my judgment.

Is this really necessary? Am I making too much out of this?

I think, in some ways, I want this to be true. I want it to be a big joke, a school wide hazing experiment. *Haha! We got the new teacher! She really thought you had it in for her...*

I feel the heaviness of my limbs and know the toll this is taking on me. I know I haven't slept well in days and I'm coming across as flighty and distracted. I make my way to my desk and am putting my bag in the drawer when I see a piece of paper sticking out from my planner. Even from here I recognize the handwriting and I fall into my chair in disbelief.

He just won't stop.

A familiar bubbling rises to the surface and I recognize the anger for what it is — a recognition. For the first time, I don't even read the note. I don't have to in order to know that I am absolutely done with this — whatever it is.

Fuck this, I think.

I push the planner away and stand up, my hesitation from earlier completely gone. I set my shoulders back and make my way to Principal Stahl's office, not even looking behind me to acknowledge the persistent feeling of being watched.

.::.

HE'S NOT in his office when I get there, and I debate whether or not to wait. I hear a noise behind me, and when I turn, I see Jasper with an armful of papers. The relief I feel in seeing my friend is palpable. We both have been so busy we haven't been able to talk since the coffee shop incident, just a few stray texts here and there. His eyebrows dance up in surprise.

"Oh. Hey."

"Here early to snag the copier?"

He laughs. "Yeah. It's still jammed, though. So it's back to old-school paper and pen for their notes on *Scarlet Letter.*"

I suck air through my teeth.

"Ah. Well. I think you're forgetting we teach Gen-Z. I doubt they even own pens or notebooks. They'll have personal computers they can use."

"You're right." He snaps his fingers. "Oh — *you're right.* I can use that. Everyone in my class has their own computers, so now they're going to do the lecture. Not me."

He leans forward for a high five.

"You're the best."

I lean in to slap my hand against his and offer a smile. Checking my watch in the process.

He glances at the office door behind me and nods his head toward it.

"Waiting for Stahl?"

"Hey, about the coffee shop —"

We both start talking about the same time and laugh.

"You first." He motions toward me.

I shake my head and wave my hand in front of me as if it's not that big of deal, because I really don't want it to linger in his head for long.

"I wanted to apologize for leaving so quickly. I must have had a bug or something. Simon and I didn't get any sleep that night I was so sick. And it came on so quickly —"

He shakes his head, frowning.

"Juniper. You're fine. Please. That was weeks ago. I had forgotten about it and we'd gotten enough ideas down to make these past few weeks a piece of cake. Did you see the Slack channel with the updates from the meeting they had the other day?"

"Yeah — I think the only thing we're missing now is a caterer, right?"

He nods, excited.

"Your idea about using the parents to volunteer was genius. The kids are excited again and it's gotten the parents involved, which has seriously been lacking these past few years."

He studies me for a moment and I wonder what he's thinking.

"You sure you're okay?"

"Yeah." I try to make my voice even so he doesn't get concerned. I'm still embarrassed, but I don't let on. I feign a yawn.

"I'm tired. Talked to Lavender last night way too late and now I just need to get clearance about an idea I have for finals so I want to make sure I don't miss him when he gets back." I stretch and give him a wink. "Speaking of Lavender, have I told you lately that you'd be a good fit for my twin?"

He blushes and looks away for a moment before catching my eye and pointing at me. "And have I told you how uncomfortable it makes me to have someone try and pair me with a complete stranger?"

"She's not a stranger! She's the other half of me! We're basically the same person! She's just a lot more impulsive and drinks more caffeine and likes to run from commitment!"

He throws his head back then, laughing, and shrugs.

"Oh, okay. In that case —"

Tracey walks in then and pauses mid-step, raising an eyebrow.

"Oh. Sorry. I didn't realize...."

She trails off and waits for us to respond and when we don't, she adjusts her shoulders and looks at me.

"Are you here to talk with Principal Stahl about the gala?"

Jasper maneuvers himself behind Tracey and I'm envious of his escape plan. He looks at me and rolls his eyes, mouths goodbye, and I smile and send him a wave before turning my attention back to Tracey.

"I'm here to talk to Principal Stahl, yes."

She waits again, thinking I would fill in the gaps and tell her more information, but my lips are sealed.

She sighs then, looking around the office.

"Well you clearly didn't have an appointment, because he's out all day."

I look at her.

"He's out?"

She nods, a look of smug satisfaction stretched in a smirk. "Stomach bug."

Well, shit.

She gasps, and when I look at her, I realize I said that out loud.

"Um — sorry. I just. I needed to run something by him. I can just come by later."

"Or I can help—"

"No, that's fine." I cut her off and get up, walking past her in a rush. "Thanks, Tracey." I don't even really wait for her to respond. I don't want to deal with her right now. I continue down the hall, feeling her eyes on my back, and I know she's thinking of a million different reasons why I could be wanting to chat with Stahl. It also probably drove her crazy she walked in on me and Jasper and didn't catch us in a scandalous conversation. She had to know everything about everyone. It drove me crazy.

I think of a conversation I had with Lavender at the beginning of the year when I was telling her about Tracey and she smacked her lips and declared, "I don't trust that bitch."

I smile, thinking of how quickly Lavender sized her up and called her unworthy.

At the time, I defended Tracey, thinking it was a rash judgment on someone I had really just met.

"You haven't even met her, Lavender." I chastised. And she had laughed at me.

"I don't have to meet a bitch to know whether or not they can be trusted," she said. And now, I am understanding just how right she was.

I return to my classroom and am pleased to see some of my students already there, studying for their exam later in the week.

"Look at you guys!" I exclaim as I walk in between the rows of desk. "You're making me feel bad that I haven't even finished grading the last exam!"

They chuckle to themselves and I feel my phone vibrate. My heart leaps. Simon. I smile at the students and pull my phone out of my pocket, checking the text.

I have three.

One from Lavender, telling me she would call me tonight.

One from Simon, including a morning selfie with groggy eyes and a smile.

And one from Silas.

DID YOU GET MY GIFT?
LET IT BE A REMINDER, JUNIPER.
SIMON CAN DISAPPEAR IN AN INSTANT.
LET'S NOT BRING PRINCIPAL STAHL INTO THIS.

DESPITE MY HEART pounding against my chest, I'm confused. A reminder for what? Another threat toward Simon? And again: how in the hell did he know I was going to talk with Principal Stahl?

I remember the note in my planner and I walk behind my desk, pulling out the piece of paper that turns out to be an envelope. I see my name on the front, which was the handwriting I spotted this morning. I tear it open, pulling out what's inside. When I register what it is, I collapse into my chair. I can see my students watching me out of the corner of my eye but I can't manage to hide my reaction to this one.

It's the Death card, from my mom's tarot deck.

The meaning is clear, and now I have proof that he really was in my house. My hands are shaking when I stand up, and I push my chair against the wall behind me with the force of my body's motion. I startle my students and try to laugh it off.

"Oops," I whisper, my voice strange against the silence.

They look at each other and I take a deep breath.

"I um—I will be right back. I need...I need to make a phone call."

The look at each other, raising eyebrows and beginning to whisper. I can't care. There was no way for me to know this card was missing, but I know my mom's deck. This is absolutely from there. I know because the scent of jasmine is still attached to the card — my mom's perfume. I swat at my cheek, frustrated at the display of emotion. I rush out of my classroom and down the hall, passing Tracey on my way outside.

"Juniper! Class is about to start!"

She calls after me and I can only wave my hand above my head in response with a strangled, "I'll be right back!" over my shoulder. It's enough for me to see her look of distaste and the hatred I feel for her escalates times 3000. I make a mental note to tell Lavender that she was right — that I will trust her taste in others for always as long as she will listen to me about men — if I ever get out of this alive, and then I stifle a sob because the thought of me not making it through this has never even been a thought until now.

I've experienced fear for being hurt. And terror because my boundaries were crossed. But the text echoes in my head and I can't help but understand the implications. His threat is clear, and I have no idea how I'm going to move on from here. I walk into the courtyard, gasping big gulps of air into my lungs. The tarot card is still in my hand and I look at it again — studying the detail. There's a woman at the center, head thrown back and facing north. Her leg is kicked up behind her as if she's in the middle of a dance. A snake wraps around her and behind her is a background of peonies and a skull.

Life and death. Beginnings and endings.

A cicada and a butterfly crown the top of the card, and I am reminded of a conversation with my mom about this card back when I was younger. She was the one who taught me that this card most often looks like letting go of control, allowing the cycle of life to move through every piece of who we are — every area of our life that we tend to hold tightly for fear of losing it. Intrinsically, I know this is the intended meaning. Intellectually, I know this card doesn't actually mean *death*.

But I also know the way in which Silas meant for it to be received.

I pull out my phone and glance around to make sure I'm alone.

Forget Principal Stahl. It's time to call the police.

27

W e're less than 20 minutes from first period starting, so I don't have much time. I glance around the courtyard and am relieved to see I'm by myself. The last thing I need is wandering ears hearing this conversation, but I'm surprised there aren't any lingering students trying to get their last few moments of freedom. Normally the courtyard is bustling with activity.

I take what I can get. I search for the local police station on my phone. My hands are still shaking, but I manage to find the number. I work through how I'm going to approach this conversation. I have no idea what to expect on the other end of the line, but I'm out of options. I feel the edges of the card in my pocket and it bolsters my resolve.

After a few rings, I hear a gruff voice answer the phone.

"Providence Police."

"Hi, um. I needed to talk with someone about a stalker."

"If this is an emergency —"

"It's not. I mean, it's serious, but I'm not like in danger right now."

There's a pause.

"Okay...." the voice levels off and I can hear the confusion. "So what can I do for you?"

I wait for a beat and then dive into an explanation. I feel the thread of dissonance weave itself into my own brain and I struggle to articulate my thoughts.

"I'm not sure if this is where I would even call — I don't have like any investigators' phone numbers or really know what my next steps should be...."

"How about you tell me what's going on, miss, and I can let you know whether next steps are warranted."

I frown at his tone.

"I need you to take this seriously."

He stifles a chuckle and I can hear him chewing on something. I grimace.

"I can't take anything, sweetheart, until you talk to me."

I pull at my ponytail, my frustration growing.

"For the past few months, I've had a stalker. Recently, it's gotten—well it's gotten scary. He leaves me these notes, and I think he's been in my home."

"In your house?"

"Yes — he's been in my house. I think. I mean, I know." Ugh. My hand comes up to my forehead and I close my eyes to collect myself. I'm getting twisted trying to explain this and I hear a frustrated sigh on the other end of the line and I know he's now trying to find a way to get me off the phone.

"Let me start over. I have a stalker. He's been leaving me notes everywhere, texting me, he threatened my boyfriend in one of them and today he left me the Death card from my mother's tarot deck. This is how I know he's been in my house. The tarot deck is at home and a few weeks ago—"

"Wait." There's a small laugh and I bite my lip in anger. "Let me get this straight. You have someone leaving you notes and sending you texts and you say he's threatened by your boyfriend..."

"Yes, well — no. He's not *threatened by* my boyfriend. He's the one who is threatening us.and like I said, his behavior has turned erratic over the last few weeks and it's concerning."

"This isn't CSI, ma'am. You don't have to tell us about escalated behavior. We can spot that on our own when you tell us what's going on. So outside of notes and your boyfriend feeling threatened, what else has happened?"

I swallow frustration and force myself not to correct him — I realize now that won't get me any further. Whether Simon knows about this or not isn't relevant to this guy. I need to just share the basics.

"The notes are constant and have increased with threats. I never gave him my number, and yet he texts me all the time. He knows everything I'm doing. A lot of warning me not to talk to anyone or reminding me what he is capable of or that he won't ever stop regardless of me asking him to leave me alone."

"Hmmm." He clicks his tongue and I hear a quiet snap as if he's trying to get the attention of someone. "Have you received any other threats? Any damage to your property? Anything making you feel as though you're in danger?"

"Well, yeah. These notes don't make me feel like puppies and rainbows. Jesus Christ. How many times do I have to repeat that he *threatened my boyfriend*." I feel the heat rising in my chest and I have to fight from raising my voice.

He clears his throat.

"Ma'am. I understand this is a scary situation, but I need to ask that you keep your tone at a professional level. There's no need to get belligerent."

My eyes grow wide and I begin to regret calling.

This can't be happening.

I look around again, making sure there wasn't anyone who'd come out since I started talking on the phone. I walk over to a corner that will allow me to see the entire area and lower my voice to a more acceptable volume.

"I'm not belligerent — I just need help. He's threatened my boyfriend. He sends me notes and texts even when I've asked him to stop. He knows what I'm doing even though he's nowhere around — or at least I don't see him. And he also told me in a text today that the Death card was a reminder of what he could do and to not get the principal involved...."

"Death card?"

"From my mom's tarot deck? What he took from my house? I know it was from her deck because it smells like jasmine."

He makes a noncommittal grunt and I know it's lost on him why this is a big deal. I hear him sniff and let out a sigh. I roll my eyes. He's just placating me.

"Ma'am how old are you?"

"I'm 27. Why?"

"There was something you said earlier — he told you not to tell the Principal."

"That's right. He saw me waiting this morning to speak with the principal about it and that makes no sense either because I got here early *specifically* to catch him before everyone got here and yet still he knew—"

"Is he a coworker?"

I hesitate for a half a second.

"...No. He's not a coworker. It's a...it's a student. I teach seniors in high school."

He laughs then, a full-throated laugh that escapes unbidden.

"Ohhhh. Okay. This makes more sense. You have a student admirer, ma'am. Not a stalker." He laughs again and I bristle. I refuse to accept this as a workable excuse.

"He might be a student, sir, but he's 19. Definitely old enough to know whether or not what he's doing is wrong." I feel like I need to clarify this. I want them to know this isn't an elementary crush.

"Yeah, and I was 17 when I fell in love with my English

teacher and followed her to the local movie theatre one night. Your point?"

I sigh.

"Frankly sir, that's concerning. I imagine you made her feel uncomfortable. Listen. I had crushes too but I didn't text them constantly. I didn't ignore their pleas for me to stop talking with them. I didn't spy on them while they were at home by themselves. I didn't break into their houses or threaten their partner." My breath is coming out in short bursts, and I know I sound unhinged. The slight quiver in my voice gives my emotions away.

"Are you saying you've had these type of relationships before?"

I clench my fist, my nails digging into the skin of my palm. This man. This misogynistic dumb ass. I turn for a moment so I can rest my head on the brick wall behind me and wonder just how much it would hurt if I kick it.

"Sir. No. That is not what I'm saying. I was simply responding to your excuse that you once had a crush on your English teacher. Just because this is a trope doesn't make it *right*. And honestly, that's beside the point. The point is that I am concerned about an individual who is continuing to make it known that he will never give up trying to win me over. He threatened harm to my boyfriend. He leaves me these notes that tell me I can't get away from him and he knows things like my walking into my closet to change or the fact that I'm talking on the phone with my sister." Just voicing what I've been through makes my skin crawl. I wrap my arm around my stomach as if protecting myself.

"It's fucking creepy. It's like he's spying on me somehow. I know it. I just can't prove it and I need your help. That's all I'm asking. That's why I'm calling."

I take a breath and send out a prayer, hoping against hope that he's understanding the severity.

"Can you help?"

"We would need evidence proving this would be the case, ma'am. And with all due respect, you're the adult here. Lay down some expectations. Get his parents involved. Make it abundantly clear this behavior isn't acceptable."

"I have."

"Well clearly he's receiving mixed signals because it sounds as if he is still pursuing you. And I'm not entirely sure that qualifies as *stalking* rather than a *hopeful* romantic thinking he has a chance with his teacher."

"This is unbelievable."

"Get more evidence. Talk to his parents. See if there is a pattern. Bring back a little more than witchy assumptions and complaints. Stalking is a serious offense and we take it seriously — but we have to have something to go off of first. You can't just tell us someone has been in your house. We need proof."

"I have texts!"

"We would need more than that. Pictures. Proof that he's actually dangerous. Again: a crush on teacher is nothing new. And again: if I know teenage boys like I think I do, I was one after all, I would venture to say you probably said or did something that made him think this was encouraged."

I laughed, the disbelief evident in my voice.

"You've got to be fucking kidding me. What about him being in my home? Is that not enough?"

"We don't know if that actually happened, and the evidence you suggest is weak at best. If it helps, it might be worth installing a security system. Get some cameras. Find out if he's actually breaching your property."

I hang up on him, not willing to continue listening to something that ridiculous and unhelpful. I look down at my watch, knowing I'm pushing the tardy bell. I rub my face a few times, trying to gain control, when my phone rings. I look at the screen and see Simon's number. I answer immediately.

"Simon." My voice is haggard. I know he knows it and hears it because he pauses for a moment before he speaks.

"You okay?"

I shake my head, clearing my thoughts so I can focus on him.

"Yeah! Yeah I'm fine. What's up? I got your text earlier but I haven't been able to reply. I was going to ask if you wanted me to pick something up for dinner on my way home. I know you you have a short day today so we can eat together..."

"Sure. That sounds good. Your choice."

I've started walking back to my classroom, but his voice stops me in my tracks. He sounds distracted. Disjointed.

"Everything okay on your end?"

"Um. Not really."

My heart sinks and a plethora of possibilities run through my mind.

"What is it?"

"Did you notice anything this morning when you left the house?"

My heart rate increases. I think about all of the things he could have found — everything that could have happened — and remember Silas' text. I also hear the hesitation in his voice. There's a hint of anger — frustration — and definitely confusion. Whatever it is, it isn't good. I decide to go for the obvious, prompting the bandaid to be ripped off quicker. I'm not used to hearing anything other than complete connection in his voice.

"Simon? What happened? I didn't see anything."

"Someone slashed my tires. All of them. They're completely mutilated. I'm going to need to have this towed to a shop or something."

"What?!" My hand flies up to my mouth before I can

remember I was still fingering the card. It flies through the air and lands a few feet from me. I stand there for a moment before walking over and picking it up again, shoving it back in my pocket.

"They keyed my car, too. It's bad, Juniper. They really dug in — whoever did this was pissed. I have to call an Uber for work. I can't be late today. I have that pitch I'm giving to our angel investors...."

"Shit. Simon, I'm so sorry." I open my mouth to tell him everything. It would be so easy to let him know and have him take care of it for me, but something stops me. I can't bring him into this. Not any more than he already is just by being with me. And clearly, Silas is intent on making our lives a living hell. I can't believe he keyed Simon's car.

"It's fine — I'm okay and insurance will cover it. It sucks, though. What's crazy is the message. It makes no sense."

I freeze.

"The message?"

"Yeah there was a typed note in the windshield that just said *told you*."

"W-what?" I choke out. I check my watch. Five minutes to the tardy bell. I can leave. I can be home in 40 minutes if I hurry. I can tell Tracey there's been an emergency —

Simon sighs. "Listen. It's fine. I'm fine. Promise. Don't worry about it — I just wanted to know if you noticed anything off before you left, but this must have happened after you left."

My voice comes out in a whisper.

"I don't know who could have—"

A lie.

"I said don't worry about it, Juniper."

It's too late, but he doesn't understand the depth of this fear. The tears have started flowing now and I wipe them away from my cheeks. I see a student run by and slow when they notice me and I wave them off, knowing they must think I'm on tardy sweeps. I check my watch again.

Two minutes.

"Let me come home. You can take my car."

"No."

"Simon—"

"Juniper." Simon answers quickly with an abundance of kindness in his voice that makes the tears spring fresh. "I can hear you stressing about this. It was probably just a case of mistaken identity. Some breakup gone rogue. There are plenty of houses on the street. Just an unfortunate accident. I'll take pictures and let insurance take care of it."

I think about the process of that, and feel the anxiety begin to surface again. I also think about the pictures and hear the voice of the man I spoke with today.

We need proof. Pictures.

I wonder if this would be enough.

"Will you need to reach out to the police about it?"

I wonder if there would be any way to link the two — if they would figure out this was the house of the crazy woman who called in this morning about her student stalking her. As much as I want proof, I also don't want them talking to Simon about my call before I can let him know what's happening. He doesn't need to hear from someone else.

I feel the control slipping from my hands and I stifle another sob.

It feels like Silas is winning. Once again, I'm on that damn never-ending train. I bite at a knuckle, the anger simmering deep in my bones. I refuse for this to be my story. I refuse to let him win.

And yet.

I hear Simon suck in his lip and I can picture what he's doing: on our porch, leaning against the railing, hands in his hair. I take a quick breath because I realize I just thought of it as *our* porch—not *mine*. The pain in my chest is back and I place my hand there to keep my heart from breaking in two.

"I don't think I would need to outside of just filing a report. I'm not concerned about there being a repeat occurrence. I do want to install a security system, though. All of this would have been captured by a camera if we had one — that would have made things a lot easier."

"Yeah. Okay." My agreement comes quick, but it's only because I now need to get off the phone before he hears me losing it. I'm not ready for that yet.

"Hey listen, if you're sure you don't want me to come home, I need to go because first period is about to start and Tracey was already on my ass for being late this morning."

"Late? You get there before dawn."

"I stopped by Principal Stahl's office this morning and ran into Jasper. Long story that ultimately ends in Stahl not even being here today and my needing to run out of the room to catch this call and Tracey seeing me. I'll tell you about it later?"

"I can't wait," he says.

And we say our goodbyes, with me knowing deep in my bones the severing between us has just escalated beyond my own control.

28

I 'm late for class but I don't care. I call Lavender and get her voicemail.

"Hey. I need to talk with you — please call me tonight. And, if you don't call me, I'm going to be blowing up your phone right around the time you like to go out and forget you have a twin so please call me. Please."

I try to keep the shaking from my voice, but she'll know it's urgent. I don't leave those types of voicemails — that's her space. She is the ocean: volatile and unpredictable in her energy. I am the stream. Quiet in my undoing and consistent.

When I was in grad school, I had someone tell me I was the most composed person they'd ever met. "Does anything ever rattle you? You're not stoic, but you're close." They laughed about it, and I smiled in response, knowing what they were talking about because it'd been true my entire life.

"Things rattle me," I said. "I freak out about a lot more than I let on, but it's all internal."

They looked at me confused, not understanding. And honestly, I didn't blame them. I didn't understand it myself.

"It's more of a survival technique than a strategy," I said.

"Basically, I don't want to let on just how much the current atmosphere or situation is freaking me out, so I push it inward. On the outside, I look fine. On the outside, I might even be laughing. But on the inside? It's a fucking hurricane."

"Sounds exhausting," they suggested.

I nodded. "It is. And very much not sustainable. Eventually, it all comes crashing down. You can only pretend for so long."

I could probably take some notes from how Lavender handles traumatic events. I start pacing, trying to figure out what to do next. I look at my watch again, and see that I am now seven minutes late to class. I'm surprised Tracey hasn't come looking for me.

I sigh and pull at the ends of my ponytail again. Regardless of what I need to do next about Silas, I still have an obligation to at least *show up* to my job. I sneak in the back door of my building and quietly make my way to my classroom, feeling myself fall apart one step at a time. I have to get through the day first. I pause at my classroom door for just a moment before walking in, starting class as soon as I crossed the threshold. No hesitation, no opportunity for curiosity about where I've been.

"Good morning! Thanks for holding tight while I handled a small family emergency." My voice wasn't coming out as firm and confident as it normally does, and I can tell the class notices the shift in my tone, which only makes it more difficult. I make a sharp pivot in my lesson plans for the day, knowing I won't be able to stand in front of my classes today and engage with them like everything is normal.

I hold my hands up in assurance. "Everything is fine. Don't worry. I just needed to make a quick call. Now, I'm here! I trust y'all are ready to learn?"

There are a few glances across the classroom and smiles of encouragement are thrown my way. I know there are a lot of assumptions about teenagers these days, but by and large these students continually show me how versatile and resilient they are — and how ready they are to accept messiness as a part of life. I smile at them in return and lean against my desk, folding my arms across my chest.

"Today, we're tapping into the literacy curriculum. You'll be researching a mathematician and writing a one-page abstract on their influence on the world and how they came to understand their particular field of study." This was very much a thrown together lesson, and I was again nervous about them spotting the pivot from a mile away. They probably did, but they made no obvious motion of letting me know. Still, I'm nervous again, and I feel my hands drop and reach for each other. I glance around the room one more time, my hands clenched as tight as possible. I see Madison, a quiet student who sits in front of my desk, notice the way my fingers are turning white and she frowns. I unclasp my hands and shove them in my pockets.

I'm fine. I'm FINE. Smile, Juniper.

I smile, and point around the room.

"I'm assuming everyone has a means to research, but we also have the two classroom computers if you forgot your device today."

The class is silent and I look at them, questioning.

"Does everyone understand?"

A hand raises in the back and I lift my chin to acknowledge the student.

"Yes, Valerie?"

She drops her hand and looks around the room.

"Um. While you were gone—"

The entire class turns around then, their eyes threatening and a small *hush!* vibrating across the classroom.

"Read the room, Val. Fuck." someone whispers from the back. I recognize this group think and wrinkle my nose in disagreement.

"Folks," I warn.

She leans back again, suddenly, face full of an apology. She catches my gaze and offers a half smile and a shrug.

"Oh. Um. Nothing. Sorry. I was just going to say there were some questions about last night's homework?"

I blink and raise an eyebrow. I don't buy her cover up for a second. I look around the room, expectant.

"Is that true? There were questions while I was gone...."

I repeat, leaving the end of the sentence hanging empty, waiting.

Another student sighs and looks back at Valerie before turning back to me, rolling his eyes.

"It's nothing, Ms.. Reese. We had no questions. But one of the office ladies just came in and started rummaging around with the papers on your desk. She told us not to say anything, but it was weird." He shrugs again and returns his focus to the iPad in front of him.

I jerk my head back, trying to keep my reaction as even as possible.

"Oh. I see. Okay. Well, thank you. I will make sure to touch base with her later. I'm assuming it was Tracey?"

I only realize after asking the question that I didn't use her last name, but they knew who I was talking about — they nod, slowly at first, and then it's like someone breathed life into their bones and brains. Now that the *secret* has been revealed, they can return to their job of writing the essay and talking about last night's basketball game in quiet tones. Shuffling and a low chatter takes over and I wait until I see computers and iPads and notebooks pulled out of backpacks and a sense of focus take over before breathing a small sigh of relief and turning back to my desk.

I look at the papers, knowing Tracey came in to the class-room thinking I would be late, but I don't know why she decided to go through my desk. I don't see anything, but I notice my planner open and I frown. I know I closed it when I got the envelope from Silas. There's nothing there for her to find, but why would she worry about what was in my planner? What was she expecting to find? I look at the week and remember that I have a hair appointment this weekend and make a mental note to tell Simon so he doesn't plan on anything.

And that's when I pause mid-thought because this is the part of whatever is happening that makes no sense to me. I can be terrified and frozen with the fear of thinking I will never get away from Silas' attention, or filled with a boiling rage about the authorities not taking it seriously, and then simultaneously acting as if nothing is wrong and everything is normal with Simon.

Haircuts.

Date nights.

Talking about the future.

And doing all of this when I know damn well that none of this is probably going to happen. I know it in my bones. It's why I'm beside myself trying to come up with what I need to do next because I feel the ticking of an invisible bomb and I have no idea when it's going to detonate but when it does?

My entire life will be up in smoke and I will be among the ashes.

29

I manage to get through the rest of my classes without any other incident, but while I am running through the essays after school, I hear a noise at the door and look up. It's Tracey.

I sigh and lean back into my chair. I know I'm not in the right mental space for this conversation, but I also know she is going to do whatever it is she wants to do. I can't at this point care.

"Hey, Tracey. Can I help you?"

She walks in slowly, eyeing the classroom and running her finger along the metal of one of my desks. I wrinkle my nose, noticing she's trying to intimidate me. Her chin is tilted upward, and the air of authority she's trying on for size is ill-fitting and hanging off her like an aura.

She stinks of suspicion and I suddenly realize why she was in my planner. She was looking for proof of me being with Silas. Her voice cracks against the silence and I look at her, expectantly.

"It looks like you finally showed up for your students this morning. How late were you?"

I almost roll my eyes and stop myself. I let myself wait for a minute before responding, knowing she is chomping at the bit for any and all information.

"Have I ever left them hanging? Plus, I don't think it matters how late I was — last time I checked I still submitted attendance within thefifteen-minute window."

She sniffs and looks away and I know I caught her by surprise.

"Because I know you're probably thirsty for the reason why, I needed to handle a small family emergency and was only a few minutes late. My students still got the majority of a period with me, and they all completed their literary practice for our class this week." I motion to the stack of essays on my desk.

"A family emergency?" She prods, her interest piqued again.

I look her in the eyes. "Simon had all of his tires slashed and his car was keyed."

Her twists her lips in surprise but can't hide the smirk. "That's horrible. I hope he's okay."

"He's fine."

She leans agains the desk nearest to her and I lean forward, my elbows resting on the desk. I decide now is as good a time as any to ask her about going through my things.

"You know, I'm glad you stopped by. I was going to come find you after I finished this work." I wait a beat, watching her face. "Did you find what you were looking for earlier?"

She swallows, and I realize she wasn't expecting me to call her out on coming into my classroom.

"Your students told you."

"They did."

She makes a noise of distaste and I cock my head in curiosity.

"You're mad? Like most people, my students find it weird when someone comes into a classroom and starts rummaging through the papers on a desk that doesn't belong to them." I cross my arms. "So again — did you find what you were looking for?"

Her shoulders stiffen and I fight a smile.

"Your attendance was late. I needed it —"

"That's bullshit Tracey and you know it."

Her eyes widen in shock.

"We submit attendance online and I submitted attendance within the fifteen-minute window. You came in before that — probably even before the tardy bell." I notice a flush spreading across her neck and I know I'm getting to her. I feel the instability of this morning coming to the surface again and let myself ride the wave.

"I don't have any copy of my roster in paper form. And you weren't looking for attendance. You were looking in my planner. Again: were you looking for something specific?"

"It doesn't matter," she mutters.

I stand then, walking toward her. She stutters backward, and I can feel the intimidation vibrating off of her.

Good.

"But it does matter. It matters because you walked in here, knowing I wasn't going to be here, and decided to go through my personal things in order to find something clearly incriminating."

She starts shaking her head and I raise my eyebrows.

"No? You weren't trying to find something that would prove I was having a relationship with one of my students? You thought you would find something, didn't you?"

She starts stammering and I roll my eyes.

"You're really something, Tracey. You've had it in for me from the very beginning, when I was trying to help you in any way I could. And now this. Refusing to believe me. Determined to find dirt where there is none. What if I showed you the texts of Silas admitting he's been watching me? What if I showed you the threats he's made against my boyfriend? Would you believe me then?"

I am breathing heavy now, gesturing wildly as she flinches with every word.

"Juniper—"

"No. No, you can't take it back now. It's done. Fuck, Tracey. How hard is it to believe someone when they tell you things?"

I raise my hands to my forehead as if I'm trying to figure out a problem.

"I wonder what Principal Stahl would think about all of this? You're so close to him and seem know things." I snap my fingers. "Maybe that's it. Maybe you're projecting your obvious feelings for Stahl in what would be an invisible relationship between me and a student."

She steps back then, shaking her head.

"Juniper — you can't...."

"I wonder what he would think about you having access to private information because you were putting your nose where it doesn't belong?"

"Private information shouldn't be on your desk." She shrugs, and I can see the desperation on her face. I've hit on a truth I wasn't even trying to find.

"Neither should you." I step closer to her, feeling myself break apart from earlier. "And that's the whole fucking point."

She gasps then, the shock radiating off of her in waves.

"Ms.. Reese!"

I turn around, ignoring her, and walk back to my desk.

"I'm done, Tracey. You can see yourself out. Go find Stahl." I glance back at her and wait until she looks at me before studying her closely. "At least now I know why you've been so obsessed with what I'm doing with my free time." I smile. "Don't worry. Unlike you, your secret is safe with me."

She takes a deep breath.

"Juniper. There's nothing between Stahl and me."

"Sure."

"You can't say anything."

"Whatever you say."

"I mean it. No one can know."

I look at her again. "I understand, Tracey. But you need to understand something — owning your shit is so much better than looking for everyone else's."

Her hands clasp in front of her and I realize I've never seen her this docile before — she's always over posturing, always forcing herself on to other people. I'm enjoying the change in demeanor. She starts to turn to leave.

"Oh, and Tracey?"

She looks over her shoulder at me and I notice for the first time there are tears brimming, ready to fall. She tries to wipe them without me noticing but it's too late.

I say nothing, and lean forward in my desk again, making sure she's paying attention.

"Don't ever come into my classroom again."

She stands there for a split second, unsure of what to do, and sputters something about needing to ask the librarian a question before she leaves.

I smile at her and nod. "Sounds good."

She turns around then and before she can leave my classroom I call after her, "have a great day!" I can't help but laugh under my breath at the way her shoulders stiffen all over again and it's only after she's been gone for a few minutes that I allow the revelation of her and Stahl to sink into my bones and I shake my head in disbelief.

This school.

The layers of dysfunction is a fucking onion. My phone vibrates then, and when I look down at the screen, I see Simon is calling again. I answer the phone.

"Hey. Are you on your way home?"

I hear a buzzing in the background and realize he's not in

the car but somewhere else. I try to figure out what I'm hearing when I hear a familiar beep and my spine turns into ice.

"Simon. Where are you?"

"Before I say anything, I need you to know I'm okay."

I close my eyes and let my head fall to my desk.

You've got to be fucking kidding me.

"I might need you to pick me up from the hospital."

I grow quiet, unwilling to accept the words I'm hearing.

"What?"

"I'm in the hospital. I'm fine."

Even though I knew he was going to say this, it's still a punch to the gut when I hear it. I clear my throat, trying to clear the tears that are tangling themselves in a knot.

"It was that damn curve on the way to Providence. Do you know which one I'm talking about?"

I nod before realizing I'm talking to him on the phone and he can't see me.

"Yeah — yeah I know."

"It was the weirdest thing. The driver was going the speed limit, totally safe and paying attention — we weren't even talking. And then out of nowhere this car comes into our lane and we end up swerving off the road and hit the barrier."

"Ohmigod."

"I'm okay, Juniper. I promise. They just had to check us out because it was a pretty rough crash but I'm fine. I'm waiting to be seen right now."

"Is everyone else okay?"

"My driver is, but I don't know about the other guy — I'm guessing he's fine. He never actually hit us and he actually left the scene. I don't even know if he realizes we wrecked?"

My fingers clutch the phone automatically and I feel the pressure in my knuckles.

"The other driver kept...driving? He left the scene?"

"Yeah. It's unfortunate. No one caught a license plate, either.

The road was pretty empty when it happened, so there were no witnesses."

I breathe out a deep sigh and Simon laughs quietly.

"It's been a hell of a day, right?"

"Yeah," I mutter. There's a thought I'm trying to chase in my brain — just out of reach. Something important. Something I need to know. Simon keeps talking.

"We were so lucky though, Juni," I key into him using my nickname because he so rarely uses it, knowing it was something my mom used to call me. My attention falls back to him and the thought I'm chasing disappears into the background.

"I'm so grateful fo the driver, honestly. If he would have swerved like two seconds later, we would have gone off that cliff. We were so close."

I shake my head, unwilling to let that image stay.

I feel a vibration and I pull the phone away from my ear to check the screen. It's a text from Silas. The tears caught in my throat come free then, and I tap on the message to see what it says.

NEXT TIME I MAKE SURE HE DISAPPEARS FOR GOOD.

I RUN my tongue against my teeth and nod again, closing my eyes. An understanding settles deep in my gut then and I know what I need to do next. Simon must hear how ragged my breathing is and he starts to try and comfort me again, but I hear nothing. I hear nothing because the thought I've been trying to chase cuts through and makes itself known: Silas wasn't at school today.

He wasn't at school because he was making good on his threat of trying to kill Simon and he almost succeeded.

Fuck.

I hang up on Simon, knowing he'll wonder what's wrong, but I am unable to engage anymore. I look around my class-room, expecting some type of familiarity, but everything feels foreign. Even my own skin. I choke back a sob.

The bomb just detonated, and I know now Silas has won.

30

I t's chilly on the beach, and I'm glad I thought to bring my sweater from the backseat of my car. I wrap it around me tighter, feeling the way the fabric brushes against my fingers. It's comforting.

My head rotates back and forth, expectant. My fingers move from the sweater and start drumming a rhythm on my arms. I'm nervous. No — terrified. I don't have long to do this. Simon is still at the hospital, waiting for me to pick him up. I check my watch and note the time. I have less than 20 minutes before I need to leave.

I may go down, but I will go down fighting.

I texted Silas to meet me here. I'm not entirely sure what possessed me in the moment, but I knew after hanging up on Simon that I had to do something. I needed to speak with him directly. I was tired — am tired — of the texts and threats. I straighten my spine and roll my shoulders again, the stress knotting itself into hard pressure points. When this is over, I am going to need a lifetime of massage therapy.

Now that I'm standing here, watching the waves, completely alone and vulnerable, I'm questioning my decision. I shuffle my feet a bit and feel the coolness of the sand between my toes. I took off my shoes at the car, unwilling to attempt to walk in heels. Plus, if I am honest with myself, I want to be able to make a quick get away.

I breathe once, a deep inhale through my nose, and let everything out through my mouth. I imagine Silas watching me, waiting for the perfect time to make himself known, enjoying the opportunity to once again be the one controlling the situation.

I close my eyes and shake my head, getting the image out of my head.

I might be going crazy.

I glance to the right again, watching the fishermen who set up camp for the next few hours. Their laughter echoes across the shore and I manage a small smile, thinking of easier times. At least there are other people here. I walk to the water and look out into the expanse, sending a message out into the universe.

I need you right now, Mom.

I watch the waves crash and notice a starfish by my feet. I pause for a beat, letting the sign wash over me. I lean down to pick it up and throw it back into the sea, remembering something about starfish signaling love or motherhood or something. I whisper another plea for strength, letting the waves baptize my feet, and find my place back away from the water. I hear my mom's voice coming up from inside of me, a soft whisper of recognition.

And so it is.

I feel as if I can breathe normally again. The tide is coming in and the spot I claimed is now being kissed by the waves, but I don't move. I wait, knowing any minute he'll show up out of nowhere. It doesn't take long. I see his form, walking toward me, a smile on his lips. When he gets close enough, he leans in as if to hug me, and I step back, the sand almost making me lose my balance. I steady myself and place my hand up in front of me.

This is what I was afraid of happening.

"Silas, wait."

He cocks his head, the smile unwavering.

"The wind has made your hair absolutely wild." He laughs and takes a strand in between his fingers. "It's absolutely beautiful. *You* are beautiful."

I move my head away from his grasp and raise an eyebrow.

"That's not why we're here. I need you need to stop."

He reaches for me and I back away again, my hand moving further in front of me. Confusion begins to etch its way across his face but he keeps trying.

"Silas."

He looks at me and laughs, any doubt washing away with his persistence.

"It's okay. It's okay, Juniper! You don't have to say anything. I already know."

"But you really don't."

He starts nodding his head vigorously.

"I do. We're meant to be together. I know you know that. I know that's why you texted me to show up here. It was what I did with Simon, wasn't it? That convinced you? I knew it would...." his eyes are bright and I realize just how much he believes the words he is saying. I look at him in shock.

"You *bastard*."

He flinches and then shakes his head.

"You don't mean that."

"I do."

"But—"

"You almost killed Simon."

His smile broadens and this time, there's a hardness to it. "But you know now, don't you?" His voice turns menacing. "You know what I would do for you. I would do anything!"

I look at him, my hands moving up to my sweater, wrapping it closer to my skin. I don't feel safe here. I shouldn't have come. I swallow and straighten myself as much as I can, relying on the calm exterior to stay solid —

Don't crack. Not now. Not here.

I look at him again, and see ownership in his gaze. This makes me feel brazen and firm and I let the anger course through me so he can feel it.

"You have to stop."

He opens his mouth as if he's about to speak and then looks at me, confused all over again.

"What?"

"You have to stop, Silas." I karate chop my hand into my palm, emphasizing my point. "Stop texting me. Stop leaving me notes. Stop threatening my boyfriend. It's not okay." I motion between us. "This is not okay."

"But we're meant to be together. I know you know—"

"—but that's just it, Silas." A laugh escapes my mouth and he frowns. I don't care. "We're not. We're not meant to be together. We've never been meant to be together. You're my student."

"I'm 19."

"That doesn't change things."

"I love you."

"You're obsessed with me. There's a difference."

I notice the hardening of his posture and I wrap my hand around my neck, feeling the threat. I give a quick glance around me, looking for the fishermen from earlier. I remind myself that I chose this spot on purpose, that there are people present. I knew this much. I thought this much in advance to protect myself.

He can't do anything to you, Juniper. Not here.

"I will have you," he grits out between his teeth, leaning

closer to me. I startle, his presence shocking after our constant dance during the conversation. I push him away.

"Not if I can help it, Silas." My words are soft — gentle. They fall on his shoulders and I see the impact they have on him as tears start to fall from his eyes. He wipes them away, scoffing at the wetness they leave behind on his fingers.

"You're making a mistake," he begs. He's two seconds away from getting on his knees and pulling on my dress. I step away again and he reaches toward me, grabbing my arm. I gasp at the strength and wince, trying to pull myself away.

"Let me go, Silas." I bite back the tears of fear, and wait for him to listen. Slowly, he loosens his grip, but not before running his fingers down my arm. I shudder and he smiles, seeing it as encouragement. He whips his hand back up, placing it behind my neck.

"You see?" He shivers and whispers closely in my ear. My hands shake and I close my eyes, willing this conversation to be over.

"I do something to you. You do something to me, too. Can you feel it?"

My breath hitches and I push him away all over again. This time, he's not expecting it and he stumbles backward, looking at me with a wounded expression.

"Don't ever touch me again." I raise my voice enough so that a few people, including the fishermen, turn around and watch me. "Do you hear me? Do you understand?" I point to him. "Whatever you're doing, whatever you're planning — it's over." I look him in the eyes, my voice lowering. This next part is only for him.

"I will never be yours."

I turn around then, walking back to my car without looking back. Only when I get into my car and put the keys into the ignition to I let myself fall apart.

The fissure is complete. I run my hands over the places he

touched, convinced I need to take a shower to get the feeling off of me. I brush anyway, rubbing away the feeling of his fingers and notice a red mark where he grabbed my arm.

I catch my breath and wipe the tears from my eyes. Collecting myself, I make my way from the parking lot and onto the highway toward the hospital, noticing briefly in my mirror Silas watching me from the edge of the road.

31

I get to the hospital and Simon is waiting. We check him out, getting the clearance from the doctors.

"If you have any headaches, any soreness at all, come back so we can look at you," they instruct. "Sometimes it takes a while for our body to fully process the adrenaline from the wreck."

We listen, and promise to pay special care to any symptoms that might come up over the next few days.

When we're finally able to break away and are on our way home, Simon carries the conversation, talking about everything from the police officers who stopped to help after the wreck to the meeting they had to reschedule at work to what he's craving for dinner. I speak maybe a few words over the course of 20 minutes before he keys into my silence.

"Juniper. I promise I'm okay."

I smile, the thought of him thinking my silence rests in the stress of the day because he's not wrong. It's just, not the whole truth. I look at him from across the passenger seat and reach for his hand.

"I know. I'm just a little shaken and I have a headache. I'm also trying to focus on driving. I'd be lying if what happened this morning didn't freak me out a little bit."

He makes a grunt of agreement and then keeps watching me.

"Is that all?"

I sigh.

"Outside of everything that happened today, it was a difficult day at school. Tracey was at it again."

He frowns.

"Does she ever quit?"

That makes me laugh, because I wish.

"I wish she would quit." I catch a smile before continuing. "But to answer your question, no. No, she doesn't ever quit. She's like a dog with a bone and once she gets caught on something, it's like she can't rest until she proves herself right."

I twist my lips.

"We had a pretty severe disagreement after school today and I'm probably going to have to apologize if I want to keep the peace but I'm debating if that's even something that interests me at this point."

I look at him.

"It was bad, Simon. I yelled."

He lifts my hand to kiss the knuckles, trying to hide the smirk at me yelling at someone. He knows how rare that is and how upset I had to be to actually do it with Tracey. I stare at him, considering just how different he is from Silas. How unassuming, caring, cautious. Despite him all but begging me to come work with him, even that is wrapped up in this notion of him wanting to take care of me.

When we get to the house, the first thing I notice is the door wide open. We pull into the driveway and stare at the door for a moment, both of us trying to make sense of what we were seeing. I decide to venture into the obvious.

"Did you....did you lock the door this morning?"

I know he did. Simon is notorious for being the one who remembers the locks and lights and everything else I've left unattended before leaving for school.

I put the car in park and turn the ignition, looking at him for what to do next. He's still staring at the door, completely quiet.

"Simon?"

"Juniper, I have to be honest. I'm beginning to think today wasn't just a really bad day."

I choke back a response, letting him connect what he needs to connect and trying to figure out exactly what he means by this.

"Okay...."

He motions to the door.

"My tires get slashed. My car gets keyed. I'm literally run off the road by some asshole who keeps driving. And now your door is wide open."

"It's a lot," I say, not wanting to focus on what really caught my attention — him calling the door *my* door. Not *our door*. He's probably just stressed. But still. My brain captures the information and files it away for later.

"Maybe it's just all a coincidence. When it rains it pours! It's been windy today. The foundation needs to be looked at, and you know how many times the door just pops open when we're home. Maybe that's what happened." I know it sounds ridiculous. I also know I sound as if I absolutely don't believe the words coming out of my own mouth.

He looks at me dubiously and then looks back at the open door, considering. I place my hands in my lap, the keys jangling together and clattering against the silence. I can see the wheels turning in his head. He's not stupid. He has to know something is wrong.

"I mean, if it's not a coincidence, if someone really did do all of this, do you have an idea of someone who could have done it?" I manage in between trying to remind myself to breathe. I'm hoping for suspicion. I'm hoping for an *I don't know — it would probably take a lot for someone to think of all this....*

"I didn't want to stress you out even more." He goes quiet and sighs, rubbing his face with his hands.

My heart crashes against my chest and I know that he knows. I know it like I know how much I love him.

He looks at me, leaning against the window.

"We've been getting notes at work. Random calls. The other day some guy showed up and threatened our secretary if he couldn't see me. They're all connected. I know it. For the past few weeks it's just been getting worse." I balk.

"You didn't tell me any of this."

"I didn't."

"Simon."

"I thought it was just some guy trying to put pressure on us — someone in the security field who was using tactics hackers use to secure jobs from government agencies? Like, oh he found some weakness in our security infrastructure so we need him on our team to boost the capability."

I'm so confused. I literally had no idea this was happening and the entire time I was trying to keep things from him.

"Have you gone to the authorities about this?"

He shakes his head.

"No — and I won't. I know this type of person, Juniper. They're dangerous. Volatile. One wrong move can provoke them."

I stare at him, my own thoughts careening.

"So what are you going to do?"

He rubs his lips with his fingers.

"I'm going to go check the house. Stay here. Once I know it's clear, I'll come and get you."

"But what about the guy—"

"I don't know, Juniper. I don't. I've been trying to figure it out for weeks. Give me a minute, and I'll come and get you when it's safe."

He looks at me.

"Okay?"

"Okay."

He moves to get out of the car and then stops himself.

"Since I told you everything — can you actually tell me what's been going on with you? I know you've been dealing with more than what you've told me. If I'm connecting the dots, it all fits."

My mouth moves but no sound comes out.

How does he...

He reaches for my hand.

"I know you, Juniper. I knew you were hiding something, but it just makes sense. You've been getting notes too, haven't you? And texts?"

The relief I feel that pushes through my veins is surprising.

He knows. He finally knows.

"I have," I whisper.

He nods and looks down, wincing a little bit as he unbuckles himself and gets out of the car. The soreness is kicking in and he rubs at a spot on his neck.

"Give me five minutes," he says, turning back to the house and pausing at the doorframe before stepping into the darkness.

.::.

HE DIDN'T FIND ANYTHING. He comes and gets me, and we call for Thai delivery while he showers and I change into sweats, throwing my hair into a high bun after brushing out the residual sand from earlier. I hear the water turn off and collapse into the couch, waiting for him.

Butterflies jut up against my ribcage and I worry about his reaction. Even though he knows and even though he hasn't run yet, will he believe me?

Like really?

He walks into the room and I inhale the scent of his body wash — citrus and sandalwood. He sits next to me, reaching for my hand.

It's my cue.

"I've been receiving notes from one of my students — Silas — since shortly after the school year started. At first, I thought it was just infatuation. A lack of social skills or boundaries, whatever. I just didn't think it was that serious and so I would throw the notes away. But then they started coming more frequently. And being left in more places — even outside of school. Like on our windshield while we were on a date."

His eyes widen in recognition.

"That one night—"

"Yeah. I grabbed it before you could even know what it was....but it was definitely from him."

I tell him everything. He sits there, next to me on the couch, holding my hand the entire time. Nothing surprises him, and he even interjects at certain points, filling in holes for himself or letting me know why he acted a specific way.

Like the night of the storm when he came over with pho.

"I had a feeling someone had been in your house," he told me. His face was matter of fact. "It's part of why I wanted to move in with you. I mean I wanted to move in — *want* to move in — outside of that, but knowing I could be here and help protect you? I wanted to catch the bastard."

"You knew?"

"Not for sure, no. I just had a *feeling*. You were super jumpy and things in the house looked...everything was clean but a few things had been moved? It was weird, but I couldn't prove anything and I definitely didn't want to freak you out. He used that window," he points behind me and I look at him with wide eyes. "How?"

"It was cracked open, and there was snow on the sill. That lamp was moved juuuuuust enough that I noticed the shift."

I smile at the slight nod to my own specificity of where things are located. I probably would have noticed myself had I not been beside myself with terror.

"And you didn't say anything?"

"Would it have helped you?" His eyebrows are raised now, a questioning look on his face. "I had nothing to go off of outside of my gut."

"No. No it wouldn't have — I was — am — terrified that people won't believe me or think something else was going on...."

He squeezes my hand.

"I believe you."

I take a breath then, knowing there's more he needs to know.

"He started threatening you recently. Telling me he could *make you disappear.* That's part of why I wanted to meet with Stahl this morning, but he wasn't there. But then he left me the Death card from my mom's tarot deck in my planner...."

"He did what?"

"Yeah. It was definitely supposed to be a nod at what he was capable of even though the card might not have been the best one for his symbolism." I shrug. "Death doesn't necessarily mean death in tarot."

"Oh."

"It still scared the hell out of me though."

"Well, of course."

"So I called the police."

His eyebrows skyrocketed then and he leans closer. "You called the police?"

"Well, I called the station. I didn't really want to call 911 since it wasn't an emergency, and I just needed to know what to do next, so I called to see if they could give me any guidance."

"And?"

"They laughed about it. Said I was obviously doing something to make him think there is a chance between us."

His neck turns red and he shakes his head, pinching his lower lip with his fingers. He's pissed. "Of course they did nothing. Of course they did."

I nod. "And then you called about your tires and then the wreck and so — I seriously thought I was losing my mind, Simon. It's why I hung up on you when we were talking earlier. I couldn't take any more."

I stare at him a beat before continuing.

"So I texted him."

He blinks and I know he's trying to determine if he heard me correctly.

"You did what?"

"I texted him. I told him to meet me at the beach. That was the errand I had to run before picking you up. I met him at the beach and told him to leave me alone."

He stares at me for a beat, still unsure of what he just heard.

"You went to meet him. By yourself." His questions come out as statements and I know by the storminess in his eyes he's trying to control his emotions.

I nod.

"Juniper..."

I squeeze his hand.

"I was fine. He was upset but maybe it worked? I haven't gotten a text in hours and —"

He starts shaking his head.

"It didn't work. I know it feels that way because he hasn't tried to talk to you in a few hours but...not for this guy. He's only planning his next layer of attack. We need to be smart about this." He takes a deep breath.

"You can't be alone. Ever."

"What about work? I get there early —"

"Not anymore."

I know there's no use in arguing. I'm just going to have to rework my schedule.

"Maybe I can talk to Jasper about meeting in the morning about the gala?"

He nods.

"I'm okay with that. I just don't want you to be alone."

I take a bite of my food and wait, knowing he's thinking about something because I see him open his mouth as if he's about to say something and stop himself.

"What is it, Simon?"

He shuts his eyes and places his hand on his forehead, thinking.

"There's another thing. It's crazy. But. I have an idea. I need you to trust me."

I look at him, curious.

"Of course I trust you. What is it?"

At first he doesn't respond. He simply sits there, thinking.

"Simon?"

He gets up then, and walking to the television, turns it on with the volume all the way up.

"Simon!" I put my hands over my ears and look at him in confusion. "I can't hear you — what are you doing?"

He holds one finger up and walks over to me, kneeling in front of where I'm sitting on the couch. He grabs my hands and returns my gaze, and I see every ounce of love I've ever received from him in one look. I smile, wondering what he could be doing, and then he leans forward and whispers in my ear, dropping a weight I wasn't expecting.

"Don't react. I turned on the TV because I know he's probably watching, listening, or both. But, I need you to break up with me."

32

The next day, I call out from work. After yesterday, it feels as if it's the only option. I wake up before dawn, like always, but I can't find it within me to get out of bed. I blindly feel for my phone on the nightstand and with one eye cracked open, call the sick line. It's an automated system, and for this I am grateful. There's no talking with Tracey or another human — no explaining exactly what's wrong with me and why I can't come in to teach. All I have to do is select the substitute for my class and I'm good to go. I'll do that later, though. I still have a few hours before the cut off when they'll default to whomever is available.

I glance next to me at the empty space where Simon would normally still be sleeping. I frown and run my hand along his indention in the sheets from a few nights ago. Leaning over, I cradle the pillow he uses and inhale his scent.

He went back to his condo in Providence last night in order to make the fake breakup appear more real whenever it happens. I bite my lip, already nervous about his plan to temporarily and *totally unofficially* break us up in order to get Silas' attention.

I still don't fully understand it, but I know one thing is for sure: Silas will know. He probably already knows Simon didn't stay the night. I glance around my room with a snarl on my face. I throw up my other hand and point it above my head.

Fuck you, Silas. I know you're watching me. Somehow.

It's dark outside — a new storm system is blowing in from the south. It makes this entire plan that much more nerve-racking because I know the next few days are going to be rainy. I've seen the movies. How many times does the bad guy capture the heroine when it's bright and sunny outside?

Yeah, zero.

How many times does the weather depict the mood? *It was a dark and stormy night.*

Yeah. I know. The limit does not exist.

I groan. I'm not looking forward to this at all. And yet, I know Simon has a point.

Us breaking up will push Silas into action.

We're not going to actually break up. Not really. I mean, we'll put on a good show and everyone will think we officially ended things, but we'll still be together.

Just no talking or seeing each other — not even a phone call.

"He's probably tapped your phone somehow," Simon told me last night.

"Are you sure we don't need to just call the police? Again?"

He shook his head and grabbed my hips to pull me closer. He was still leaning in front of me. I placed my hands on either cheek.

"They told you to bring evidence, right?"

I nodded.

"This will be our evidence."

I throw my phone across the bed in disgust, frustrated. I'm so ready for this to be over. Imagine a world where a woman is just...believed.

No proof necessary.

No good boys' club protecting their own.

Instead, we're going out of our way to play detective in order to catch a stalker who's turned dangerous. Makes zero sense.

I think over our plan.

Tonight, Simon is coming over. At first, it will be normal.

We'll grab something to eat. Maybe start watching a movie. And eventually, we'll start to fight. Eventually, I'll throw him out of the house.

Last night, I asked Simon if he could be the one who broke us up. Even if it's fake, I don't know if I can do it myself.

"It has to be you. He has to think you are choosing him."

"Simon, I just told him he has was basically delusional — that there was nothing between us."

He nodded. "Yes. I know. But what *he* heard is that you've gotten distracted. What he heard is still completely different than what is actually happening in reality."

I told him okay, that I would try.

"If we do this, and do it well, he'll act. He'll do something — show his hand."

He moved one of his hands and placed it palm up in between us. I grabbed it.

"And then we'll have our evidence."

Simon nodded.

"And then we'll have our evidence."

Here's what I can't stop thinking about: we still don't know *how* he will act. Hell. We don't know how he's planning on acting after I met with him yesterday. For the first time in weeks I'm not in constant terror thinking about doing this on my own and that maybe, just maybe, I might get out of this in one piece. But even still — there's a fear we're missing something pivotal. That I'm putting myself in danger by provoking him.

I massage my forehead, thinking.

It doesn't really matter. He's going to do whatever he's going to do regardless. What we're doing is just capturing the data. Allowing ourselves proof. Even when Silas showed up at Simon's work, he had thought enough in advance to rig the security cameras so they captured the sun beaming in through the windows rather than him berating the secretary. So he's smart. Calculated. Everything you don't need in someone who is determined to have you.

I need to call Lavender. I wish I could call her and tell her everything — that's what I was planning on doing yesterday when I left her that message. But when she called me back last night, Simon and I were talking and by the time we finished I was too exhausted to call her back. I look at the time. 7am. She will definitely *not* be awake right now, but at the very least I can leave a message so she's not freaking out about me disappearing or something. Maybe I'll send her a quick Marco Polo.

And then, when we finally are able to connect, I'll tell her about Simon. I'll pin it on him, so she has no choice but to hate him, and there will be no questions. As far as she will assume, Simon and I won't be together anymore.

I grab my phone and pull up her profile in the app. Before I press the button to start recording my face, I close my eyes and think about Mom. Just for a moment — just enough time to bring the tears right up to the surface — and then I sniff and open my eyes and press record.

She'll need to see me teary.

.::.

SIMON GETS to the house right on time. I've already spoken with Lavender, and she was beside herself with shock at the audacity of Simon all but forcing me to leave teaching to work for him. I hated lying, but she played right into the narrative I concocted. We've been texting all day and she hasn't once asked me anything more about him.

I know what this means.

To Lavender, Simon is dead. Done. Out of the picture. Gone.

She didn't even mention him when she called me crying about one of her projects at work. I tried to listen to the situation, giving her advice where I could, and apparently I said something of value because at one point she sniffed and said how grateful she was for me — "how are you always so practical, Juniper? You always know what to say."

I hummed a response, and she took that as exhaustion, apologizing for the call. I told her it was no worries — that she could call any time.

"I know, Juni. But you've had a week and here I am centering myself. I'll let you go get some rest. I love you."

I didn't correct her, just responded in the way our mother always did.

"....to the moon and back."

I heard her breath catch and she laughed. Like me, she never gets over hearing the words.

I sigh. I will have a lot of explaining to do on the other side of this.

"You okay?"

I blink and come back to the world around me, only now realizing I was completely in my head. I grab Simon's elbow, giving it a squeeze. Looking at him, I smile.

"I'm fine. I was thinking about Lavender. I told her. She is... not your biggest fan right now." I turn and lean on the counter as he dishes out our food. "I will have a lot of groveling to do when this is all said and done."

"Maybe," he says. And then looks at me out of the corner of

his eye. "Or maybe she'll understand where you were coming from and give you some grace?"

I laugh.

"Oh, Simon. That's cute. You don't know Lavender. She is — she is a pistol. Nothing stands between her and family....unless it's some hot guy she found in a theatre or the water cooler at work..." I smile to myself. "But even then, all I would have to do is tell her I need her and they would be a distant memory. It won't be that I lied that I have to account for — it will be that I didn't let her know that I needed her."

He stops cutting the steak and really looks at me. Placing the knife on the counter he wraps one arm around my waist.

"Do you need her?"

Tears pop into my eyes and I have to fight back a sob.

"I miss her."

His face tilts upward and he studies me.

"I can fly her out. We can have her come visit."

I start shaking my head.

"No. No. I don't want her here. Not right now. Not when Silas is still doing his thing. I remember when he found out I was a twin. He couldn't stop talking about it for weeks." I shudder. "You mean there are *two* of you?!"

I stare off into space and tap Simon's arm still around my waist.

"It was as if he won the lottery but couldn't believe it."

I take a breath, shaking off the thought.

"Anyway. No Lavender. Let's finish whatever this is first and then we can fly her over later. When life is...normal."

He raises an eyebrow and we break into a moment of laughter.

I know. *I know.*

After you've been through something like this, what even is *normal*?

.::.

We start fighting an hour later.

We're on the couch watching a movie and he taps my knee. I look at him and he mouths *are you ready?* I take a breath and stand up, turning to look at him.

"Simon. I don't know how many times I have to tell you. I'm not coming to work with you. I love my job. I love teaching."

His eyes sparkle for a brief moment before he purses his lips and his face transforms before my eyes.

"Juniper. I understand. I just want to take care of you."

"You're not taking care of me, you're trying to control me. There's a difference. What don't you understand about me loving my job?"

"But you're always so stressed!"

"I want to do a good job."

"But you are doing a good job. You don't have to try so hard. You shouldn't *have* to try so hard." He runs his fingers through his hair, clearly frustrated. "You would be fantastic working with me. I would create a role for you — it would be perfect."

"Simon, I think you need to go."

He looks at me confused. "What? Juniper. I'm just trying—"

I shake my head, closing my eyes. It doesn't take much for the tears to come because all of this is excruciating for me. It's not a real break up, but it's definitely *something.* I won't have his steadiness around me for who knows how long. I blink away the tears and look at him.

"No. I — I don't think this is working for me anymore. I don't like the way you refuse to see how much I love my job and it really feels like you're trying to control me by having me work with you."

He stands up then, his eyes flashing love before clouding

over. "Do you know how infuriating it is to see you waste your intellect on something as simple as *teaching*?" He sneers. "Babe, these kids aren't even going to remember you!"

I breathe in quick then, because these words in any other situation would legitimately sting. Even though we've rehearsed them, imagining the impact is easy.

"Leave, Simon."

He stands up straighter.

"No."

"Simon. *Leave.*" I raise my voice. He reaches for my arms, tries to pull me close.

"Juniper—"

I break away and grab a book off my coffee table, throwing it across the room.

"LEAVE!"

My voice startles even me. We stare at each other, our breath making our chests rise and fall in tandem. I see a moment of pride in Simon's eyes before he looks down, away from me. He starts nodding his head as if he's accepting my ultimatum.

"Okay. Okay." His voice is quiet now.

"But if I leave, this is over, Juniper."

I stand up straighter, fingering the edge of my shirt. We watch each other for a moment, unwilling to let the conversation end because we know it means we're moving to the next stage of no contact.

I swallow. Wipe tears from my cheeks. Straighten my shoulders.

"Bye, Simon."

And then I turn around as he waits for just a moment and walks out the door. After that, there is no faking the heartbreak that takes over my body. I walk into my room and collapse onto the bed, sobbing. My entire being aches.

This is what I was afraid of this entire time. This is why I didn't want to get too attached. Because even though, intellectually, I know Simon and I are still together, that he still loves me, that one day I'll feel his arms around me again, to my body this feels all too familiar.

Lost time. Lost love. Lost everything.

I let the grief flow through my body, and only after managing to collect myself do I notice my phone lighting up in front of me.

It's a text.

I stare at the phone for a beat, trying to figure out if I want to see it or not. I doubt it's Simon. He was pretty clear in the no-communication rule, and texting me right after we broke up would completely annihilate everything we just did.

Lavender told me she was giving me a few days to recover.

That leaves only one other person who would text me. My hands shake as I reach for the phone and flip it so I can see the screen. I unlock it and stare at the message in front of me, my blood running cold.

I KNEW YOU LOVED ME.

NOW THAT SIMON IS OUT OF THE PICTURE, WE CAN BE TOGETHER.

FOREVER.

THE CHILLS CASCADE down my spine and I fight the bile rising in my throat. It took him less than 30 minutes to reach out to me once Simon left my house. I glance around me, suddenly feeling vulnerable and very, very, alone — the one thing Simon said he didn't want. I realize only now the huge flaw in his plan of us breaking up.

Simon was right. We pushed him. But now I am facing him alone.

And I don't know what he plans on doing next.

33

The next day, I struggle to make it through my classes. Mostly because I'm just exhausted. I stayed up most of the night, thinking I heard things. And who knows, I probably did. But I'm trying to play the role — both for Simon (and others thinking we're done) and for those at school (and hopefully them thinking I'm not completely losing it).

My students, still feeling the weird energy from a few days ago, watch me the entire time, waiting for something to happen. I remember this feeling from high school. I remember knowing something was about to happen — something juicy — something I could talk to my friends about for weeks. The inevitable train wreck making an appearance.

I don't like that they're waiting for it to be me.

I walk down the halls before my planning period, trying to make it to the lounge before the rush of other staff. I see a few teachers waiting by their door for the classes and I smile and wave, providing the standard niceties expected. When I finally get to the lounge, I breathe a sigh of relief. For a moment, the crowd and buzz of noise lessens and I'm grateful there aren't very many people, most likely because most of them are waiting for their lunch.

Our lounge is absolutely ridiculous. It's always been over the top, but a few months ago one of the parents, an interior designer, came in and redid the entire thing for some hopeful exposure. I'm guessing it worked. Last time I checked she had a waitlist that was pushing a year. The entire room is painted a rich emerald and there are professional candid photos of the entire staff in a grid on one wall. I look at my picture and notice the ease of how I'm standing in the classroom, laughing with another student. It was two weeks into the school year, and I honestly thought I had stumbled into my dream job. I purse my lips and look away. I can't think about that right now.

A leather couch lines one wall — the plush kind that makes you feel completely enveloped. I've seen multiple teachers crashed out and snoring after school a few days when we were in the midst of testing or curriculum planning. For other seating, there are multiple chairs big enough for two people that face each other and three solid wood tables that have the comfiest seats I've ever experienced. I once did some digging, trying to figure out where they came from, and stumbled on a version of them at Restoration Hardware.

They are $1000 each.

For dining chairs.

Needless to say, I stuck to my original idea of finding mine at IKEA.

Most teacher lounges have coffee makers or, if they're lucky, hidden French presses other teachers have left in cabinets. This one though? It's a legitimate coffee shop.

As in, there is a guy who runs the counter where they have standard espresso drinks, some customized and seasonal like a *bacon latte* and small sandwiches. He's one of our chefs in the cafe, and when he's not working with students in nutrition for college or creating menus that fit within the weird national guidelines for school cafeterias, he's behind the counter keeping us caffeinated. We all call him chef, and he is a school-wide treasure..

We still have the freshly brewed coffee in those brown standing containers and the standard cluster of fridges for those who bring their lunch, but most people will grab a salad or banh mi because they can. And I mean, who wouldn't skip Starbucks in order to have a freshly brewed latte in between classes? I see Jasper in line and I walk up behind him, leaning forward to catch his attention.

"What's your poison today?"

He turns around and smiles.

"Ah. I'm going with draft Kombucha today." He puts his hands up. "I know. I know. Such a stereotype. If it helps, I had too much scotch last night and it's to help ease that horrible decision?"

I grimace and shrug, my hands palm up. "I don't know. It seems pretty fitting. English teacher, scotch, resetting with kombucha..."

"Okay, then. What about you?"

"Mmmm. It's tough, you know?" I look at the menu. "I might get adventurous and double fist today."

He raises an eyebrow and I roll my eyes.

"Drinks, dummy."

He chuckles and I groan.

"Unbelievable. *Anyway.* I need all the energy I can get today, so I am probably going to get a double shot and then the Sparkling Twilight."

"Impressive. Save one for later?"

I shake my head and motion my two hands pouring an imaginary liquid into one container.

"Imma mix it."

"Brave."

"Reckless? Maybe might a better word? I don't know. Check back with me at lunch and see how I'm faring."

We laugh and I tap his arm. And for a moment I'm proud of myself for being able to communicate normally.

Look at me. Engaging with the public, acting like everything is okay.

"Hey. What are you doing after school? Do you want to meet and touch base about the gala? We need to go over the menu, right? I know we snagged Tiffanie's dad for the catering, but he gave us a few options for the food?"

He nods.

"We did. But I won't be able to make it today. I have a deadline with these essays and I have to grade." He separates his hands to indicate how large his stack is of papers and I laugh. "When was the last time you graded? Last semester?"

"No." He looks at me, wrinkling his nose. "Last week."

I groan.

"That's why I'm a math teacher."

"Yeah, well....I'm going to be only grading intros or picking apart the basic structure of their writing. There's no way I can read every single word of every single paper before tomorrow's deadline for grades."

I widen my eyes, understanding.

"That's a lot."

"Yeah."

I grab my coffee from the chef, throwing him a smile of appreciation, and turn back to Jasper, who is taking a sip of his kombucha and trying to hide his facial reactions.

"Bitter?"

"Mmmm. It's uh. It's something."

"Well good luck with that — and good luck grading. I'm going to go back and see if I can finish my lesson plans for the next few weeks. Mattham has been down my throat since I'm normally much more ahead than I am right now."

"Ah. Yes. You would think the department heads remember what it's like to balance all the things but every year, they forget."

"Encouraging." I hear the door open and Tracey walks in, spying me from across the room. My cue to exit. I step away from Jasper. "I'll take a look at the menu options and write something up for you to glance over. We can meet up tomorrow?"

He nods. "That's perfect."

I walk right past Tracey, catching her shoulder as I try to open the door.

"Oh!" she exclaims. "I'm so sorry."

I look at my blouse and am relieved to note that I didn't spill any of my coffee. I stare at her then, not breaking eye contact as I open the door and maneuver past her.

"Tracey. We're always running into each other, aren't we? Do you know if Principal Stahl is in today? Or is he missing again? You would know, right?"

Her eyes widen just enough I know I've reminded her of our conversation the other day. I rub my tongue along my teeth, grateful for the ability to side step her. This time. I take a sip of my drink and feel the fizz run down my throat. I close my eyes and sigh.

I'm also grateful for caffeine.

34

W hen I think about that night, I will think about all of the ways I should have seen it coming. I don't know why I ended up staying. I promised Simon I would only stay late if Jasper was with me, but that also meant I would be home alone.

At least being alone in my classroom meant other people were most likely here working? At least for a little bit. Still. I remember thinking it was safer than my house.

I hadn't heard from Silas in almost 24 hours and the silence gave me too much confidence. I wasn't as hyper-vigilant as I normally am. I should have texted Jasper. Met him at a coffee shop for a co-working session. I should have called Lavender instead of sending her a Marco Polo. I should have broken my agreement with Simon and texted him to come sit with me. I should have done a lot of things, but instead, I sat at my desk and pretended not to hear the noises that were slowly making their way closer to me.

I tried to tell myself it was the custodian, knowing we had a few who worked overnight with the security guard. At first, it was. He came in the the classroom and I startled him.

"Oh. Sorry. I can come back — I didn't realize you were still here."

"No! No. It's fine. Come on in. I'm just....finishing up."

Another body this close felt comforting. Safe. Even if I wasn't entirely sure whether I was allowing my fear to get the best of me or tapping into a very real intuitive hit of danger being imminent. I talked myself out of it so many times. Surely I couldn't be in danger.

Not me.

Not now.

I tried to tell myself it was the tree knocking against the window next to my desk. Too afraid to actually get up from my desk, I wondered if the teacher's lounge was unlocked and what it would look like if I just stayed overnight on the couch.

That would take walking down a dark hallway, though.

But so would me leaving.

I turned on my lamp, hoping more light would make it less foreboding. It only cast more shadows than before and I couldn't shake the feeling in my body that something was coming.

Or someone.

When I finally decided to leave, I had my keys in between my fingers like we do. Makeshift claws. I'm guessing I thought I could use them as a shank if something happened.

But what I didn't know is that someone had been watching me, toying with me, the entire time. I almost made it to my car. I remember seeing it in my vision and feeling a deep sense of relief.

I made it.

But then, I didn't. I never got there. Instead, my keys fell from my hands and I was overtaken by a familiar scent. I heard him laughing under his breath before anything else. By the time I turned my head, my fist poised to strike, he had me. The last thought I had was one of Lavender, and her thinking this was all her fault. I hoped she knew there was nothing she could've done. I hoped Simon would be able to tell her how much I loved her. And then, despite how much I attempted to fight, the blackness took over and there was nothing.

Like a mouse in a game, I had completely underestimated the cat toying with his prey.

LAVENDER

35

We walk out of the hotel and I can barely feel my limbs. I have no idea what he gave me, but it's made me loopy at best and completely reliant on him to keep moving at absolute worst. I look around me, trying to find one familiar face, but there's no one. The sun is blinding and I have to squint against its ferocity when we cross the parking lot.

"You're not...you're not...."

I try to speak but his hand grabs my arms and squeezes tight. The vice makes me breathless and I inhale, trying to breathe through the pain.

"Youcantgetawaywiththis." I throw all of my words into one gasp as he pushes me into the passenger seat of the car and leans his entire torso in after me, reaching for the seatbelt. He pauses for a moment, staring at me.

"It would benefit you to stop talking," he says. I give him a snarl, at least that's what I'm thinking I'm doing to my face, but I have no idea what it actually looks like.

His eyes brighten, delighted.

"Just like Juniper. Beautiful when spicy."

I bite my tongue and taste the metallic undertones of blood. I want to fight. I want to kick free and run across the parking lot to safety. I want to know if Jasper is okay.

I think about the perverted since of reality this guy has and it makes me wonder what he believes about the situation. Now I have a face for the one terrorizing my sister — and know what he did to Simon — the lengths he went to try and separate them. Even still, I can see how Jasper and I played into his hand. Just like them. I remember Simon's words and a chill rushes through me.

"During those last few days we thought we were three steps ahead of him, but in reality, he knew everything. He knew every move. He's a master. He's done this before, Lavender."

The seatbelt clicks into place and he runs a finger down my arm and I lean my entire body away from him, trying to avoid his touch. It doesn't work. Whatever he gave me has completely disconnected my brain from my body. I can think and process and know exactly what's happening, but I can't do a damn thing about it.

It's terrifying.

A single tear falls from my cheek and he notices, wiping it with his finger and then bringing it to his mouth.

"You sister does the same thing, you know. Cries as a way to get my attention. As a way to prove her love and devotion to me."

He straightens and adjusts his belt and I glance away with just my eyes, my head now stuck in his direction. He laughs then.

"Don't worry, my love. We'll have plenty of privacy later."

I send as many subliminal signals as I possibly can to Dan and Simon, begging them to hurry and find us. What no one knows is that before Simon and I got off the phone, before Jasper came and interrupted our conversation, he told me he was going to drop something off at the front desk of the hotel.

"Please trust me, Lavender."

I told him I did, but only because Juniper trusts him, and I trust her more than anyone.

"It's not going to look like much, and that's on purpose. Just stick it in your pocket and find a way to discreetly pull the sticker off before throwing away the paper."

It was a tracker. I knew it. I picked the envelope up from the front desk and knowing I was being watched, made a show about pulling the paper out of the envelope and reading it, smiling as though it were a secret message. I took my hand and scratched my neck, and then slowly, almost imperceptibly, I slipped the tiny piece of sticker backed by metal into my pocket when I was thanking the front desk clerk.

It was our ticket — our escape. I only hoped it worked.

Silas shuts the door and walks over to his side of the car and gets in, starting the ignition. I open my mouth to try and speak and nothing comes out. He's timed it perfectly. We're not even out of the parking lot before the darkness takes over and I am completely gone.

I'm coming, Juniper, is the last thought I remember.

JASPER

36

I opt for cheeseburgers and milkshakes for lunch, knowing Lavender will probably want comfort food. Either that or she'll take one look at what I got for us and decide that she can't eat because she's too worried, nervous, embarrassed because of the kiss.

God, that kiss.

I pull into a parking spot at the hotel and close my eyes, leaning my head against the steering wheel. I'm falling for her. No — it's not actively happening anymore. It *already* happened. I am on the ground, struck dumb by this woman, completely enamored with Lavender Reese.

Damn.

I'm...in love with her?

Maybe. I don't know. Possibly?

What are you doing, Jasper.

I suddenly remember a conversation I had with Juniper before the school year began. She was talking with me about Simon, and I was completely enamored with how she absolutely glowed whenever his name left her mouth.

"How did you know?" I asked her.

She looked at me, confused.

"How did I know?"

I nodded.

"Yeah." I drew a circle in the air around her face. "This whole vibe you have going on right now? Total love. Endgame type shit."

Her eyes brightened. "Oh. Yes." A small bit of laughter escaped and she scratched at a spot on her neck. "Um. I know it's cliché. But I really did just....*know*. From our first date, actually." She shrugged and gave me a small smile. "He was - *is* - it for me."

I groan against the steering wheel again and hit it with my hand a few times.

Impeccable timing, Jasper. As always.

I take a deep breath and compose myself while gathering the food and drinks and make my way to the hotel room. As I walk through the doors, I hear something behind me. Turning my head to look over my right shoulder, I see a man helping a woman into their car. She says something to him, I can't make out the words, but she sounds feisty. I laugh as he leans in and drops a kiss on her forehead. I pause though as he turns and faces me.

That look...the smirk.

My blood runs cold as I turn my body to get a better look in the car. I drop the bags of food on a bench nearby and struggle with pulling out my cell phone. I call Lavender.

No answer.

I call her again.

No answer.

I forget about the food and run up to the hotel room, begging my imagination to be working overtime.

Please answer the door, Lavender.

"Lavender! Lavender - answer the door. I'm serious. Lavender. Lavender this isn't funny."

A head peaks out from a room across the hall and I ignore the stares. I'm about to shoulder through the door when I feel my phone vibrate and I look down. It's Dan.

I answer it and continue to pound on the door, my prayers hitting the ceiling and falling around me, my emotions warring for control.

"Dan." I say.

"Listen, Jasper - I need your help."

"Dan," I repeat. He goes quiet.

"Jasper. What is it."

I stop pounding on the door and pull my shirt up to wipe the tears that have fallen. I kick the door out of anger this time, knowing there's no one in the room now. Knowing she's gone. Knowing he has her and I just missed them and if I would have gotten out of my car one minute earlier, I would have seen him. I could have done something. I kick the door again.

"He has her. He has Lavender."

LAVENDER

37

I wake up and I'm back in San Francisco. Juniper and I are at the beach with our friends and there's a bonfire. We're sitting next to each other for warmth, fighting over a blanket that's about two feet too small for the both of us.

We can't stop laughing.

Juniper turns serious then and I look at her.

"What is it?"

She looks at the ocean for a bit, and I can tell she's nervous.

"I think—I think I need to move, Lav. All I've ever known is this," she motions between us as if it's a bad thing and I shake my head, not following. "I need to find out who I am on my own."

I adjust myself so I'm able to fully face her and not be shoulder-to-shoulder.

"I don't understand."

She turns to mirror me, and I am once again taken by just how much she echoes my own being. Looking at her, I see who I am in completion.

"I'm moving, Lavender. I found a spot on the east coast."

I start shaking my head, afraid to accept this harsh truth

that runs cold down my body. It doesn't feel good. It feels dangerous. We're Lavender and Juniper. We come as a set. We're not meant to be separated. I tell her this and her eyes widen.

"That's just it, though. I need to know that I am my own person. Don't you want to know that for yourself?"

The tears are falling and I can't make them stop. My hands are frozen in front of me so I can't even wipe them off my cheeks, I just sit there, staring at her, unable to move and unable to believe the words coming out of her mouth.

"You're breaking us," I whisper.

And then before she can respond, her eyes grow wide with disbelief. I follow her gaze. It's Mom. She's walking toward us, her hair flowing in the breeze behind her. I stare at her, shock running through my body. How — how is she —

"Mom?"

She walks up to us and kneels in front of us and suddenly it's just us three and we're in a tiny basement that's cold and sterile. The walls are a musty blue and the fear radiating off Juniper and myself is thick.

"My babies," she says, pulling us close to her. I breathe in her scent and am immediately transported to a time of safety and knowing and certainty and magic. We collapse against her chest, each of us sobbing. She kisses us both on the crown of our heads and then leans back so she can look at us.

"You need each other now," she whispers.

We look at each other. What does she mean? Of course we need each other. We always need each other.

"Juniper's moving though," I manage in between sobs. Mom rests her hand against my cheek and smiles in understanding.

"Give it time. You both will know just how much y'all mean to each other. Lavender, you can't run anymore. And Juniper, my love. Stop hiding." She stands up then, slowly backing away from us. An ethereal glow surrounds her and she slowly fades into the ether. Juniper and I start wailing, reaching for her, desperate to have her back. We grab onto each other, the mirror of our individual pain, and let the other bear the brunt of our devastation. We melt into each other then, becoming one and our tears become the sea, surrounding us with waves cascading in the rhythm of our pain.

.:::.

IT's the crying that wakes me up. I open my eyes slowly and for a moment, I'm disoriented. All I see is a blinding light positioned right above me. Slowly, I come into awareness. That was a dream. A dream of when Juniper told me she was moving and then — Mom.

Mom visited us.

I take a breath and let my eyes focus, looking around me. I recognize the room as the one in my dream and realize either I've come in and out of consciousness or something very supernatural just happened. With our mom, either way could have worked.

And then why I'm in this room fully sinks into my bones.

Silas.

I go to wipe the tears from cheeks and realize I can't move and that my skin is dry. It's not me crying. It's someone else. I can hear the sniffing to my left and I try and move my head without success. I know this sound. I grew up with this sound.

I open my mouth and try to speak for a few moments before sound comes out as a squeak first, and then words.

"Juniper? Is that you?"

My voice is raspy and I hear a small gasp.

"Lav-Lavender. Yes. It's me. I'm here. Ohmigod, I thought you would never wake up."

I do blink away tears then, growing emotional from hearing her voice and knowing she's still alive. I smile and know we're going to be okay. We're together now.

"Well I can't believe you lied to me about Simon."

She laughs then, a tiny hint of her joy, and it washes over me like balm.

"So he told you."

"He loves—."

"No," she interrupts me, her voice getting almost too quiet to hear.

"Not now," she says, even quieter. And I understand. I can't talk about it here. Not with Silas.

I grow quiet.

"I had a dream about Mom."

She sniffs.

"Lavender —"

I talk over her.

"It's okay. It's okay. It was good. She visited us and we were here — in this room. She told us we needed each other."

I hear her crying again.

"I'm so sorry," her voice is broken.

I blink.

"Why? For moving here? Juniper, I get it. I do." I can feel the emotion building. "I didn't at first — it pissed me off. But I get it. You have nothing to be sorry for —" my voice dims and I think back on that night so many years ago. The decision that led to Mom's death.

"If anything —"

"—I killed Mom, Lavender."

There's only silence.

"Wait, what? No. No."

"I know. I'm horrible. I was pissed and angry because you

went to the movies with Thad and she knew it and was trying to make me feel better and went to go get ice cream....."

"Juniper."

"If she hadn't left—"

"JUNIPER."

She pauses.

"She left to come get me. She had to come get me. Thad-Thad raped me that night. I ran. I ran, and called her, and she was on her way to get me."

A small whimper grew into a muffled sob.

"Thad raped you?"

I breathe deep.

"Yeah. Yeah. And I called Mom totally beside myself and she didn't even hesitate. Grabbed the address and said she would be right there. And then she never showed."

"Ohmigod,"

I wince.

"I know. It wasn't — it wasn't ever your fault. It's mine, Juniper. I killed Mom. I was so selfish and I didn't listen to you and —"

"No, no. Lavender. Stop."

We both grow quiet then, thinking about the revelations we just shared. The weight we'd both carried for so many years.

"Wow," I sniff. "We're both really, really fucked up aren't we?"

She laughs then, and I hear her trying to catch her breath through the tears.

"Don't ever run to Mexico without me again," she whispers.

"Yeah, well don't ever move across the country, bitch."

We both laugh, and it feels good. I can feel Mom.

"She's here with us, isn't she," Juniper says. I smile.

"Look at you, witchy twin. Who even are you?"

"Apparently someone who pulls tarot cards now. I don't even know."

"Wow. You've changed."

"Having a stalker does that to you."

Silence again.

"Where is —"

—I don't know. He left a while ago. I was awake when he came and dropped you off and I've been sitting here, waiting, hoping — we have to get out, Lavender. We have to get away."

I think for a moment.

"Are my hands tied or am I still drugged?"

I tried to send awareness down to my wrists, but nothing pops up. I must still be drugged.

"Your hands are free," Juniper confirms. "But you're tied down like me and wearing a gown."

"I'm wearing a gown?"

"Yeah." She clears her throat. "These are...um....our wedding gowns?"

I choke and she hums.

"I know," she says.

But I'm not thinking about him changing me into a fucking wedding gown. I'm thinking of him changing me. Taking off my jeans.

My jeans with the tracker.

"Hey, Juniper?"

Before she can even respond, we hear a roar from another room and the tumbling of footsteps down the hall.

She whimpers and I cringe.

"Nevermind," I whisper. I think he found it.

38

I watch both of you, and I can't believe my good fortune.
Finally.

I have you.

Juniper *and* Lavender.

I can see you laughing, your eyes squinting in the same way, and joy rushes through me. Both of you are so happy — so free now that I have brought you here. It's going to be us. Forever.

I cannot wait for it to truly begin.

But for now, I let you have time to reconnect and I resist turning on the volume to listen in, knowing you need a bit of privacy.

I grant you that one thing, but the entire time I watch the curves. Juniper rolls like the ocean, but Lavender is still choppy, trying to embody herself again.

Soon, those curves will be against my skin. My hands will know what it will feel like to possess two pieces of perfection at the same time. I salivate at the thought, and force myself to break away from watching you to focus on something else just as important.

I text my dad to let him know I am working late again and he tells me how proud he is — how hardworking I am.

He has no idea.

I smile and look at the setup that's gotten me through to this moment. Monitors line the wall and it's like my favorite show I won't ever have to stop binging. At any moment, I could tap in and watch both of you. Until now. Now there's no need, because I have you. I look at the monitors and the different areas I have surveillance going until I see movement. My eyes catch on something and I lean in.

Simon.

I bite the skin on my thumb and feel the blood break through. What is he doing? Why is he still here? Doesn't he know Juniper doesn't love him anymore? He looks around and then what happens next has me standing up quickly, the chair rolling backwards and crashing against the wall.

It's Jasper.

"What the fuck?" I whisper.

I watch as Jasper walks up to Simon and shakes his hand and I shake my head. I almost had him. When I came home I noticed he was at Juniper's place. It was the perfect moment to catch him by surprise. I gathered my tools - conveniently disguised weapons of singular destruction - and walked out the door, but by the time I crossed the short distance, he'd already left.

I'd stood in Juniper's living room for a solid three minutes, trying to figure out where the hell he'd gone.

I had to have missed him by seconds.

I came back then, rewinding the tape and trying to figure out what spooked him. Enough time had passed that he had to have known Lavender was already gone from the hotel. I watched as he walked around, looking for something, and then walking out the back door. I fast forward the tape a few minutes. He pulls his cell phone out of his pocket and answers the phone call. I stop the tape then and lean in as if I can hear, but remember the speakers I impacted into one of the lights had been taken by the feds. I hit the desk in front of me with the palm of my hand and wince. But then he does something that has my blood running cold.

He looks at the screen of his phone once, confused, and then realization crashes into his facial features. He keeps talking, clearly getting more animated.

He just found something out. He freezes, listening.

And then, he looks right at me.

Or rather, right at the camera, which is in the direction of *this* house. The small abandoned rental no one ever notices because it's in an alley way. I sit back in my chair and watch.

What did you find out, Jasper?

And who called you?

That's what I'm doing now, trying to figure out what's happening. I'm pulling at the hair in my eyebrows and I know I won't have any left by the end of this. I move to my lip, plucking the dead skin around the edges, and move my attention back to Simon and Jasper.

Why would they be together? What would they be doing?

"I won, bastards. What game are you playing?"

Dan pulls up then, parking next to Simon. He gets out of his car and walks up to them and I lean on the table, not believing my eyes. I'm on the edge of my seat but this is not the show I'm wanting to watch. This is a nightmare. A horror film.

Simon pulls something out of his pocket. It's something tiny. Metal. Realization dawns.

I put my hands in my hair and back away from the computer as I see Jasper clap his hands together, clearly excited about something and Dan putting up his hand to calm him down.

They found me.

But how?

I've been so careful —

And then I remember Lavender, that bitch, saying something about me not getting away with this. I think about fucking *easy* it was to catch her by surprise and bring her back here. I turn around, my breath quickening, and pull at her clothes.

No no no no no no no no no no.....

When I find the matching chip that Simon is holding in the feed, the betrayal hits me like a knife. I scream and punch a hole in the wall.

And just like that, the ax falls and the love I had for these two has turned into hate.

JASPER

39

Dan drops a string of profanity and starts screaming at his team.

"We need a SWAT team over at Juniper's house. Now. *Now.*"

I'm leaning against the door now, waiting for direction. Once I hear where he's going, I turn and start running down the hall.

"Jasper, how quick can you get to Juniper's?"

"I'm already on my way."

"Okay. Simon will meet you there and fill you in on what he's been doing."

I hang up before he can say anything else and am on the road, food completely forgotten, within minutes. I dial Simon's number and he answers on the second ring.

"Hey."

I swerve to pass a line of cars and ignore the honking.

"Hey. I'm on my way to Juniper's. Are you there yet?"

"No. But, Jasper - "

"He has Lavender, Simon."

Simon grows quiet.

"Simon?"

He sniffs and I can tell he's not saying something.

"Simon, so help me - "

"I knew he would take her, Jasper. I-I planted something on her to help us track in case this happened, but I knew it was only a matter of time."

I hit the steering wheel so hard I bruise my palm.

"What the fuck, Simon."

"He has Juniper too, you know. You can't forget that."

I laugh, the anger rising in my chest. "So you figured you would give him two for one?" I know most of my anger isn't directed *at* Simon. Not really. But his carelessness feels incredibly short sighted.

"We were supposed to protect her."

"We are."

"We were supposed to keep him from taking her, too."

"That wasn't an option. This was always his plan. As soon as she landed here, as soon as he saw her, she was a mark. And he's too smart, Jasper. It was either lose both of them completely or try and play his game. And we have him. We just have to be smart about it."

I pull in to Juniper's driveway and get out of the car, slamming the door behind me.

"I'm here," I growl. I'm pissed. I don't care what their plans were for saving Juniper, I don't like that Lavender was used as bait. I walk into the house and pace the living room before the energy is too much - too volatile. I run out to the back so I can watch the waves crashing on the shore. Right now, the chaos of the ocean is just what I need to bring me back to center. At one point, I think I hear something and I turn my head, my ear pointed toward Juniper's house. The noise stops, and I assume it's her AC kicking into gear.

I thought I turned her AC off...

I walk over to the unit and realize it's not on. I let my hand rest against the edge.

It hasn't been on, either.

I frown and look around again, seeing nothing, and take my spot on her patio. The waves are whitecapped today because of a storm brewing off the coast. They whip and tangle with each other before crashing into the rocks on the shore. My heart begins to return to a normal rhythm.

It really is an incredible view.

My phone rings. It's Dan.

"Hey. Are you there?"

"Yeah I'm here."

I get up from my spot and start pacing, but the reception is bad so I walk inside to better hear him.

"Listen. We know who it is now. And he's close."

"Close?"

"He's across the street, Jasper."

I freeze.

"And he's probably watching you right now. We know he has a massive surveillance system going."

I throw my hand up into my hair.

"You've got to be shitting me." I look around me and land on a spot on the wall. It's a framed picture, but there's something off about the framing. It's...uneven. I stare at it for a moment until Dan's voice breaks through and captures my attention.

"Jasper."

"Yeah. Yeah I'm here."

"You have to wait for my team. We're almost there. I'm going to park in the driveway, but the team is parking out of sight so he doesn't know what's coming. You can't just go banging down doors. I need to know you're not going to do anything stupid."

I hear gravel crunching underneath tires. Simon's here.

"I won't do anything, Dan. Just...hurry. Please."

I hang up with Dan and walk out to meet Simon as he's getting out of his car.

"Jasper."

"Simon."

He shakes my hand and looks around, his eyes resting on a worn down rental in the back of an alleyway. My blood runs cold.

"That's where he is?"

Simon turns and looks at me, nodding slightly. I stare for a moment, every fiber of my being wanting to *do something stupid* as Dan would say.

Simon clears his throat. He doesn't want to say anything, because he knows I'm still pissed.

"I'm still pissed," I say.

"I know." He responds. "Have you spoken with Dan?"

"He should be here soon."

Like clockwork, he pulls up next to Simon's car. When he walks up to us, all three of us look at each other and take a breath.

"This is it boys." He mutters. He takes off his sunglasses and wipes them clean. "My team is taking their places as we speak. I cannot stress this enough - you have to let them lead."

Simon and I nod. My hands clench into fists at my sides.

Dan looks at Simon.

"Are we still connected?"

He nods, pulling something small out of his pocket.

"It activated this morning, right when she picked it up in the lobby. I don't know if it's still on her person, but it hasn't been found yet. Or destroyed."

Dan nods.

"Good. Good."

I point, my finger shaking.

"What is that - is that - is that a tracker?"

Dan and Simon's silence tells me everything I need to know.

I run my fingers through my hair again and pace to control the wild energy coursing through my veins.

We're almost there.

We almost have you.

You're almost safe.

Hang on, Lavender, I beg. *We're coming.*

40

I run into the room where they are being held and hold the chip in front of Lavender.

"You *bitch*. You betrayed me. What the fuck is *this*?!"

The intimacy is gone. In front of me is a stranger. The betrayal runs deep.

She watches me for a moment.

"Hello, Silas. It's nice to see you, too." She looks down at the dress I had lovingly placed her in just a few hours before. "Thanks for this great gown, by the way. Juniper tells me we're getting married?"

Rage runs through me and I spit in her face and grab her by the hair, wrenching her neck in an awkward position and getting so close to her face I can see the way her skin dimples and folds in a slightly different way from her twin. Two completely different cartographies from the same country and I won't ever be able to discover them now because of my disgust. It makes me angry all over again and I pull Lavender's hair and feel satisfaction when I hear her grunt under the pressure. Juniper cries out behind me and for a moment I remember her

— *you* — the original portrait of perfection — and begin to question everything. Is it worth this anger?

But then I see Lavender's lips curl into a half smile and she raises an eyebrow.

"What are you gonna do? Kill me?" Lavender whispers so quiet only I can hear. "They'll get here before you can do anything."

She tricked me.

How can something so close to you go so wrong, Juniper? How can you be so perfect and she be so...not?

I let her go and watch as she tries to collect herself, her hands clumsily crashing into her face as she slowly comes back to life under the drugs. I walk over to you and get close enough to smell your breath. Your eyes grow wild under my study and I smile.

I will miss you.

"I make you nervous, don't I? You've never seen me angry."

"I don't—I don't know why you're angry. What happened?"

I take the chip and run it down your cheek and then walk behind you, making sure I have Lavender's attention.

"It seems your sister decided to turn against us, Juniper."

I watch Lavender's face, looking for any clue that she knows. She gives away nothing. She stares at you instead.

"I have no idea what he's talking about. Is this normal? Does he do this all the time?"

She looks concerned and I see your chest bounce with quickened breaths. I press up against you, reminding you of my presence.

"You see, Lavender — to answer your question, I could kill you. But that wouldn't be any fun. I wouldn't be able to see you squirm under the grief and devastation of watching what you love the most fall away from you." She starts shaking her head, realizing what I mean — what my intentions are. I pull my knife from my pocket and run a small trace across your collarbone.

I catalogue your whimpers into my brain to obsess over later.

You are so, so beautiful when you are in pain.

"It's such a shame, too. The beauty you two possess takes my breath away. I dare say you're even perfect. But I just can't get over the betrayal."

Blood begins to trickle from the cut and I am struck for a moment at just how much you look like art. Red streaks running into the white gown, puddling and turning into something pink and splattered.

Lavender kicks and sputters in between Juniper's cries.

"Juniper. Juniper, I'm so sorry." She turns to me. "You *monster*. What are you doing?!"

I smile and take the knife to the other side of your collarbone.

"Well, right now, I'm making art of your sister. Don't worry. You're next." I look up and wink and Lavender grimaces and avoids my gaze. You are gasping under the pain and I'm having to do everything I possibly can not to take you right here, right now.

Ohmigod seeing blood is such a high.

"You tried so hard, you know that, Lavender? I have to give you and Simon credit." I pull out the chip again and let it dangle, frozen on my finger, before dropping it on the floor and stomping on it.

"What...is....that?" Your voice comes out uneven and I can see your skin has turned even more porcelain. I imagine you are only a few minutes from fainting from loss of blood. I'm about to answer you, but I hear something in the distance and I pause, knife posed mid-air.

It's helicopters. Helicopters and a lot of sirens.

Shit.

Fuck.

Lavender starts giggling when she realizes what it is and she looks at me and attempts to spread her hands wide but instead, still under the influence of the cocktail I gave her, they fall at her side.

"Lavender?" You mutter and then go quiet. I feel you give next to me and I look down, seeing that you've finally given into the loss of blood. Instinctively, I place my finger at your pulse point and feel a slight flutter underneath my skin. I lean down to kiss you.

You're here, but barely.

"JUNIPER!"

Lavender bucks and kicks, throwing threats my way of what she would to do me if you died. I stop listening. I know you won't die. But not because of any weakness on my part. As much as I love you, I couldn't reconcile your sister's betrayal and there was a large part of me that planned on doing away with both of you. That is, until I knew there was a better way.

It was good though, wasn't it? What we had? Around me, everything grows quiet because there is a sudden peace of what's next. I tried, and for a time, I succeeded beyond my wildest dreams.

But now, what I accomplished won't matter. Lavender reads my expression, my focused intent, and her eyes grow wide.

"No no no no no no no no...." she throws her arm toward me in an attempt to stop me and I'm struck by how angelic she looks floating toward me, the gown flying up behind her like wings.

I realize, as the knife slices into my skin and I felt the life leave me, that maybe I was too quick. Maybe, she was trying to stop me because after all of this, she actually did love me.

Did you love me, Lavender?

I crash into the floor and hear the booms of a SWAT team bursting into the home as everything fades to black.

LAVENDER

41

What happens next feels like a dream.

"Lavender?" I hear Juniper whisper my name and I look at her right as she fades away, her head drooping in front of her and her weight resting on Silas.

No no no no no no no no

Not now. Not after all we've been through.

I see him notice her, and pause for a moment as he checks her pulse.

He never tells me if she is still alive. I cannot get to her. I watch her skin turn pasty and I am trying my hardest to kick my way over to her.

And then Silas turns to me and lifts the knife as the sounds of the SWAT team get closer. I know what will come next, but I do not believe it. My hands reach out to stop him and I notice three things all at once.

- The way I can feel my body now. The grief of seeing

Juniper lifeless and leaning on Silas pushes me to access a strength I did not know I have and I know with certainty it's Mom holding me up and out and carrying me to where I need to be: with Juniper.

- Silas' eyes as they latch on to me. He slices his throat and I can't even think about what's happening because all I see is the blood pool at his feet and him watching me. His mouth moves and I swear he tells me he loves me as the life leaves him. I see an intensity that will forever be etched into my memory, his blood cascading around the room and my gown as he stumbles to the floor. I cannot catch him, and I don't even try to, because my focus is on Juniper and making sure she's okay.

- Without the barrier of Silas standing next to her, she begins to fold in on herself, the weight causing her to crash to the floor — on top of the man who kidnapped her under the faulty notion that they belonged together. No. No. I will not let this happen. I catch her in my arms as her blood mingles with Silas' and I slip and fall, crashing into the arms of Simon, who is running into the room behind the SWAT team.

I HAND Juniper over to him, and notice his distress and the way his mouth moves in the motion of Juniper's name but I can't hear him — I can't hear anything, and I see Jasper walk in and catch my gaze and I see my entire future in one breath. I collapse into his arms, my sobs racking my entire body, unable to speak or answer any of his questions.

EVERYTHING FEELS LIKE A DREAM.

Nothing makes sense.

AND THEN, in a moment where I am able to take a breath and look at him, I swear I see the image of a woman leaving the room, her blonde hair flowing behind her like a crown.

MOM.

EPILOGUE

"Juniper? Have you seen my red heels?"

She walks into my room, the shoes in question on her *feet*. I balk at her smirk and point.

"Are you — are you wearing my heels? My red stiletto heels?"

The shock is limitless.

She laughs and does a twirl.

"Do they look okay with this dress?"

I sit back on the bed and watch her and grow emotional all over again. She catches the shift in energy and stops mid-twirl, pausing only to lean against the doorframe.

We stare at each other.

"You're here," I say.

She nods.

"I'm here."

She points at me.

"You're here too."

I take a breath.

"I am."

She walks over to me and sits next to me on the bed, laying

her head on my shoulder. Since Silas, we're doing remarkably well. But there are moments, like now, where we have to remind each other we are here — we made it — we're through it.

"Tell me again about Mom," she whispers.

And then there's this.

I've told her the story a hundred times already. How I couldn't feel anything and then I felt everything. How I knew Mom was with me. How I saw Mom leave the room as I passed her off to Simon.

How she saved us.

I won't ever get tired of telling the story. I reach for her hand and squeeze it, but before I can start talking, a knock sounds at the door and a tall lanky guy peeks in. I smile.

Jasper.

Since moving to Providence, Jasper and I have been inseparable. He is everything I never knew I needed. More than once I've had to acquiesce Juniper's knowing looks and reminders that she knew — she knew even before everything happened — that he was for me.

Simon juts his head in right next to Jasper and they stand there waiting for us to move.

"Sooooo are we going or not?" Simon asks, looking to Juniper for a cue. I love the way he loves her. He holds her in a way that I will never be able to, and it's been wild to see that relationship solidify. Juniper stands up and reaches for my hand. I walk over to my closet on the way out the door and pick up a spare pair of heels and stick my tongue out at Juniper.

"Those heels look amazing on you, but I need you to know I'm settling in order for you to look amazing."

She laughs and Jasper turns and looks me up and down.

"I see literally nothing wrong with what you're wearing."

I don't even look at him.

"Yeah, you wouldn't. That's the point."

I keep holding Juniper's hand and squeeze Jasper's arm with my other one.

"How are we getting there? Two cars? One?"

And Simon groans.

Juniper laughs.

I know the question irritates him since they live in Newport and Jasper and I live in Providence, but I ask it anyway. Every week. Every double date.

What's love if not persistent annoyance?

That night, we're headed to a karaoke bar downtown. When we get there, Juniper and I find a table while the guys go and find us drinks. A song comes on and we see a few people take the stage for their turn and Juniper straightens.

"Ohmigod."

I look at her, then look at the stage. I can't quite see it.

"What is it? More sorority girls? A bachelorette party? Some tourists." I guess everything I possibly can think of but nothing has me prepared for what I see when the crowd parts and I notice Jasper and Simon, grooving to the opening beats of The Weeknd and Daft Punk's I Feel It Coming.

"Ohmigod," I echo.

Juniper looks at me and we bust out laughing and then stand up in tandem, dancing to the sound of our men taking the small world of this karaoke bar by storm.

I wrap my arms around my sister and she holds on as we sway and tears come to my eyes all over again.

Jasper catches my gaze and points at me.

YOU'VE BEEN SCARED *of love*
And what it did to you.
You don't have to run
I know what you been through.

· · ·

I SMILE AT HIM, making my hands into the shape of a heart, and continue to sway with Juniper. They step off the stage then, making their way toward our table, and we stop dancing, confused at what's happening. Simon hands his mic to Jasper as the chorus kicks in and looks at Juniper before kneeling in front of her.

"Ohmigod," I repeat, my hands flying to my mouth.

Her eyes widen and she puts her hand out, unsure of what was happening. The spotlight turns and shines on our small group and Simon looks up at my sister, his face expectant.

I hit her arm then with my hand and she blinks and crashes into Simon, her squeal echoing across the bar.

"I think she said yes!" Jasper calls out and I throw my hands up in the air and jump into Jasper's arms. The beauty of the moment only heightened by what we'd all been through a few short months before.

Juniper pulls herself from Simon's arms and looks for me, her face streaked with tears. When she finds me amidst the cheers and calls for shots, we fall into each other's arms, crying and jumping up and down and soaking in the moment.

You guys need each other, Mom had said.

I knew what she meant now.

My mirror. My twin. Forever here.

ACKNOWLEDGMENTS

Seven years ago, I woke up from a dream and immediately grabbed my phone. I opened up my Notes and wrote the first sentence introducing me to Lavender and Juniper. I wanted to keep writing - to follow through with this idea. Instead, I focused on finishing *Secrets Don't Keep* and kept this one close. I remember talking with my Story Sisters about the premise, and then letting the idea rest.

When I started writing the story three years ago, these were the women who championed me from the beginning. So thank you Amy, Rachel, Laural, and Vicky. Your constant excitement in those early days kept me moving.

Charlie, thank you for being my beta reader and recognizing the small breadcrumbs I would drop along the way for my readers.

Lindsay, thank you for being the best critique partner and editor a girl could ask for — you stay saving me from embarrassing mistakes and massive plot holes. You pushed these characters to be who they are and I am so grateful.

Janell and Barb - my Pleasant Bitches. I am better for your sisterhood and so much of the bond between Juniper and

Lavender I gained because of our friendship. Thank you for keeping me sane and honest.

To my Patreons, thank you for believing in this story first. By simply signing up, you gave me the confidence to keep writing and sharing, regardless of the messiness of plot and organization. I'm so grateful you let me share a piece of the process with you and I can't wait to see what's next.

Russ, you always wonder how I can watch those creepy-ass shows on Netflix and Hulu. This is why. It's all compost, love, and you put up with my deep dive into psyche and why people do what they do and the hours I spend writing about them. You champion me in so many ways. I love you.

And Jubal, my little lion man, this is the first book your mama has been able to finish since you came earth side and so much of this accomplishment is shared with your magic and curiosity and determination to live life according to your terms. Keep pursuing what lights your fire, moon baby. I'll do the same.

To my readers, every single one of you makes me absolutely humbled to be able to do what I do. I'm so grateful. Every review - every email - every comment - they all take up such a huge piece of my heart. I love y'all. Here's to many, many more books.

ABOUT THE AUTHOR

Elora Ramirez has been telling stories her whole life.

It started when she was four, when she taught herself how to read and write as a way to entertain herself while her grandmother kicked and danced in aerobics class. She cut her teeth on books from Dr. Seuss and writing anywhere she could find the space -- including her Fischer Price kitchenette, the pages of picture books, and Highlights Magazines.

She's matured a bit since then, now choosing to write in the margins of her books.

Intuition and hustle get her through the day, as well as her chef-husband Russell who always greets her with a kiss and their little lion boy who makes it a habit to roar from the front porch.

Stay up to date with new releases and her musings on creativity here.

ALSO BY ELORA NICOLE RAMIREZ

Every Shattered Thing

Somewhere Between Water and Sky

Secrets Don't Keep

Indie Confidence

Join her Patreon community and read her latest manuscript as she writes.